Dial C for Chihuahua

Waverly Curtis

KENSINGTON PUBLISHING CORP.
http://www.kensingtonbooks.com

KENSINGTON BOOKS are published by

Kensington Publishing Corp.
119 West 40th Street
New York, NY 10018

All Kensington Titles, Imprints, and Distributed Lines are available at special quantity discounts for bulk purchases for sales
promotions, premiums, fund-raising, and educational or institu-
tional use. Special book excerpts or customized printings can
also be created to fit specific needs. For details, write or phone
the office of the Kensington special sales manager: Kensington
Publishing Corp., 119 West 40th Street, New York, NY 10018,
attn: Special Sales Department, Phone: 1-800-221-2647.

Kensington and the K logo Reg. U.S. Pat & TM Off.

ISBN-13: 978-0-7582-7495-3
ISBN-10: 0-7582-7495-5

First Mass Market Printing: October 2012

10 9 8 7 6 5 4 3 2 1

Printed in the United States of America

To Shaw Fitzgerald,
who made this book possible

Chapter 1

Apparently the fad was over. All those actresses and models who thought a miniature dog stuffed into a Versace shoulder bag was so cute were now abandoning their furry "accessories" in record numbers. The Los Angeles shelters were so full of Chihuahuas they had to fly them to other parts of the country. My new pet was one of forty Chihuahuas who had been shipped to Seattle.

At the Humane Society, the Chihuahuas were all in one cage. Most were milling around or throwing themselves at the bars, barking. One dog sat by himself, away from the others. A ray of sunlight fell through the opening high in the cinder block wall and illuminated his white fur.

I knew as soon as I looked into his big, dark eyes that he was mine. He held his head high but he looked forlorn. It was a feeling I could totally understand.

My divorce had just become final. My ex had already bought a new three-bedroom house with his fiancée, while I was scraping by in a one-bedroom condo with his cat. To make things worse, the real estate market was crashing, and my career as a stager was in jeopardy. After suffering through a series of disastrous dates, I decided to adopt a dog. I was in need of some unconditional love.

My new pet was quiet during the drive home but he turned into a little white tornado when I set him down on the carpet inside my front door. He raced around the living room, sniffing around the edges of the furniture. Luckily I had locked Albert, the cat, into my bedroom before I went to pick up my new companion.

While he was exploring, I went into the kitchen to set up a water bowl and food dish for him. I opened a small can of Alpo Gourmet, hoping he'd like beef and vegetables with gravy. At the snick of the can opener, he scampered around the corner, his nails clicking across the tile floor, before I could even spoon the food into his dish.

Poor little guy, I thought, he must be terribly hungry. But instead of wolfing down the Alpo, he paused in front of his dish and just stared at it.

Maybe he didn't like beef and gravy. Maybe he didn't like vegetables. But I'd been in a hurry to get to the Humane Society before they closed and had just picked up the first can of dog food I saw at Pete's Market. Maybe I should have bought an assortment of flavors.

I was about to tell my new companion that I'd get

him a flavor he liked, when he looked up at me and said, "*Muchas gracias.*"

"*De nada,*" I replied as he began gobbling up the food like he hadn't eaten for a week.

Wait a minute . . . he couldn't have spoken to me. And in Spanish, no less. I'd been alone too long. That was it. I was under a lot of stress. I was late with my homeowner's dues and late with my mortgage payments. I had started looking for work on Craigslist, but so far I wasn't making much progress. Thirty resumes out, but only one interview. That interview was with the owner of a private detective agency. Jimmy Gerrard had a sleazy appearance, a shabby office, and a weird way of talking about himself in the third person. Still, I was desperate and had tried to convince him I would make a good investigator. I have an eye for detail, I'm a good judge of character, and I speak a little Spanish.

The dog had emptied his food bowl and was licking his lips with his long pink tongue. He looked out toward the living room. "*Tu casa es hermosa, muy hermosa.*"

"What?" I agreed that my home was pretty, but I didn't expect to hear it from him.

"*Tu casa es mi casa,*" he said approvingly. He got it backwards, but I got the point: he felt at home.

He trotted into the living room and started looking around, more slowly this time. I poured myself a glass of Chardonnay and followed him. He seemed to like what he saw, his head bobbing up and down as he poked his nose into the corners. I sank down on my chocolate brown sofa and set my wineglass on the end table. Before I knew it, I had a Chihuahua in my lap. He proceeded to give my crotch a series of vigorous sniffs.

"Stop that," I scolded.

"I am a dog," he said. "What can I do?"

I was about to shoo him away, when he lay down in my lap and curled up, snug as a kitten. He was so soft and cuddly, his short fur like warm velvet. His long ears were shell pink where the light shone through them.

I mused aloud, "What shall we call you?"

"My name is Pepe," he answered in Spanish.

"Pepe?"

"*Sí.*" He got off my lap and stood on the couch beside me, his huge brown eyes looking directly into mine. "And your name, senorita?" he continued, still speaking Spanish. "How are you called?"

"I'm Geri Sullivan," I told him.

"*Bueno,*" he said, with a wagging tail. "I am now, with great pride, Pepe Sullivan."

I took another sip of my wine. This was too much.

Pepe looked me up and down. "You are *muy bonita,* Geri!"

I blinked. "Really?" It had been a long time since anyone had complimented me on my appearance.

"*Sí!* Your dark, curly hair gleams like the wing of a raven. Your lashes are as long and thick as a camel's. And your curves are as sultry as the Yucatan."

"Pepe," I said, "you are quite the flatterer." Although I was still pondering the comparison to a camel. Was that a compliment?

"I do not flatter," he said. "I speak only the truth. I can recognize a hot mama when I see one."

"Well, thank you." I said. They say dogs are man's best friend, but this one was definitely woman's best friend. He made me feel way better than any of the losers I had dated since the divorce.

"Geri," Pepe asked, "have you any other dogs?"

"No, I don't." I said. For some reason, I was reluctant to tell him about Albert. Just as I was reluctant to let Albert know about the dog.

"*Buenísimo!*" He nodded approvingly. "That makes me *el jefe.*"

I didn't think Albert would agree with that and was about to tell him so, when my cell phone rang. I got up and fished it out of my brown leather purse.

I expected it to be my best friend and business partner, Brad. I had promised to stop by his shop to show him my new pet. So I was shocked when the caller introduced himself as Jimmy Gerrard, the owner of the Gerrard Agency.

"Jimmy G. has good news!" he said. "You're hired."

It had been three weeks since the interview. I had long since given up hope that he would hire me. So it took me a moment to recover. "Great! When do I start?"

"Right now!"

"What do you mean *right now?*"

"Jimmy G. means what he says. Right now. We've got a case!"

"OK," I said. I really wanted to spend my time getting the dog settled but I couldn't afford to pass up this opportunity. "Do you want me to meet you at the office?"

"You're on your own for this one," he said. "Jimmy G. is in Portland. On another case. Tailing a suspect. But we got a call from a woman who lives on Capitol Hill. Her husband is missing, and Jimmy G. needs someone to get over there to interview her. She's expecting you. Told her you could be there by 4 PM."

I looked at the clock. It was 3:30. "But I've never done this before," I said. "I have no idea what to do—"

He cut me off. "You'll be fine. Find out what she wants. Take some shorthand." I wanted to tell him shorthand went out in the fifties, but he kept on going. "We can go over your notes when Jimmy G. returns."

Pepe was still standing on the sofa, listening to me as I spoke on the phone. After I hung up, I turned to him and said, "That was good news, Pepe. I've got a job. I'm a private investigator, and I'm going out to interview a client." It seemed OK to brag a little, especially to a dog.

"I will go with you," he said.

"No, you have to stay here," I said as I slid my cell phone back into my purse.

"*Por favor?*"

I shook my head. "I'm not going to blow this chance just because I'm hallucinating a talking dog. You are a figment of my imagination."

"I am no figment," Pepe told me. "I am flesh and fur and blood. Am I not standing here before you?"

"Yes, but—"

"Oh, so you bring me home only to deny me." He turned away and walked to the other end of the couch, where he stopped, his head hanging low. "I am offended."

Poor guy. I went over and stroked his smooth back. "Pepe," I said, "I'm sorry. But it could be dangerous." I didn't really think so, but it made my life seem more glamorous. Although I wasn't sure why I was trying to impress my dog. But don't we all want to impress our dogs?

Pepe perked right up. "Dangerous, eh? I could be of help."

"You're just a little Chihuahua."

"I am full of machismo."

I smiled. "That's all well and good, but—"

"Trouble is my middle name," he told me. "Do you know that I have faced the bulls in Mexico City?"

"No."

"*Sí.*" He paused. "Well, truth be told, I only by accident fell into the bull ring—but I dodged *el toro* better than the matador. The entire crowd cheered for me."

"Really?"

"*Sí.* Now can I go with you?"

"No, Pepe. You have to stay here." I headed for the door. But I hadn't gone more than a few steps, when Pepe scampered after me.

"I have also worked as a search and rescue dog in Mexico City."

"You?"

"It takes a small dog to search small spaces after an earthquake. Tight places, dark places, dangerous spaces. But I am very brave."

"That's fine, but—"

"So now can I go?"

"I'm sorry," I told him. "I'll be right back. I'll only be gone about an hour."

He planted himself in front of the door.

"Additionally," he said, "I have worked with the federal authorities in the battle against the Mexican drug lords."

"Cut it out, Pepe. How could you have done all that? How old are you anyway?"

"Old enough to have done these things, and many more," he said.

I shook my head.

"You doubt me? I will show you. I have a good nose."

He headed for the living room and went straight to the black lacquered Chinese cabinet underneath my TV. I followed him.

"Here," he said, standing on his hind legs and scratching at the dangling gold tassel on the cabinet doors with his tiny pink paws. "Drugs."

I was stunned. "There aren't any drugs in there."

"No?" He sniffed at the drawer, his nose quivering. "I beg to differ. *Sí*. It is marijuana for certain."

"Oh, all right. But it isn't mine."

"Whatever."

"Really. Jeff must have been left it behind—"

"So," Pepe interrupted, "I have proven myself. Now you must take me along."

"Fine, fine," I said. "I give up. I'll go get the leash."

"No leash."

"There's a leash law, Pepe, we—"

"How can I protect you if I am all tied up?" he asked. "Do not worry. I promise to walk only at your side. To heel, as it is called."

"OK, OK," I said. "But we have to go right now or we'll be late."

"*Sí. Vámonos,*" he said, leading the way to the door. "But I have to do one thing before we get into the car."

"What's that?" I said, as we went outside.

"I need to mark my territory."

Chapter 2

A cold, wet breeze was blowing from the south as we approached my green Toyota sedan, which was parked on the street. The day, like most April days in Seattle, had been fickle: rain showers alternating with sun breaks. But now a huge, black cloud hovered over the gray waters of nearby Lake Union, promising to fulfill the weatherman's prediction of a cold and stormy night.

"Are you sure we are in Seattle?" Pepe asked, as he sniffed at a dozen different spots on the grass of the parking strip. "It feels more like Nome, Alaska," he added with an extended shiver.

"I suppose I should get you a rain coat," I told him, fishing my car keys out of my purse. It was one of the things I was anticipating with pleasure. Chihuahuas look so cute when they are dressed up.

"No." His tone was authoritative.

"Why not?"

"Real dogs do not wear coats." With that, still

shivering, he went to my car's rear, curbside tire, lifted his hind leg and peed all over the hubcap.

"Pepe! Stop that!"

"I had to mark my territory," he said, walking up to me.

"Fine," I said. "But you didn't have to do it on my tire."

"It is the very best place, Geri."

"Why is that?"

"It is a little trick I picked up from my cousin, Chico," he explained. "If you park your car near our hacienda, all the senoritas in the neighborhood will soon know that I live here. But your car, it also gets around—this means that senoritas all over town will know of Pepe el Macho. It is simple."

I couldn't argue with his logic, but I told him, "Don't do it again."

"If it makes you unhappy, I will not do it anymore. I solemnly promise." He said this with an overblown sincerity that made me nervous. "Now can we get in the car already?" he asked, shivering mightily. "I am freezing my tail off."

I opened the rear passenger door for him, but he didn't budge.

"I ride only in the front," he said.

I didn't have time to argue with him.

I closed the rear door and opened the front one. "OK, you win. Just get in," I told him, then remembered how short he was. "Here," I added, bending down, "I'll help you."

"I can do it myself." With a mighty leap he

launched himself from the pavement to the floor-board of the car, and from there another jump took him to the passenger seat.

I got in and started the engine. As I put on my seatbelt, I looked over at my canine passenger and had to say that he looked quite handsome. He sat up straight, his head lifted, though I doubted he could see over the dashboard.

"Well," I asked him. "Ready to go?"

"*Sí*," he answered. "But there is just one thing."

"What's that?"

"Crack open my window a bit, *por favor*," he said. "I get carsick."

The woman I was supposed to interview, Rebecca Tyler, lived on Fourteenth Avenue East, a street also known as Millionaire's Row, because it's lined with huge, turn-of-the-century mansions built by Seattle's early merchants and timber barons. It was a wide, stately street, lined with tall elms and horse chest-nut trees. The houses were set back behind mani-cured lawns and wrought-iron fences, all well preserved in styles of the past: Southern colonial, Tudor revival, neoclassical. The people who built them had big money back then; the people living in them now had big money today.

I didn't know much about my client, just that her husband was missing and instead of calling the police she had called Jimmy Gerrard. Perhaps her husband had run off with another woman, and she didn't want to expose herself to the public scrutiny a police investigation would involve.

As we pulled up in front of the Tyler residence, Pepe, who had been talking non-stop the whole way there, said, "Are we here? Is this the place?"

"I think so." I took out my notes to double-check the address.

Pepe stood, putting his forelegs on the armrest so he could see out the window. "The house number—what is it?"

"It's 640," I told him. The house sat behind a wrought-iron fence with pointed barbs. Huge stone pillars flanked the driveway with the house number displayed in tile on either side.

"*Sí*," Pepe told me. "*Seis cuatro cero.* This is the correct casa."

Casa seemed a misnomer, I thought. It wasn't just the biggest home on the block, it was a gigantic white wedding cake of a mansion. Four huge white Corinthian columns on either side of the entryway supported a gracefully curved upper deck. Gold-painted lion statues guarded the wide stairs leading up to the front door.

"I do not like those big lions," said Pepe.

"They're not real."

"Still, they give me a sense of unease."

"Fine. Just be quiet for a minute," I told him. "I want to make sure I'm prepared." I grabbed my big brown leather purse and rooted around to find my pen.

"You tell me to be silent? I am insulted."

"Look, Pepe, your mouth hasn't stopped during

this whole trip. You talk more than any dog I ever knew." I stopped, realizing how absurd that sounded.

He hung his head. "Perhaps it is because you are the only person who has ever listened to me in my whole life."

That stung me—I certainly knew what it was like when nobody would listen to you. I gave him a gentle pat on the head.

"I apologize," I told my tough little *hombre* with the delicate feelings.

He perked right up, his tail wagging. "Then I can talk?"

"Yes, you can talk."

"Look there, Geri," he said, looking out at the house again. "The front door—it is ajar. Is that not strange?"

"Yes, it is," I said. I watched the door for a minute, but saw no sign of activity. "You stay here." I opened the car door. "I'm going to check it out."

"Me, too." Before I knew it, Pepe had scrambled across my lap and out of the car. He ran up the stairs and into the house in a flash.

"Pepe!"

Chapter 3

How could such a tiny dog run so fast? And how would I explain his presence to the client? I scrambled to catch up with him.

I paused at the open front door and caught my breath, hoping Pepe would appear in the entryway. The foyer was all white marble and crystal chandeliers, with a huge semicircular staircase as the centerpiece. I rang the doorbell, which produced a mournful series of chimes but no human response. I didn't know if I could just walk in. What were the rules about that?

I rang the doorbell again. Still no answer. But this time I did hear a faint and distant yip coming from somewhere to the right. It was the first time I'd ever heard Pepe bark. Although it didn't really sound like a bark. More like the sound a tiny Chihuahua might make right before being gobbled up by a tough pit bull.

That thought got me moving. I dashed through the foyer and headed right, finding myself in an all-white living room, one of the largest I had ever seen. The carpet was a snowy white, the walls were papered in white damask, the curtains were clouds of white satin. Even the grand piano in the corner was white. It desperately needed a spot of color, something like the bright red throw rug under the glass coffee table.

It took a second before it sank in. That wasn't a rug, but a pool of blood. As I got closer, I saw that it surrounded the body of a man who lay face down on the white carpet. Pepe was sniffing the bottoms of his shoes. The man wore Birkenstocks, those clunky sandals so popular in Seattle, over green socks.

Pepe lifted his head. "You should not be here," he said. "We must leave right now." He headed toward me, leaving a trail of tiny red footprints behind him.

"No, we can't leave!" I said darting toward the prone figure. I bent over and put my fingers against his neck. "What if he's still alive?"

"Believe me, he is *muy muerto!*" Pepe said. He was right. The man's skin was gray and felt cool beneath my fingertips.

I willed myself to study the corpse. He had sandy-colored hair pulled back into a short ponytail at the base of his neck. He wore a pair of khaki pants and a yellow T-shirt with some sort of lettering on it, hard to read now because it was mottled with brown stains.

"Who is he?" I asked.

"I do not know," said Pepe. "All I know is we must

get out of here! Something stinks about this situation, and it is not just the smell of death." He wrinkled his nose expressively.

A gun lay a few inches from the man's right hand. "This must be the murder weapon," I said, picking it up.

"Do not touch that!" said Pepe. "Do you not know anything about crime-scene investigation?"

Too late. It was already in my hand.

"How do you know about crime-scene investigation?" I asked, turning the gun over to examine it.

"I am a big fan of TV crime shows," he said. "*CSI. Forensic Files.* I watch them all. *CSI: Miami* is the best. Now put that down!"

But before I could put it back, somebody behind me yelled, "Drop it, lady!"

"Set it down nice and slow," another voice commanded.

I turned and saw two uniformed policemen. Both had pistols trained on me.

"I said drop it!"

Without even thinking, I did as they said. The gun slid from my grasp and fell onto the glass coffee table, which shattered into a million pieces.

"*Policía* . . ." I heard Pepe mutter as he slunk underneath the sofa.

In no time, the police had put me in handcuffs. They had taken a quick look at the corpse and then called for backup. Soon the room was full of policemen, four or five in blue uniforms, two in suits, and three or four in white jumpsuits and blue paper booties. A pair of detectives (the ones in suits) took me into the dining room, which was just as huge as the living room, but all done up in gold, from the gilded coffered ceiling to the bronze satin on the chair seats. I shuddered to think about the rest of the color scheme in the house. I was willing to bet there was a bathroom done all in shades of purple.

One of the men looked a bit like my father, with his wire rim glasses and thinning brown hair combed over a bald spot. He wore a rumpled navy suit. The other one was a handsome black man with a shiny, shaved head. His suit was gray, paired with a blue silk shirt and silver cufflinks. The older man said his name was Detective Earl Larson; the other guy was Detective Kevin Sanders.

"Did you find Mrs. Tyler?" I asked. It occurred to me that she might be somewhere in the house, perhaps in one of the upper rooms, as dead as her husband. (I had learned from overhearing snippets of conversation that the body in the living room belonged to David Tyler). But the police had fanned out and searched the house and grounds without finding any other bodies or any trace of Rebecca Tyler. "She was supposed to be here."

"Why were you meeting her?" Larson wanted to know.

"I'm a private investigator," I said. I didn't want to say more. I knew from reading detective novels that PIs had the right to keep their conversations with their clients private, just like priests and lawyers.

Larson asked to see my license.

"I don't have one yet," I explained. "I was just hired. This is my first assignment."

"Who's your boss?"

"Jimmy Gerrard of the Gerrard Agency."

"Why isn't he here?"

"He's in Portland right now, working on another case." I thought it sounded good that he had trusted me with such an important assignment. But Larson shook his head. I could tell he didn't believe me.

"We're going to have to take you down to the precinct for questioning," he said. Sanders motioned for me to get up, and they walked me towards the front door, one on each side as if they were afraid I was going to make a dash for it.

"I'm not leaving without my dog," I said. I hadn't seen Pepe since the police had first burst into the room.

"What dog?" Sanders asked.

"He's a little white Chihuahua," I said. "He was in the living room with me. Maybe you missed him because he's the same color as the room." That was supposed to be a joke but apparently they didn't think it was funny. It's one of my faults, at least according to my ex, that I tend to make jokes when they're not appropriate.

Sanders went into the living room and talked to some of the other men there. A man with a large camera was wandering around, taking photos of the shattered coffee table and the gun.

One of the guys in the white jumpsuits pulled aside one of the white satin curtains and came up with a small white object. He held it in front of him with gloved hands, as if it were contaminated.

It was Pepe! I could tell he wasn't happy. He pedaled his feet in the air, as if trying to find firm ground.

"That's my dog!" I said, rushing towards him. But Larson blocked my way.

The photographer stepped forward and snapped a photo. The flash went off in Pepe's face and he flinched.

"You can't touch him, ma'am," the technician said. "He's evidence." He pointed to Pepe's paws, which were caked with blood. "We're going to have to take him to the lab to be processed."

"No way, José!" I heard Pepe mutter. He squirmed around and bit the technician on the wrist. The man dropped him with a cry of pain, and Pepe hit the floor, making his own little yelp as he landed. Then he dashed between Larson's legs and darted out through the open front door.

Chapter 4

I dashed toward the door, but Larson and Sanders kept pace with me. Sanders grabbed me by the elbow just as I was about to plunge off the front porch.

"Catch that dog!" Larson shouted as Pepe scuttled through the high yew hedge that bordered the yard.

One of the policemen made an attempt to penetrate the hedge, but he couldn't part the heavy branches. Another cop, noticing the delay, took off around the hedge, but he came back a few minutes later, shaking his head. "That pooch is gone," he said.

"That's my new dog," I said. "I just got him today." I turned to Sanders whose fingers were pinching my elbow. "I've got to go after him. He doesn't know his way around Seattle. He's from L.A."

He rolled his eyes but called one of the uniform cops over. "Have your guys canvas the neighborhood. We need to know if any of the neighbors heard or saw anything out of the ordinary. And tell them to keep an eye out for the dog."

"But warn them, he's vicious," said the technician, who had come out on the porch and was holding his wrist.

"Go and have that looked at," said Larson.

"Probably need a rabies shot," the technician muttered as he headed towards the red-and-white emergency vehicle that idled on the street. It was too late to be of any use to David Tyler.

"He's current on his vaccinations," I called out as he passed by. Just then, a sleek, black Lincoln Town Car drove up the street and coasted to a slow stop beside the cluster of blue and white squad cars in front of the house. A woman got out of the car and came rushing up to the yellow crime-scene tape that cordoned off the front yard.

"Who's in charge here?" she asked. A tall, slender woman with long, dark hair, she wore a pale blue linen blouse, which beautifully set off her tan. Combined with her beige linen skirt and gold high heels, she looked dressed for Beverly Hills, not Seattle. Which turned out to be the case.

"I'm in charge," said Larson, heading down the stairs to meet her. "Who are you?"

"I'm Rebecca Tyler," she said impatiently. "I live here. What's going on? Was there a burglary?"

Surely she knew the police didn't use crime-scene tape for burglaries. Even I knew that, although I was only a private detective in training.

"You're just the person we need to talk to," said Larson. He motioned for Sanders to bring me over.

"This woman claims she was supposed to meet you here."

Rebecca looked me over. I could see the disdain in her startlingly blue eyes as she scanned me from the tips of my scuffed black cowboy boots peeking out from under my jeans to the hand-crocheted beret crammed over my unruly curls. A tall man in a dark suit had gotten out of the Town Car and was opening the trunk.

"I certainly didn't have an appointment with this woman," she said. "I don't even know who she is."

"I'm Geri Sullivan—" I started to say, but Sanders stopped me.

"Don't say anything," he said.

"Besides, I've been out of town," said Rebecca. "I've been in L.A. meeting with studio executives. So I couldn't possibly have made an appointment to meet her."

As if to back up her claim, the driver approached with two large blue suitcases that matched the color of Rebecca's blouse. I was impressed. I had never thought of coordinating my attire with my luggage.

"Where should I put these, ma'am?" he asked.

"Let me get this straightened out," said Rebecca. She turned to Larson. "Who is she? And what's going on here?"

I tried again. "Geri Sullivan," I said. Perhaps Jimmy Gerrard hadn't passed along my name. "I work for the Gerrard Detective Agency."

She looked like she was trying to frown but couldn't manage it. "Never heard of them," she said. She turned back to Larson. "You haven't answered my question."

"Ma'am, I have some bad news for you," he said, his voice soft. "I think we should talk about this in private."

Her smooth composure cracked. "Oh, no!" she cried out. "He can't do this to me! Not now!"

Larson put his arm around her shoulders and steered her towards the house. The guy with the suitcases followed. Sanders delivered me to one of the uniformed policemen and told him to take me to the East Precinct station. I tried to object, but they told me they could hold me as a material witness at the very least. It was raining as we drove away. I began crying as I thought of Pepe out there alone, cold and lost.

They put me in a little interview room with several orange plastic chairs and a linoleum-covered table bolted to the wall. They removed the cuffs and brought me a cup of bad coffee.

I used my cell phone to call Jimmy Gerrard, but his voice mail picked up. "You've got to get me out of here," I said. "I'm about to be arrested." I thought about calling someone else, but who? My sister would just sniff at me and tell me it was probably my fault. My ex would laugh. Anyway, his fiancée would probably answer the phone. Amber had an annoying habit of forgetting to tell him I had called.

Every once in a while one of the detectives would

come in and pepper me with questions. They asked me what I was doing at the Tyler residence. They asked about the location of the gun. They asked about my affiliation with the Gerrard Agency. I kept asking them if they had found my dog.

They seemed really puzzled by Pepe.

"Tell me again why you brought your dog with you," Sanders was saying, when the door flew open and a tall, imposing man entered the room. He had broad shoulders and a pale, round face, with a hint of five o'clock shadow around his jowls. He wore a black hat and a long, black wool coat.

"I'm Sherman Foot," he said, holding out his hand to Sanders. "I've been hired to represent Miss Sullivan."

"Don't say another word," he said to me.

Then he turned back to Sanders and asked, "Are you charging my client?"

Sanders shook his head. "She's free to go."

"Fine. We're leaving," Foot said to me.

"Just don't leave town," Sanders said.

Foot offered me a ride back to my car, which was still at the Tyler residence. He had a very nice black Lexus.

"How did I become your client?" I asked as I slid into the front passenger seat.

"Mr. Gerrard called me and told me of your plight," he said. "I'm his personal lawyer."

"Thank God," I said. "They didn't seem to believe me when I said I worked for the Gerrard Agency."

"Well, that is a problem," he said, as we took off into the night. The car practically purred. The rain had stopped but the streets still glistened. He drove slowly as if he had all the time in the world.

"Why is it a problem?" I asked.

"Well, technically you don't work for the Gerrard Agency."

"That's not true. Jimmy hired me!"

"I don't work for James. I work for Stewart Gerrard."

"Who's that?"

"Stewart actually owns the agency. James is his employee. So if Stewart says you don't work for the Gerrard Agency, well then, you don't work for the Gerrard Agency."

I pondered that as the big, black car nosed up the hill.

"James should not have sent you out without proper training. So Stewart will have to deny that you have any connection with the agency."

"He can't do that!"

"You've got to understand. Stewart must protect his business investments."

"But what about me?"

"Stewart will take care of you. That's why I'm here."

I didn't like the sound of that at all.

"So what's my defense?"

"You don't need a defense," Foot said. "You didn't commit any crime. Did you?"

I was about to reply, when he cut me off. "Never mind. I don't want to know. We'll come up with a plausible story that fits the facts."

"I don't want to come up with a plausible story," I said. "I want to tell the truth."

"You'll find out soon enough," he said, "that the truth is usually not the best defense." That was a sobering thought.

We pulled up in front of the crime scene. That's how I thought of the Tyler house now. There was still yellow crime-scene tape festooning the yard, but the house was dark.

Foot pulled a card out of his pocket as I opened the door to get out. "Give me a call tomorrow and we'll talk." I took the card and tucked it into my purse. Foot drove away but I wasn't going anywhere without my dog.

I wandered up and down the block, calling Pepe's name. I don't know if you've ever done this but it's one of the worst feelings in the world. You're pouring your heart into those two syllables and all you hear is silence.

The night was dark and cold and I was drenched. A bitter wind was blowing. There was no sign of a little white dog, but I did hear other dogs barking inside their warm houses. Occasionally people would peer out from their lighted windows. One man even came out to ask what I was doing.

After a while, I was afraid that one of the neighbors would call the police, and I certainly didn't want to end up back at the police station. So I got in my car and drove around. I had the heater up full blast, but I was still shivering.

At every corner, I rolled down the window and called Pepe's name. I drove in wider and wider circles. The only animal I saw was a raccoon waddling across the road near the park. Which really scared me when I thought about how small Pepe was. An encounter with a raccoon would probably be the end of him.

Around 11 PM, I gave up and headed home. I had adopted a dog and lost a dog all in one day. Maybe the whole thing was some elaborately staged April Fools' prank. I parked down the block and trudged through the rain towards my home.

I live in one of eight adjoining units in an old brick courtyard building that was turned into condos. I'd fallen in love with its retro charm. My unit is the first on the right as you enter the courtyard, with the front door hidden behind a juniper bush. And there, to my surprise, was Pepe sitting on the welcome mat at the top of my front steps.

"Pepe!" I shouted. I gathered him up in my arms and covered him with kisses. He didn't seem to mind. Gave me a lick or two with his pink tongue.

"I've been looking for you everywhere," I said. "And here you are."

"I have been waiting for a very long time," he said, shivering. "It was most unpleasant. I suggest you install a dog door."

I wasn't sure the homeowner's association would approve of that, but I agreed. I was just so happy to see him. I unlocked the door and we tumbled into the living room together. Pepe headed straight to his bowl, which was empty, so I went to the refrigerator to get his food.

"I've heard of dogs returning to their homes, traveling thousands of miles," I said, as I spooned out the Alpo, "but how do you do it? Is it smell?"

"Perhaps for some dogs," Pepe said, as I set the dish on the floor in front of him. "But for me, it was easier. I simply memorized your address."

Chapter 5

Pepe wolfed down his food like he hadn't eaten for a week. I ate the rest of last night's Thai takeout (basil fried rice) straight from the container while leaning against the kitchen counter, watching him.

As he slurped the bowl clean with his long, pink tongue, I said, "Pepe, I'm so glad you're all right. When I thought I'd lost you, I just didn't know what I'd do." A tear rolled down my cheek, and I brushed it away, saying, "I love you, little guy."

He looked up at me with those big dark eyes, and I thought he was going to say something equally mushy. But instead he said, "What is that noise?"

"I don't hear anything."

"Listen." His long pink ears swiveled towards the bedroom. "Do you not hear it?" He walked out of the kitchen and into the hallway. I followed. "There!" he said. "It is coming from behind that locked door."

"Oh, my God," I said, finally recognizing the

scritch of claws against wood. "It's Albert!" I exclaimed.

"Albert?" Pepe asked.

"My cat."

"*Un gato?*" His tone was a cross between disdain and disbelief.

"I locked him in my bedroom before I picked you up," I said. "I wanted you to get used to each other's scent before you met. I can't believe I forgot him."

"You forgot him?" Incredulity.

"I know," I said, "but it's not as bad as it seems. I put his food dish and his bowl of water in there with him and he has access to his cat box, which is in the bathroom."

Pepe stopped in his tracks and looked up at me. "How could you forget to tell me about *el gato?* You told me I was the only animal."

"Dog. You asked if there were any other *dogs* and I told you 'no.' I was completely truthful."

"That is parsing the question, if you ask me," he said.

I was impressed by his vocabulary and was about to say so, but the scratching intensified. Now that Albert could hear my voice, he was more insistent. Or perhaps it was because he smelled Pepe.

Albert is a big cat, and when he's unhappy he can do a lot of damage. Jeff and I never got back our security deposits after Albert shredded the curtains and the carpet of every apartment we rented.

"You stay here, Pepe," I said, turning to the little

dog who was sitting in the hall staring at the door. "It's too soon for you to meet Albert. Especially when he's in this mood."

I opened the door just a little, planning to slip into the bedroom and close the door behind me. But Pepe was too fast. He darted around me. By the time I got into the room, Albert had jumped up on my bed and was standing in the middle of my pink chenille bedspread staring down at the small white dog who stood at the foot of the bed looking up at him. Everything in Albert's demeanor read *outrage.*

Did I say that Albert is a big cat? Eighteen pounds of pure muscle. He is an orange shorthair with powerful hind muscles and an extra-long, fluffy tail. I could see his tail swishing back and forth behind him, but I wasn't sure Pepe could see it.

"*Hola, el Gato,*" said Pepe. "I have come to introduce myself to you. I am Pepe but you can call me el Jefe."

"Do you speak Cat?" I asked Pepe.

"Of course, I do," said Pepe.

"Well, then can you tell me what Albert is saying?" I asked. I could hear a low rumble emitting from the cat's throat. It was not a purr.

"He is saying, 'I will obey your every command, O noble and magnificent Dog,'" said Pepe.

It was true I didn't speak Cat, but I was pretty sure that wasn't what Albert was saying. My foreboding was quickly confirmed, when, with a mighty roar, Albert launched himself off the bed and landed on top of Pepe.

The next few minutes were pure pandemonium. I caught glimpses of white fur and orange stripes, heard yips and yowls, saw claws slashing and fur flying.

"Stop it, Albert!" I said. "Come here, Pepe!"

They both ignored me, but the fight was over almost as soon as it began. Albert leaped back on top of the bed and licked his paws, while Pepe trotted over to me, shaking himself off. I saw spots of blood on his white fur, right behind his right shoulder, and there was a red stripe across one of his ears.

"Well, I certainly showed that cat who is boss," Pepe said, before exiting the room. I followed behind him. He was limping a little.

"Are you sure you're all right, Pepe?" I asked. "Let me check you out." He jumped up on the sofa and I looked him over. He had a few superficial cuts and a lot of damaged pride.

I got the rubbing alcohol out of the bathroom and checked on Albert at the same time. He seemed unscathed but annoyed. Thank God, he couldn't talk. I really didn't want to hear what he would have said.

Back in the living room, I applied rubbing alcohol to Pepe's injuries. He winced at the bite of the liquid but didn't complain.

"Are you sure you'll be all right?" I asked. "Maybe I should take you to the vet."

"I will be fine, *senorita*," he said. "I have endured much more. In the Everglades, I fought off an alligator."

"An alligator? Pepe, that's ridiculous. Why would you be in the Everglades?"

"On a film shoot," he said. "But that is another story for another day."

"Well, if you're fine, I am going to bed. I've had quite a day," I said. "Are you coming with me?"

Pepe looked down the hallway at the bedroom. I think he was thinking of Albert. "I will stay out here to guard you," he said, but his voice trembled a little.

"I appreciate that, Pepe," I said, dropping a kiss on the top of his head. If he wanted to play the macho role, I would have to let him. I went to turn off the lamp.

"Do you think you could leave that on, Geri?" he asked, in a forlorn little voice. "I like to sleep with a night light."

To my surprise, I fell into a deep sleep. Perhaps it was knowing that Pepe was on guard. Albert seemed to have suffered no harm from their encounter. He was already fast asleep in his usual spot at the bottom of the bed.

I've had Albert ever since the divorce. He was my husband's cat, but his fiancée is allergic to cats so now he's mine. Albert always liked me more than Jeff anyway. He lets me pet his tummy. I'm the only one that can get that close to him. And Albert lets me sleep in his bed. At least that's how I think *he* thinks of it. Because by the end of any night, he's taking up two-thirds of the space and I'm clinging to the side. Which is very similar to the way things were with Jeff, actually.

* * *

I woke up as the gray dawn light began to filter in through the rose-colored dotted swiss curtains over the bedroom window. I could hear the patter of raindrops against the glass. Albert was sprawled out on the other side of the bed snoring.

And then I heard voices coming from the living room. Instantly I was on alert, although Albert continued to slumber. Two men were arguing. They spoke so rapidly, I couldn't make out their words. But their voices were rising in volume.

Who were they? What did they want? How did they get in? I didn't remember locking the door the night before, but surely Pepe would have alerted me if intruders had come into the house. And why wasn't Pepe barking? He barked once yesterday, why not now when it counted? Then I thought about how very small he was. It would be easy for a burglar to hurt him, kill him even. Maybe that's why he hadn't barked.

I leaped out of bed.

Chapter 6

Pulling on my bathrobe, I looked around for a weapon. The only thing I could find that seemed useful was a bottle of hair spray from the bathroom counter. I grabbed a nail file, too, just in case. Then I slipped through the door and whisked around the corner, hoping to surprise whoever was in the living room.

I was the one who was surprised. The living room was empty, except for Pepe. He was sitting on the chocolate brown sofa, directly in front of the TV, which was turned on to the Spanish channel.

He looked up at me and said, "Do you think Conchita will ever find true love with Hector?"

I was so relieved that I almost dropped the hair spray. Pepe had somehow switched on the TV and was watching a soap opera.

"You scared me to death," I told him.

"*Shhhhh!*" he said, turning back to the TV. "This is a juicy part. I do not want to miss it."

I was about to ask how he managed to get the TV

going, when I noticed the remote control on the carpet. He must have knocked it off the end table and manipulated it with his paws.

On the screen, a lovely woman wearing a tight red satin dress was pressing herself against a dangerous-looking dude with a mullet and a leather jacket.

"*Oooo*," said Pepe, looking up at me again. "I told you it was going to be good. Sit down, Geri, watch the show with me. They are playing two episodes back to back."

"I need some coffee," I told him.

"*Bueno*," he said. "Make your coffee and come back. I will fill you in on what has happened so far. *Paraiso perdido* is not to be missed."

I'd been wrong: today *was* starting out as crazy as yesterday. But I was too tired to worry about it. I made some coffee, extra strong, and then sat down to watch the Spanish soaps with Pepe.

"You just missed the end of part *uno*," he told me. "While the commercial is on, I will catch you up. Here is what happened. The beautiful Conchita was upset because handsome Hector did not invite her to the big dance as she expected, so she fell into the arms of Armando, the dangerous hombre with the mullet, to get back at Hector. At the end, Conchita was slow dancing with Armando, but secretly yearning for Hector, who was deep in the arms of Consuela, while he secretly yearned for Conchita. You follow?"

"Yes, I get it."

"OK. Get ready, it is coming on again." He

hopped into my lap and made himself snug and cozy in the folds of my bathrobe, settling down with his ears perked forward. "Part *dos* is the finale. It promises to be *muy dramático*."

The finale was *muy* dramatic. Hector asked Conchita to dance with him, but Armando objected. They got into a fight, and luckily Hector prevailed. But not Conchita. A ricocheting gunshot struck her down, and she died in Hector's arms, with one last, lingering kiss.

Pepe gave a deep sigh. "Of course, she is not really dead," he said.

"She looks pretty dead to me," I said, as the camera panned in on her pale face, and Hector's hand, as he gently drew her eyelids down over her staring eyes.

"No, the show cannot go on without Conchita. Believe me, next season it will be revealed that she was rushed to the hospital and saved by the handsome new gringo doctor. Meanwhile, Hector, believing she is dead, will kill Armando and go to jail." He jumped off my lap and went into the kitchen, sniffing his empty food dish.

I opened the refrigerator door to get the Alpo.

"Speaking of jail," said Pepe, "how did you escape? I heard the police say they were going to take you there. Are you a fugitive now? That would be *muy dramatico!*"

"No, I'm not a fugitive," I said. "And how do you know what the police were saying?"

Pepe sat down and gave me a chiding look with his big brown eyes. "Geri," he said, "are we not partners? I stayed near the scene of the crime so I could investigate."

"OK," I said, as I spooned the Alpo into the bowl. "What did you find out?"

"I found out there was a bitch in the car," Pepe said.

I was so startled I almost dropped the spoon. "Pepe, I know Mrs. Tyler wasn't a very nice woman but that's not an appropriate word to use."

"No, not the woman," he said impatiently. "A she-dog. A bitch. Is that not the right term?"

"Oh, yes," I said.

"Do you not think that is unusual?" Pepe asked. "Why take her dog along if she was going away for a week? And how did she know her husband was missing, if she was gone?"

"Good questions," I said, putting the dish of Alpo on the floor in front of him.

"You know, Geri," said Pepe, looking up at me, "I prefer bacon for breakfast."

"You can prefer anything you want," I said. "But I'm a vegetarian. No bacon in this house."

"I suppose I should be glad you don't try to make me a vegetarian," Pepe grumbled. He took a few licks, then walked away. "Caprice tried that."

"Caprice?"

"*Sí*, Caprice Kennedy."

"The famous actress?"

"*Sí*," Pepe sat down by the refrigerator and chewed on his hind leg.

"You know Caprice?"

"I lived with her for a year."

"Wow! That must have been awesome," I said. Caprice was one of my favorites among the young L.A. actresses. She had blond hair and big brown eyes and a talent for comedy. She was always playing a goofball or a ditz.

"*Sí*," said Pepe. "She took me everywhere with her. I had my own chef and chauffeur and a maid to . . ." His voice trailed off.

"To what?"

His voice was more subdued. "Dress me. She liked to dress me up in little outfits. You would never do that to me, would you, Geri?"

What could I say? I was so tempted. But I had to respect his wishes. "Of course not, Pepe."

"It is not dignified for a dog to be dressed up like a doll. Or a cat." He said that just as Albert strolled into the kitchen looking for his own breakfast. Despite his earlier rejection of the Alpo, Pepe now went over to stand in front of it. Albert just made an expressive sniff and walked on by.

"What happened to Caprice?" I asked. "Why don't you still live with her?"

"I don't want to talk about that," Pepe said. He sounded like his little heart was going to break.

"OK, we won't talk about it," I said, although I was dying to know the inside scoop on Caprice Kennedy's life. Did she really date Justin Timberlake? Was it true she had been in rehab five times? "Did you see anything else while you were investigating?"

"Oh, yes," said Pepe, perking up a little. "I sniffed around the perimeter of the house. There was a horrible smell underneath a bush along the side of the house. Do you think it came from the murderer?"

"I don't know Pepe. I suppose the murderer could have been lurking in the back yard, waiting for Mr. Tyler to come home."

"Well, it was an awful smell, something like a cat box." Pepe glanced at Albert who had jumped up onto the cushions of the breakfast nook and was preening himself. "I would recognize it anywhere. Can we go back and look at the crime scene? I will show you what I discovered. And maybe we can talk to that bitch—I mean, female dog."

Chapter 7

"Are you not ready?" asked Pepe, coming into the bedroom where I was sitting at my makeup table. I have one of those old-fashioned make-up tables, with a circular mirror and two drawers on either side. It fits perfectly in my bedroom, which I've decorated in a thirties theme, complete with a pink chenille bedspread on my bed and ruffled, dotted swiss curtains.

"I'm just doing my lipstick," I told him. "We'll go in a minute. Don't be so impatient."

"So you keep saying." He cocked his head to the side and studied me. "May I offer a suggestion, Geri?"

"Sure."

"I think that color is wrong for you."

"What color?"

"Your lipstick."

I glanced in the mirror. It was a slightly darker red than I normally used, but I thought it looked just fine.

"How would you know?" I told him. "Dogs are color-blind."

"Not so," he responded. "We see many colors."

"OK," I said. "Prove it. What color is my lipstick?"

"Black."

"*Black*?" I had to laugh. "It's *red*, Pepe. *Red.*"

"Oh, *sí,*" he said, somewhat sheepishly. "It is hard for me to tell the difference between those two colors."

I went to my closet to find a coat to go with the plaid dress I was wearing. I chose one of my favorite Value Village finds—an A-shaped red cloth coat—and pulled it on. Pepe watched me, his head cocked.

"The silhouette is all wrong! The A-shape does not flatter you."

"You're as bad as Jeff!" I said, annoyed. I studied myself in the circular mirror. It looked fine to me.

"Who is this Jeff?" he asked. "Is he another animal you have concealed from me?"

"Jeff's my ex-husband," I said. "He was always telling me what I should and shouldn't wear. That's why I got rid of him."

Pepe trembled. "So you would throw me out for offering constructive criticism?" he asked in a small voice. "As you did with this Jeff?"

"Oh, Pepe, don't worry!" I said. "I didn't really throw Jeff out." My voice quivered a little, too. "He actually broke up with me!"

"*Pobrecíta!*" said Pepe. "You have been abandoned, but I have adopted you. You will never be alone again. I will never desert you, no matter how you dress."

"That's very sweet, Pepe," I said bending down to kiss him right between his ears. I left a little lipstick smudge. "*Gracias.*"

"*Da nada,*" he replied. "And I will do my best not to offer any unsolicited advice on fashion. Even though I was well known in Beverly Hills as a fashionista."

"A fashionista? You?" I had to laugh again.

"I know all the shops on Rodeo Drive," he said with dignity. "Caprice took me with her whenever she went shopping. All the designers knew me. They catered to me. They knew I could make or break them."

"How was that?"

"I was the one who made the decisions. They would hold up two choices and I would point with my paw. I chose the dress Caprice wore on the red carpet at the Oscars!"

"Wow!" I said, remembering that dress, a frothy white concoction that made her look like she was emerging half naked from sea foam. "Fashionista, bullfighter, drug dog, search-and-rescue dog—is there anything you *haven't* been in your short life?"

"Well," he said, "I have not yet been an astronaut."

"Well, if you don't get out of here, I'll launch you into outer space right now." I made as if to kick him with my foot.

"The boots are wrong, too!" he said, as he scooted out the door.

Perhaps he was right. My bright red cowboy boots might be too whimsical for a confrontation with Jimmy Gerrard. I had placed a call to him right after breakfast and told him I needed to meet him in his office, first thing this morning. He agreed to meet me at ten. I decided to change into my black leather boots and my gray wool coat. A little more subdued than my usual look but Pepe approved when I emerged from the bedroom.

"*Me gusta* very much," he said.

Pepe made a beeline for the front door, where he danced on his hind legs and scratched at it. As I unlocked the door, Pepe turned around to glare at Albert, who was sitting on top of the sofa. "You'll get yours, *gato*," Pepe said, then barked twice for emphasis.

Albert was unfazed. His only response was to lift one of his huge forepaws, spread it wide, extending his long sharp claws, and calmly clean between his toes.

It was raining fairly hard when we got to the car. Hard enough, in fact, that it made the day seem colder than it actually was. I cursed a little under my breath as I fumbled in my purse for the car keys.

"Don't be peeing on my tire again," I told Pepe.

"*¡Madre de dios!*" he said, dripping and shivering beside me on the parking strip. "That is the last thing on my mind. It is too wet to add to it."

He settled into the passenger seat and shook himself off, spraying me and the upholstery and dashboard in the process.

"Good grief," I said, brushing at the water he got all over me. "Why couldn't you do that outside?"

"Because it is wet outside."

Well, duh, I thought. Unable to argue with his logic, I started the car.

Chapter 8

We found parking on Stewart Street near the old Camlin Hotel. It was an older area, about five blocks east of downtown proper, which had been undergoing a lot of renovation before the Great Recession hit. Now it was a wasteland of stalled construction projects and empty lots. The Hidalgo Building, which housed the Gerrard Agency, was the only building still occupied. Brick, with soot-stained terra-cotta trim, it looked like it had been due for a facelift for decades.

"That is a sad-looking building," said Pepe, standing up at the passenger window, his forelegs on the armrest. "Are you sure this is the right place?"

"This is where I came for my interview," I told him.

"It is kind of a dump. It makes me wonder how successful is this private investigating business."

"Lighten up" I said, trying to stay positive. "You better hope it's successful enough to keep you in dog food."

"Oh," said Pepe. "That is a point well taken."

* * *

The long halls inside the building were covered in carpet with a dizzying geometric pattern of gray and blue, which showed the faint impressions of old water stains. Pepe trotted by my side, sniffing along the edges of the walls and under the doors.

The building seemed to be empty, although there were signs on the frosted glass of the doors advertising the offices of a tax preparer, an importing firm, and something called Center Star Productions. But I heard no voices, saw no lights. The office of the Gerrard Agency was on the third floor at the end of the hall.

Jimmy Gerrard was on the phone when I burst into his office.

"Do you realize the trouble I'm in because of you?" I asked.

He put the receiver down quickly. He had been leaning back in his chair, his feet up on the desk, but now he sat up straight and put his feet on the floor.

"Hey, doll! Don't get all hot and bothered," he said. "Jimmy G. hates to see a pretty dame all upset."

He dressed like a private eye from the forties. He wore a brown herringbone sport coat with wide lapels over a blue-and-white-striped shirt and a fat tie adorned with a pinup girl, her legs in the air. There was a yellow stain, which I hoped was mustard, on the arm of his coat. The open sport coat also revealed a tan leather shoulder holster, worn on his left side, with the grip of a huge pistol sticking out of it. A tan trench coat hung on the back of the door.

Somewhere in his forties, he had a dark, pencil-thin mustache and black hair, greased up and combed straight back under a brown felt fedora that was tilted back on his head. He wasn't hand-some, wasn't ugly, was just rough-looking—the kind of rough-looking that might be attractive if you were in the right mood. Maybe after spending all af-ternoon drinking in a dive bar.

His big brown eyes bulged a little, making him look a bit like a toad. Or maybe a Chihuahua? I looked back and forth between him and Pepe. Pepe was definitely cuter.

"What the hell is that?" he said, squinting at Pepe who stood beside me.

"That's my dog, Pepe," I said. "Pepe, Jimmy Ger-rard, my supposed boss."

"Now wait a minute, kiddo," said Jimmy. "Jimmy G. is not your boss."

"How can you say that?" I asked. "You sent me out on an assignment because you were in Port-land. On a case."

"Oh, yeah, Portland," he said. He searched around on his desk for a pen. The surface was covered with papers, newspapers, paper bags, paper cups, and an ashtray containing the end of a big, fat cigar. "Let Jimmy G. make a note of that before he forgets." He pawed through the papers but couldn't seem to find what he was looking for.

Pepe clawed at my leg. "Stop it, Pepe!" I said.

"Looks like a rat," said Jimmy, getting up and

peering over the edge of his desk. "What kind of
dog is that anyway?"

"He's a Chihuahua," I said.

"Ha, that explains it," he said. "Jimmy G. heard
Chihuahuas were the result of crossbreeding between a rat and a dog. Kind of hard to imagine, a
dog wanting to hump a rat, but Jimmy G. supposes
that might happen in Mexico."

Pepe began growling. I'd never heard him growl
before. It was a menacing sound, though small.

"Be quiet," I said, though secretly I approved of
his disapproval. I was getting a different picture of
Jimmy G. with Pepe at my side. I picked Pepe up,
hoping that would stop his growling. It helped a
little—his growling was more subdued—but he
kept his eyes trained on Jimmy G.

It was obvious that Jimmy G.'s gray metal desk
was purchased from Boeing Surplus and the credenza against the wall (also heaped with papers)
was one of those cheap knockoffs one could buy at
any furniture warehouse. The blinds on the window
behind the desk were caked with dirt. There was an
aquarium in whose cloudy water I could see a few
rather large goldfish. The air stank of stale cigar
smoke.

"What you really need," I said, looking around,
"is one of those desk lamps with a green shade."

"Hey, thanks!" Jimmy G. said. "You've got good
taste, doll!"

"What can I say?" I responded. "I'm a stager."

Jimmy G. looked puzzled.

I was just about to explain my job, how I prep

homes for sale to make them more attractive to prospective customers, when Pepe whispered in my ear, "Ask him why he sent you to the Tyler house!"

"Oh, yes," I said. The purpose for my visit. "Why did you send me to the Tyler house?"

"Because Rebecca Tyler called Jimmy G. and asked Jimmy G. to find her missing husband."

Pepe whispered in my ear again. "Then why did she say she didn't know you?"

I repeated his question to Jimmy. "Then why did she say she had never heard of me?"

Jimmy's big brown eyes got bigger, and his face turned red. "Why do women act the way they do? It's a mystery to Jimmy G."

Pepe prompted me again. "Ask him how she knew her husband was missing if she was out of town."

"How did Rebecca know her husband was missing if she was out of town?"

Jimmy held out his hands, as if appealing to me to be reasonable. "How would Jimmy G. know?" he asked. I saw a stray thought cross his face. One thing I will say about Jimmy was that you could read emotions in his face more clearly than you could see fish in his aquarium. He would be a lousy poker player. "Ah, the mystery is solved!" he declared. "Jimmy G. wraps up another case."

"What are you talking about?"

"Don't you see? Rebecca went out of town after she called Jimmy G., thus when Jimmy G. called her back to set up the appointment, and left a message on her phone informing her that a certain Miss, uh, Miss . . ."

"Sullivan," I said in as icy a voice as possible.

"Miss Sullivan would be coming to interview her, she didn't get the message, thus she denied having an appointment with said Miss Sullivan." His face brightened.

"But why go out of town if her husband was missing?" I asked.

"Good one, Geri," said Pepe in my ear.

Jimmy's face fell again, then brightened. "Maybe she was already out of town but couldn't contact him. Thus she contacted Jimmy G. to track him down."

Unfortunately that did make sense.

"What's all this about you not actually hiring me?"

Jimmy's face fell. He looked like a school boy who was about to be scolded. "That's what Stewart wants me to say," he said.

"Why can Stewart tell you what to do?"

"He's my older brother," Jimmy's voice lost volume and confidence as he spoke. "He's the one who actually owns the agency."

"And?"

"Well, he claims I didn't have the authority to hire you. He has to be involved in any personnel decisions."

"Well, let's go see him," I said. "I want to get this cleared up right away, before the police call me in for questioning again. Do you realize they consider me a murder suspect?"

"But if you didn't do it . . ." Jimmy squinted. "You didn't do it, did you?"

"Don't be ridiculous," I almost shouted. "Why do all of you assume I would murder a complete stranger?"

"Tell him the man was killed long before you came on the scene," Pepe whispered in my ear.

"Besides the man was murdered long before I arrived on the scene."

"How do you know that?" Jimmy asked, He looked startled and upset. Maybe he was beginning to realize I was a good detective.

"How do I know that?" I asked Pepe.

"Are you talking to your dog?" Jimmy asked.

I gave him a bright smile. "It helps me problem solve," I said. "You know, talking out loud."

Pepe whispered in my ear. "Because of the rigor mortis, the dried blood, the smell!" he shuddered. "*Muy muerto!*"

"Let's put it this way, he was *muy muerto!*" I said to Jimmy.

Jimmy looked thoughtful. "Perhaps you set this up so you would have an alibi," he suggested.

"Perhaps you are trying to frame me," I replied.

"Why would I do that?" Jimmy G. scratched the back of his head.

"Never mind," I said. It was hard to believe this man had the brains to come up with such a scheme. Which made me wonder why I worked for him. But then again, apparently I didn't. "Let's go talk to Stewart and get this straightened out," I said.

Jimmy G. grinned sheepishly. "Stewart definitely

wants to see you. Came by this morning to tell me so. But you'll have to go alone."

"Why is that?"

"Stewart asked to see you, not Jimmy G. Fine with Jimmy G."

"Why is that?"

"Stewart's rude. Bossy. Thinks he knows best. Everything Jimmy G. does is wrong. Jimmy G. can't do anything right. Just because he's my older brother . . ." He realized he was babbling and stopped. "Didn't you say you had an older sister?" It was one of the many odd questions he had asked at my interview.

"Yes, I do," I said. I didn't want to think about Cheryl right now. She certainly wouldn't approve of my new job. Or my current predicament. In fact, she never approved of anything I did.

"So you probably understand," Jimmy G. said.

I nodded. An older sibling never loses the desire to boss a younger sibling around. "By the way, there's a pen under that pile of papers." I pointed to a stack that was about to slide off the corner of the desk.

"Oh, thanks!" Jimmy looked pleased as he located the pen, then puzzled as he stared at it. "Now why did I want that?"

"To make a note."

He frowned. "About what?"

"Portland."

"What about Portland?"

"That's where you were when Rebecca Tyler contacted you."

"Oh, yeah!" He grabbed the pen and scribbled a few words on a scrap of paper he tore from a paper bag. "Hey, you're good. Good observation. Good memory. Good attention to details." He leaned back in his chair and crossed his fingers over his stomach. "Jimmy G. needs a girl Friday." His voice fell. "My brother stole my last one." His voice rose again. "She was a real pistol. Took dictation. Rubbed my shoulders. Brought me drinks. Bourbon, straight up, no ice! How about it?"

"No way," I said. I had promised myself I would never work as a secretary again after putting my ex-husband through business school. "Anyway, the correct term nowadays is administrative assistant."

"So would you be my administrative assistant?" Jimmy G. asked. Was that sarcasm I heard?

"No," I said sharply. "I applied for a job as an investigator."

"Oh, yeah," he said. "And speaking of that, I've got something that will be just up your alley. Got a call just this morning from a prospective client. Want to go out on another assignment for Jimmy G.?"

"I don't know," I said. "I'm still in trouble because of the last assignment you sent me on. Plus I haven't been paid."

"Hey, no problem!" he said. He wriggled around in his chair and pulled a fat billfold out of his back pocket. He flipped it open and pulled out a huge wad of bills. Jimmy peeled off six hundred dollar bills and held them out to me.

"Five hundred for the Tyler case. And a hundred dollar advance for the new gig," he said.

"Bacon!" breathed Pepe in my ear.

I put my hand out to take the bills, then drew my fingers back. "What about Stewart?" I asked. "Don't you have to get his approval to send me out on a case?"

"Screw Stewart," he said. "He might own the agency but I'm the one running it. We'll just say you are working for Jimmy G. under the table." And he winked at me. "You'll be a secret operative."

I wavered.

"Take it! Take it!" Pepe said.

"You're awfully greedy," I said to him.

"Geri," Pepe said, "I am only looking out for you."

"Are you talking to your dog again?"

"He seems to think it's a good idea." I held out my hand, and he counted the bills into it.

"There's $200 more for you, in cash, the day the case is solved," Jimmy said.

"What's the case?" I asked.

"Oh, it's simple," Jimmy said. He started pawing through the papers on his desk. "Here it is!" He pulled out another scrap of paper. "Some old broad at a retirement home. Name is Mrs. Snelson. Here's the address." He handed it over. "A neighbor's dog is ruining her flower beds. She wants photos of the dog running around loose so she can report it to the authorities."

"We can do it, Geri!" Pepe said.

"Yes, we can," I replied.

* * *

Outside the office I set Pepe down again.

"Nice work, Geri," said Pepe, swaggering a little as we walked down the hall. "We can buy mucho bacon with that money. And the case is right up our alley. This will be easy work for Sullivan and Sullivan, Private Investigators."

Chapter 9

"You know, Geri," said Pepe, as we drove away, "you should have gotten something in writing."

"What do you mean?"

"It is something I learned from watching Court TV," he said. "You must always get it in writing. Then if Jimmy G. does not pay you, you can take him to small claims court. Maybe you could even appear on *Judge Judy*."

"That's a good point, Pepe," I said. "I'll ask for something in writing next time. But for now, I guess I'll just have to trust him."

Pepe was quiet for a few minutes. "Still, I think there is something rotten in Denmark."

I looked over at my little companion. "Pepe! You know Shakespeare?"

"Of course, I know Shakespeare," he said. "Are you suggesting I am not an educated dog?"

"Well, no—"

"That I do not have the intelligence to understand the words of the Immortal Bard?"

"Pepe, I—"

"Do you know that Chihuahuas have the highest brain to body ratio of any dog breed?"

"No, I didn't know that," I said. "Believe me, I was not impugning your intelligence. It was just that I didn't know you could read."

"Oh, I do not read," said Pepe. "How would I turn the pages of a book? I learn everything I know from watching the television. I find it *muy* informative."

I decided to ignore that comment. Pepe was quiet again, then said, "Still I think your boss is some kind of flim-flam man."

"Maybe," I said. "But he's the one keeping you in dog food right now, Pepe. So don't look a gift horse in the mouth."

"I am only a foot tall. That would be *muy difficil* for me to do." He looked up at me. "That was a joke, Geri. Get it?"

"Yes!" I laughed. He seemed pleased with himself. We needed the levity after everything that had been happening.

Jimmy G. told me that Stewart worked out of his home and gave me an address in Laurelhurst, a tony neighborhood north and east of the University of Washington. The leafy streets are lined with stern Tudors and proper brick houses set back on prim lawns bordered with perfectly trimmed laurel hedges.

I always get lost in Laurelhurst as all the streets twist and curve, no doubt in an effort to baffle those of us who don't belong there. I found the address on a street that backed up against Lake Washington. I pulled up in front of it and stopped, my breath taken away. Beside me, even Pepe was silent.

When he finally could speak, he said, "This is not a *casa*," he said. "This is a castle."

Castle was a great way to describe it. It was built entirely of dark gray stone, a building material rare in Seattle, where most buildings are made of brick or wood. It had a round tower with a conical roof and banks of mullioned windows under overhanging eaves. On one side, a wide driveway led to a three-car garage, each section with its own painted green door and gabled front. A serpentine slate path curved across a pristine green lawn and ended at a huge front door, which was barred and studded like the entrance to a medieval fortress. Two panels of stained glass framed the door: one depicted a spring orchard in bloom, the other an autumn woods. When I pushed the doorbell, I could hear sepulchral chimes echoing inside.

It was a long time before anyone answered. I don't know what I expected, perhaps a butler in evening dress or a housekeeper dressed all in black, but the person who answered the door was a lovely young woman, wearing a red, silk blouse and a tight, black pencil skirt that showed off her slim waist and long legs.

I introduced myself and Pepe, who was shivering beside me.

"Oh, this will not do!" she said firmly. "You cannot bring a dog into the house. Stewart is terribly allergic to dogs."

I couldn't afford to alienate my new boss, so I marched Pepe back to the car.

"You are not leaving me in the car, Geri," he said. "I need to be with you to advise you."

"I'm sure I can do fine on my own," I said.

"You saw how useful I was back at Jimmy G.'s office," he pointed out.

He had a good point. "Perhaps I can conceal you in here!" I pointed to my purse. It was my favorite bag: made of brown leather studded with gold brads, almost the size of a briefcase, and fairly sturdy.

"Geri, that is most undignified," he said.

"Yes, but that is the only way I'll take you with me," I said.

"Oh, very well," he stepped in as delicately as a princess, lifting his little paws high.

"Ow! Ow! Ow!" he cried. "Geri, you have many things in here that hurt!"

I pulled out my hairbrush, which seemed to be the most offensive item, and a few other nonessentials, tossing them onto the passenger seat.

"That is somewhat better," Pepe conceded. I pushed him down, slung the purse over my arm, and clamped it to my side, then hurried back to the door.

The young woman was still waiting for me. She was stunning, with long, dark hair, chopped off at shoulder length so it swung forward with the gleam and bounce I had only seen in shampoo commercials. Her nails were a bright red and so were her lips. She said her name was Mandy and she was Stewart's personal assistant.

She led me down a hallway paneled in oak, her heels clicking on the slate floor. The hallway opened up into a vast room with beamed ceilings easily three stories high. There was a huge fireplace built out of river rock in which the flames of a gas fire danced behind glass. On either side, floor-to-ceiling windows offered a view of the dark blue waters of Lake Washington.

"This is the great room," she said. Of course, it was a great room. I really hated that term. So pretentious.

The room was filled with rustic couches and armchairs plump with big cushions in a Southwest pattern. I could tell by looking at them that they were leased. All the seating faced a side wall on which hung a huge projection screen and, in front of that, a lectern stood.

"This is where Stewart does his presentations," she said. "But he'll see you in his office."

She took a turn to the right, and we headed down a flight of carpeted stairs. Stewart's office had the same incredible view as the upstairs room, but his desk faced into the room so when he sat at his desk, the light reflected off the lake seemed to frame him in a bright halo.

He stood up and came forward as Mandy ushered me in. Where Jimmy G. tried to project an aura of tough private dick, Stewart was the consummate gentleman. He wore a crisp, white long-sleeved shirt, a narrow tie with chevrons of maroon and gray, and a pair of flawlessly fitted gray wool pants. As he took my hand and patted it with his own, I got a chance to observe the silver Rolex on his wrist. It echoed the hint of gray in his sideburns.

The two brothers were certainly a study in contrasts. Where Jimmy G.'s face was round and ruddy, Stewart's face was tan and square. Jimmy G. had tobacco-stained snaggle teeth, while Stewart's teeth were perfect, straight, and flashing in a wide, white smile.

"What happened?" I asked, as I sank down into the green leather chair that Mandy indicated with a wave of her hand before leaving the room. "Your parents could only afford braces for one of you?"

I put my purse down on the matching chair beside me. I saw it wiggle slightly as Pepe got comfortable. I could even hear his mumbling inside. But I didn't think Stewart noticed. He was too busy assessing me.

"You do have good powers of observation," he said. "James told me that's why he hired you."

That made me feel good. Jimmy G. hadn't told me that when he hired me.

"I'm surprised, really," said Stewart. "My brother is not known for his good taste."

I wasn't sure what to make of that. After all, Jimmy G. had hired me. On the other hand, I had to agree with Stewart. I decided to take it as a compliment. "Thank you," I said.

I realized Stewart's desk was elevated on a dais, so I had to look up at him. The ceiling was low and crossed with massive beams. The lighting was low, too, with a few recessed spotlights here and there around the edges of the room. The whole effect was of old wealth. All the details were correct—an oak bookcase full of leather-bound volumes, dark blue oriental rugs, hunter green wallpaper hung with oil paintings of dead animals: a brace of pheasants, a limp rabbit.

Stewart continued to study me, with his fingers pressed together in a steeple and his lips slightly pursed.

"You look like an intelligent young woman," he said. "Why are you working for my brother?"

Again, with the compliment and the insult in the same sentence.

"It seemed like a good opportunity," was all I said. I was not about to explain my desperation. My purse started to wiggle off the chair, and I grabbed at it before it fell to the floor. I could just imagine what Pepe would have to say about that. I put it on my lap instead. Unfortunately, this meant I could hear Pepe's muffled comments.

"I have discovered I am claustrophobic," he said.

"Well, I understand you've gotten yourself mixed up in a homicide investigation," Stewart said with a frown.

Yes," I said. "And I really appreciate your sending a lawyer to get me out of the police station."

"Get me out of here!" said Pepe.

"It's the least I can do," he said. "I feel personally responsible."

"You do? Why?"

"Well, you wouldn't have been there if James had not sent you. And since James works for me, well, you became my responsibility."

"So you own the detective agency?"

"Yes, it's one of my many enterprises," Stewart said. "Frankly, it's just a way to keep James occupied. And he is not supposed to hire any employees without first notifying me. We have to make sure the paper work is correct. He did have you fill out the proper forms, didn't he?'

Actually Jimmy G. hadn't asked me to fill out anything.

Stewart noticed my hesitation. "I can see that he did not." He picked up a file folder on his desk, and put it down precisely at right angles to another folder. "It doesn't matter. We can take care of that this afternoon. Mandy has all the forms you need." He moved the folder again, lining it up with the edges of the desk. "Of course, we will need a copy of your resume as well. I assume you have some experience."

"No, not really," I said.

"Tell him you have a partner," Pepe said from inside my purse.

"How about training?"

"Tell him you are working with a trained professional!" Pepe insisted.

Stewart frowned and looked at my purse.

"Your purse seems to be talking," he said.

"Oh!" I gave a carefree little laugh. "I must have left my cell phone on. Sometimes it does that. I'll just check to be sure it's turned off." I peered inside my purse and shook my finger at Pepe. "Be quiet!" I whispered.

"I hope you understand," Stewart was saying, "that we cannot take any responsibility for your actions until we have received all the necessary documentation, completed a background check, processed your forms, and made sure you have the appropriate training. You do realize that training is required by the state? I'm sure the police covered that in their interview."

"Not really," I said, though it helped explain some of their questions. I wondered if they could arrest me for practicing investigating without a license.

"Do they seem to have a suspect?"

"Tell him we think it is the wife!" said Pepe. "It is always the spouse."

"Not that I can tell," I said. "But it seems to me the wife is the obvious suspect."

"But then why would she call my brother and ask him to look for her husband?" Stewart asked.

"Because she wanted someone else to find the body while she was out of town," Pepe suggested.

"Because she wanted someone else to find the body while she was out of town," I repeated.

"Well, if that's the case, I suppose the police will wrap up this investigation quickly, and you will be in the clear."

Stewart stood up. Apparently I was about to be dismissed. I stood up, too, clutching my wriggling purse.

"Meanwhile we must see that you get some training."

"But—"

"I understand the UW offers a certificate program through the continuing education department."

"I would love to take that, but I just don't have the funds right now—"

"Oh, don't worry about that," Stewart said, coming around from behind his desk. Again, he took my hand in his, and patted it with his other hand. It would have been a comforting gesture except his hands were unpleasantly warm. "I'll have Mandy set it up. We will, of course, be happy to pay for your tuition."

"That's very generous," I said.

"You have to spend money to earn money. That's what I always say." Stewart held the door open for me. I tried to squeeze by without getting my purse too close to him. Nonetheless I saw his nose begin to wrinkle. "I can tell you're going to be a valuable employee." He gave me a wink, and then the door slammed behind me. A few moments later I heard him sneeze.

* * *

"He's hiring you?" Mandy sounded both shocked and horrified. She had her own desk in a cubbyhole of a room across the hallway from Stewart. Her view was not as stunning as his. She looked out on a bank of tall juniper hedges that made the room seem dark and cold.

I had obviously interrupted her in the middle of a phone call. She was holding the receiver to her ear.

"Not exactly," I said.

"Then what did he mean by that?" she asked. I could hear a tinny voice jabbering on the phone.

"I don't know." It was puzzling.

"I think he recognizes your talent, Geri!" Pepe said.

I beamed. It's really nice to have your dog believe in you. Or, wait a minute, was that sarcasm?

"Look, I can't talk right now!" Mandy said into the phone. "Call me back in ten minutes." She slammed down the receiver. Her desk was bare except for the telephone and a gold pen. Either she was an efficient secretary or she didn't have much work to do. There was not a scrap of paper in evidence anywhere.

"He said you could give me some personnel forms," I said.

"That can't be!" she said with a frown. "We're not hiring anyone. He would have told me if we were."

"I'll be working for the Gerrard Detective Agency," I said.

"Oh!" She sounded relieved. The tension left her shoulders. "Good luck with that!"

She got up and rooted around in a tall metal file cabinet in the corner and then handed me a sheaf of papers. "You can fill them out and mail them back to me. Or drop them by."

"Stewart said you could enroll me in a training program through the UW," I said.

"Oh, really!" She sounded amused. "Like you will last long enough to make that worthwhile."

"What do you mean?" I asked.

"Jimmy G. goes through employees like"—she paused, looking for a good metaphor—"like he goes through money at the racetrack. If it wasn't for Stewart bailing him out constantly, he'd be on the streets. I don't think he's ever closed a case. And the longest anyone ever worked for him was—let me think—two and a half weeks."

I tried not to look dismayed. "How do you know that?" I asked.

"It was me," she said with a shrug. "Luckily after Stewart saw how well I was taking care of Jimmy, he decided he wanted me to work for him."

"So you were his girl Friday?"

"Oh, that's what he calls all his female employees," she said. "But he'll soon have you answering phones and typing up reports and taking out his trash."

"He's already sent me out on two cases!' I said proudly.

"Luring unfaithful husbands into compromising positions so Jimmy can take photos of them?" Mandy asked.

"No!" I frowned. Though frankly, I couldn't really brag about being asked to take photos of a dog in a compromising position. "Is that what you did for him?"

"Yes, that's Jimmy's specialty. Infidelity. Mostly wives who think their husbands are cheating. He would use the photos either to blackmail the husband or collect his fee from the wife, depending on which party had the most money."

"Very clever," said Pepe. "I would not have thought him capable of such a scheme."

"Oh," I said, "that sounds unethical to me."

"Totally," Mandy said. "That's why I was so glad Stewart hired me. He pays me twice as much and the work here is so much more uplifting. We're helping people live their dreams, not capitalizing on their misery."

Chapter 10

"Where are we going?" Pepe asked, as I pulled onto the freeway heading north. The rain had started again, and I turned on my windshield wipers.

"I figured we'd check out this Mrs. Snelson," I said.

Pepe protested. "You promised we would go back to the Tyler residence." He sounded wistful.

"I know," I said. "We'll swing by there later. I'm worried the police might still be on the scene collecting evidence, and I don't want to run into them again."

"Me neither," said Pepe with a shudder.

"Why is that, Pepe?" I asked.

"Geri, I bit one of them," he said. "They do not like me. Besides, they consider me evidence."

"That's right. I forgot," I said. "I suppose I should just head over to the police station and turn you in."

"What?" he yelled.

"Calm down," I told him. "That was a joke. I would never hand you over to the police."

"Bad joke," he said, with a shake of his head. "Not funny."

"Sorry, I couldn't resist."

"Absolutely, definitely, decidedly not funny," he muttered, lying down on the front seat. He was shivering slightly. Poor guy. I had no idea he'd take my idea of a joke so seriously.

I pulled off the freeway at the Green Lake exit. The road swerved under the freeway and then along a curved street with a broad, grassy median. Pepe sat up and looked around.

"Are we there yet?" he asked.

"Almost," I said. "We're a few blocks away."

"What is your plan, Geri?"

"My plan?"

"*Sí*, we must plan our operation. Are we going to question the suspect? Are we going to ambush this bad dog?"

"I think I need to get a little more information before I can decide on a plan," I said. "Though thanks for the suggestions." I was being sarcastic but he didn't seem to notice.

"We need to stop and get some supplies," Pepe said.

"Supplies?"

"*Sí*. It is *muy importante* to have food and drink in your car when on a stakeout."

"Why is that?"

"Geri, I am surprised at you. It is because stakeouts

can be long—very long, sometimes. One must eat after all."

"You're right," I said. I pulled into the parking lot of a convenience store.

"You've got to stay in the car," I told Pepe. "Dogs aren't allowed in grocery stores."

"An unenlightened society," mumbled Pepe. "In France, dogs can go everywhere. The bistro. The patisserie. The butcher shop." His dark little eyes seemed to glaze over with pleasure.

"How would you know that?" I asked. "TV again?"

"No, I have been to France," said Pepe. "I even *parler le Français. Et tu?*"

"Huh?" I could tell he was speaking French but had no idea what he said.

"*Quel dommage,*" he said. "We should go some day. I will show you all the best places."

"Sure, Pepe." I rolled down the window a little so he could get some air.

"Now stay low. I don't want someone stealing you."

"Get doughnuts," said Pepe. "The cops are always eating doughnuts. Also I would like some beef jerky. I love beef jerky. And some water. Not carbonated. I do not like fizzy water."

"Anything else?"

"That will do."

It took a little while before I gathered all the supplies Pepe had requested. I was standing in line to pay when I heard a commotion in the parking lot. Shouts. A spate of fierce, baritone barking. The screech of metal. And underneath that hubbub, some high-pitched frantic yapping.

"What's going on?" the checker asked a customer who was walking in, shaking his head.

"Dog fight in the parking lot," he said.

I threw my money at the cashier, grabbed my plastic bag, and flew out the door. A crowd was gathered around my car. When it parted I saw a young man in jeans and a black leather jacket holding the collar of a huge, gray Great Dane, who was lunging and jumping, trying to get at my car, where Pepe was pressed against the window barking like a maniac.

"Hey, what's going on?" I asked, shouldering my way through the crowd. "That's my dog."

"Oh, gee, I'm sorry," the guy said. He twisted around, trying to control his frenzied beast. "Sarge doesn't usually behave like this. I don't know what got into him."

I knew. I could hear Pepe shouting insults at the big dog. "*Cabrón!* You miserable excuse for a dog! Hiding behind your human! Come and get me! I can take you on!"

"Shut up!" I said to him. He continued his taunts. I was afraid to open the door, worried he'd jump out and tackle the monstrous beast.

"I'm sorry," the young man said. "We were just walking by and your dog started barking. Sarge went crazy. I've never seen him act like this."

"He wouldn't be doing that if you weren't acting like an idiot!" I said to Pepe.

The guy must have thought I was talking to him.

"Hey, I'm sorry," he said. "I just wasn't prepared for him to go off on me. He's actually a very shy dog. Let me give you my contact information. I think you're going to need some work on your car."

I could see the scratch marks where the Great Dane's claws had scraped off some of the paint. But they were nothing compared to the dings and rust spots on the body of my green Toyota. My car even had moss growing on the rubber around the windows.

"Really, it's not a big deal," I said. I stood with my back to the window so Pepe couldn't see the big dog. This seemed to calm them both down somewhat. Sarge stopped lunging and went and stood meekly behind his master.

"I'm Felix," he said, holding out a hand. His grasp was firm but warm. He had the same lean and muscled physique as his dog. And he looked a bit like the romantic hero on *Paraiso perdido*, with his high cheekbones, caramel-colored skin, and dark, wavy hair.

He pulled a card out of his pocket. "Here's my number." It read Felix Navarro, Dog Trainer and Animal Communication Specialist.

"You speak to dogs?" I asked. Had I found someone else who could hear what Pepe was saying? I could fall for him as hard as Conchita fell when the stray bullet struck her down. "Can you tell me what my dog is saying right now?"

Felix smiled. He had a great smile that lit up his whole face, which had been somber until that moment. "He's telling Sarge to stay away from his car."

Fair enough. He left out the swear words, but I think he got the message.

I dug around in my purse and pulled out one of my cards. It read GERI SULLIVAN, INTERIOR DESIGN AND HOME STAGING. Which reminded me I needed to get some new cards. Maybe, just to flatter Pepe, I would get a few that read SULLIVAN AND SULLIVAN, PRIVATE DETECTIVES.

"Here, you can call me," I said. "But I'm not worried about the damage. Really. It was all my dog's fault."

"He's a cute little fellow," said Felix. "I like Chihuahuas. They've got personality."

"Yes, he does have personality," I said, opening the door a crack. I threw in the plastic bag. Pepe flew to it and sniffed everything. That allowed me to squeeze myself in, as gracefully as I could with Felix watching me.

"I'll call you," he said.

"Good! I'll look forward to hearing from you." I gave him what I hoped was a bright smile and turned the car on. Pepe was tearing into the beef jerky and paid no attention to me whatsoever. It wasn't until we were parked outside the retirement home that I got his attention again.

"Why did you do that?" I asked.

"What?" he said. "I am only fortifying myself for the job ahead."

"No, not that. Yell at that big dog. He was twenty times your size."

"Geri," Pepe said solemnly, "it is my duty to protect you, and that means I must protect your property as well. That dog walked too close to your car. I had to warn him of the consequences. I simply did my duty."

"Pepe, it's not your job to protect me. I can take care of myself."

"So you say," he said. He went back to the beef jerky.

Chapter 11

Mrs. Snelson lived in a seven-story building designed for housing seniors. It was made of concrete, bristling with balconies, and was right across the street from Green Lake.

Green Lake is Seattle's most picturesque lake, a small, round jewel set in the heart of north Seattle and circled by a three-mile concrete pathway, always thronged with joggers and moms with strollers and dog walkers. On a summer day, it's impossible to find parking anywhere near the lake. Luckily this was not a summer day. The sky was gray, the air was moist, but no rain was falling.

Still I couldn't find parking directly in front of the building, so I pulled around to the side street. When I opened my door to get out, Pepe bounded over me and landed on the grass of the parking strip.

"Pepe," I said, "I can't take you into the building."

"Oh, you want me to stay and guard your car?" he asked, hopefully. He looked up and down the street, then strolled over to the edge of the parking strip and lifted his leg. "I will warn the other dogs that I am on patrol."

"No, I don't want you to guard my car," I said. I couldn't afford another dog-baiting incident. "Why don't you get back in the purse?" I held out my bag. It was still empty. I had not retrieved my personal items, which were now scattered all over the car, along with the plastic wrappers from the beef jerky.

"Very well," said Pepe. He seemed sulky but he stepped into it readily. I closed the flap and headed into the building.

I had to sign in at the reception desk and write down the name of the person I was visting and the reason for my visit. While I was doing this, Pepe stuck his head out of the top of my purse.

The woman behind the desk frowned. "Is that a real dog you have in there?"

Pepe looked quizzical. "What does she mean a real dog? Does she think I am a stuffed toy?" He wiggled his ears for emphasis.

"Oh, yes, he is," I said, trying to stuff Pepe back down.

"Is he a therapy dog?"

"*Sí*, I am a therapy dog," said Pepe.

"Yes, he is," I said.

"That's lovely. Our residents do so enjoy the companionship of animals. You know, studies show that contact with animals enhances emotional and psychological well-being."

"Oh, really?" I said, then remembered I was sup-posed to know this. "You can't believe what an amaz-ing impact he's had on my life. And I've only had him, I mean, I've only been working with him for a short time."

The woman glanced at the name I had written on the visitor's log.

"I'll just ring up Mrs. Snelson and let her know you're here," the woman said, setting Pepe down with a little pat on the head. "She's on the ground floor. Just go towards the elevators and turn right. You'll see her door at the end of the hall. Number 109."

"You see, Geri," Pepe said with some importance, as I stuffed him back into my bag. "All women find me irresistible."

I ignored him. "Are you really a therapy dog?" I asked.

"Don't I make *you* feel better?' he asked.

I sighed. But it was true. He did make me feel better.

The interior hallways were dim and quiet. The doors were painted dark blue and each one had been decorated by the tenant. Apartment 109 had a cheerful wreath of white and yellow plastic daisies. I rang the doorbell and a few minutes later Mrs. Snelson opened it.

She was a small woman, with curly white hair and rosy cheeks. She would have been my perfect picture of a grandmother, except for her attire—she wore pink overalls that were smeared with green and brown stains, and a pair of bright green rubber boots, decorated with frogs.

"My gardening attire," she explained, holding out a hand with a green glove on it, but then pulling it back when she realized the glove was covered

with dirt. "I was just out in the garden. Come in. I'll
show you the source of the problem."

It was clear she had an obsession and her obsession was plants. Her apartment was a jungle of
potted plants, so dense I had to stoop to get past
the fronds of the palms and push the tendrils of the
vines out of my way to get to the sliding glass door
and onto her patio. That, too, was crowded with
plants—pots stuffed with spiky grasses and hanging
baskets spilling over with colorful purple petunias
and red geraniums.

The patio looked out over the grassy hill on
which the building was perched. Mrs. Snelson was
slowly working her way outwards, creating curved
beds, filled with green shrubs and a few early flowers, daffodils with their fluted cups and a flock of
bright pink tulips. I imagined in a few years she
would have taken over the whole hill.

"This is my little yard," she said, picking up a
trowel from where she had left it. "It's all I have left
now. And this, this"—her voice quivered with rage
and the trowel in her hand shook—"is the problem!"
She waved the tool at a fluffy mound of dirt underneath a spindly rose bush.

I bent down to look at where she pointed and
saw a tower of calcified dog poop. By bending
down, I threw Pepe out of balance, and he tumbled
out of my bag. I grabbed for him but I was too late.
He landed with a little woof, then picked himself
up and shook himself off.

"Oh, you brought a dog with you!" Mrs. Snelson
said. "I can't stand them. Filthy creatures!"

"Hey!" said Pepe.

She twisted her lips contemplating him. "Anyway, it's not the dog that's the problem. It's the owner. She's an irresponsible young woman. Lets the dog out to do his business. He seems to think my flower beds are the best place."

"They are lovely flower beds," said Pepe, approaching the offending item and giving it a good sniffing.

"Stop that!" I said to Pepe.

"I am investigating, Geri," said Pepe.

"Well, don't," I said. "It's disgusting."

"It is disgusting," said Mrs. Snelson. "I called the police, and I called Animal Control, but they told me they can't do anything unless they catch the animal in the act. But by the time I call them, the dog is gone. Back hiding in his miserable home."

"Where does he live?" I asked.

Mrs. Snelson pointed to a little house just down the block. It was an anomaly among the pretty mansions that circle the lake. This one was obviously a duplex, with two doors side by side on the sagging front porch. It was a boxy wooden house in poor condition, the wood weathered, the paint faded to a mustard yellow. The yard was equally neglected; it was knee-high in weeds, mostly big dandelions.

"Renters!" said Mrs. Snelson with a huff.

"And what does the dog look like?" I asked.

"He's brown and gray with spots," said Mrs. Snelson. "About knee-high. He has a big head and a mouth full of fangs. That's all I know. I don't care for dogs."

"Does he always come over at a certain time of day?"

"No, not that I've noticed. His owner just opens the door and lets him out. And then when she wants him back, she calls his name."

"What's his name?" I asked.

"Bruiser. Or Loser. Or something like that."

Just then Pepe growled. It was a low but menacing sound. I looked up to see that the door of the mustard yellow house had opened and a brown and gray dog had rushed out. A young woman with purple hair, wearing only a large T-shirt and holding a coffee mug in her hand, stood in the doorway, watching as he headed down the steps. Then she shut her door.

We watched as the dog wandered around the yard, peeing on bushes. I took my phone out of my pocket and was ready, with my finger poised to take a picture, but Bruiser showed absolutely no interest in fouling Mrs. Snelson's flowers. I snapped a few photos of him just for practice while we waited.

"Oh, this is so frustrating," said Mrs. Snelson. "It's as if he knows we are watching for him." She stalked to the far edge of her property and glared at the dog.

"I think I can lure him here," said Pepe, who had been sitting quietly watching the whole time.

"Really?" I said. "How will you do that?"

"Watch and see," he said. He strolled out to the edge of the patio as Mrs. Snelson returned to my side.

Pepe began shouting at the dog. "Hey, Bruiser,

you really are a loser! You do not dare to step outside your little yard."

Bruiser looked up and seemed interested in what
Pepe was saying but he did not show any inclination
to head up the hill.

"I am free," said Pepe. "I can do as I please. Go
where I want." He strolled over to the corner of
Mrs. Snelson's flower bed and lifted his leg.

"Hey," said Mrs. Snelson, "stop that, you filthy
creature!"

Pepe looked offended. "I am just pretending,"
he said to me.

"He's just pretending," I told Mrs. Snelson.

She didn't seem to believe me. "I'm not sure this
is a good idea, after all," she said. "I didn't ask for
a detective with a dog. I wanted someone with a
camera."

"I have a camera right here!" I said, holding up
my little phone. "It takes pictures. We just have to
wait until the dog gets a little closer."

But Bruiser didn't move, despite Pepe's continuing taunts. We waited and waited. Bruiser lay down
on the porch and rested his giant head on his front
paws, his eyes trained on Pepe. My phone rang. It
was my best friend, Brad. He wanted to know when
he was going to meet my dog. I told him I was working and would come by later. Raindrops began to
fall, light at first, then gaining momentum. Mrs.
Snelson went into the apartment to get an umbrella.

"This is a very hard case," said Pepe. "It calls for
desperate measures." He walked out to the edge of
the garden and squatted down.

"See, you miserable Loser," he called out. "I will cover over your scent with my own. These will be my flower beds from now on."

Unfortunately, at that moment, Mrs. Snelson came running out of her apartment, moving quickly for a lady of her advanced age, and brought her umbrella down smack on the top of Pepe's head. He yelped and ran around in circles. I went to pick him up and dropped my phone, which rolled down the hill and into some bushes. While I was trying to find it, Bruiser left his porch and came creeping up the side of the hill. When I turned around, there was another steaming pile of dog poop in the flower bed, right next to Pepe's little offering.

Chapter 12

"How could you do that?" I asked Pepe as we drove away.

"I am sorry, Geri," Pepe said. "It was just a natural impulse. Once I started, I could not stop. Has that never happened to you?"

"Not exactly like that," I said.

"I will do better next time," said Pepe.

"There isn't going to be a next time," I said. Mrs. Snelson had made it clear that we were fired. Furthermore, she was going to call Jimmy G. and demand her deposit back. It looked like my career as a private investigator was already over.

"Surely you are not going to give up," Pepe said. "What do you think would have happened if I had given up when they said a Chihuahua couldn't participate in the Iditarod?"

"You never did that, Pepe!" I said.

"Of course, I did. I have done many marvelous things. More than you can imagine. But I would never have done any of them if I had given up when things got rough."

"I am happy for you," I said. "But that's not my MO." I'm the kind of person who *always* gives up when things get rough. I quit art school when my husband wanted to get an MBA. Then I had to drop out of interior design school when he wanted a divorce. I didn't even hire a lawyer, just accepted the settlement he proposed. And now I was about to give up on being a PI.

"That is why we are partners, Geri," said Pepe. "I will stick by you. We are going to go back, and we are going to catch that dog in the act."

"You might actually be a good influence on me," I said. I was being sarcastic but Pepe didn't notice that. He didn't seem to recognize sarcasm. At least, not when it applied to him.

"We must do a stakeout next time," Pepe said. "So Bruiser does not know we are watching."

"OK," I said. "A stakeout next time." That would solve one problem, since we also didn't want Mrs. Snelson to know we had returned. "Are you OK, Pepe? Did that old lady hurt you?"

"I endured much worse," said Pepe, "while performing in the Mexican circus. We will get that Loser. Do not worry, Geri!"

"I believe you," I said. Though I wasn't sure I believed he had ever been in a circus. "Now settle down."

"OK, OK," he said. "I am sorry. It has been a trying day so far." He lay down in his seat, saying, "Perhaps I need a short siesta."

"Good idea," I told him. "You rest while I drive."

"*Sí*," he said, curling up in the seat.

He was soon quiet and appeared comfortably asleep, except for occasional low growls, rapid movements of his eyelids, and twitching in his feet. I guessed he was dreaming about besting one of his adversaries. But which one? Sarge? Bruiser? Or Albert? Maybe all three.

Pepe woke up just as I was crossing over Lake Washington on the Evergreen Point Floating Bridge, which connects Seattle and Bellevue. It was a direction I don't go much anymore, although I used to live on the East Side when I was married. There is a natural rivalry between Seattle, the older city, and Bellevue, its glitzier upstart. I have friends in Seattle who have never been to Bellevue.

Unfortunately, the opposite is not so true. Because there are more jobs in Seattle, the traffic across the bridge slows to a crawl during rush hours. I was hoping to slip across and get back home before it got too bad.

Pepe looked around. "Where are we going? We are not anywhere near Mrs. Tyler's house."

"I owe my sister some money. I thought I'd drop it off before I spend it all buying you bacon."

"You have a sister, Geri?"

"Yes, her name is Cheryl."

"Do you think your sister will feed us dinner?" asked Pepe with a wistful note in his voice. "It is, after all, almost dinner time."

"It's always dinner time in your world," I pointed out.

"I am a dog," he said. "We like to eat."

"In answer to your question, no. My sister will probably not offer us dinner. And, even if she did, we wouldn't stay. She's probably fixing something disgusting like pot roast or steak."

"Steak!" murmured Pepe with a dreamy tone in his voice. "It has been ages since I had a nice, juicy steak." He glanced sideways at me. "I do not understand this human fascination for vegetables. You are omnivores, like dogs. You can eat everything. Why not eat everything?"

"I didn't really intend to become a vegetarian," I explained. "But after I read a book called *Eating Animals*, I couldn't eat meat any more." I looked over at him. "You know, the author mentions that in some cultures people eat dogs. And I read that some people believe Chihuahuas were originally raised to serve as food, just like guinea pigs."

"Geri!" said Pepe. "That is not funny!"

"I didn't mean it to be funny. I just meant to point out that different people have different attitudes about what is appropriate to eat. I would never eat a dog."

"That is good to know," said Pepe. When I didn't respond, he continued, "Geri, that was sarcasm!"

"Oh!" I said and gave a little, forced laugh.

"If I had been so particular when I was making my way across the great Sonoran Desert, I would have starved," Pepe said. "I subsisted on cactus and cockroaches."

"Ugh," I said. Then asked, "Why were you making your way across the great Sonoran Desert?"

"After my work exposing the head of a certain drug cartel, it became too dangerous for me to stay in Mexico. There was a bounty on my head. So I paid a coyote to smuggle me into this great country of the United States of America," said Pepe.

Since it was Pepe telling the story, I really didn't know if he meant a real coyote or a person. I thought it best not to inquire.

"But you must promise me you will tell no one. I do not wish to be deported."

"Don't worry, Pepe," I said. "As far as I know, we don't deport dogs. Just humans." That was meant to be sarcastic, but, as usual, sarcasm rolled right off him.

"*Bueno,*" he said.

"Wow!" said Pepe, as I pulled into the driveway of my sister's house.

My sister and her husband live in a new development in the Issaquah Highlands. The streets have names like Stonybrook and Fairmeadow, although there is not a meadow or a brook in sight. All of the houses are brand-new, multistoried with gables and porches, painted in discreet shades of brown and green, and stacked up next to each other like so much firewood.

"That is quite a house!" said Pepe.

"Really?" I was a bit miffed. I didn't think Pepe had very good taste if he was impressed by this monstrous McMansion. But then again I'd been in a million of these while working as a stager, and I knew how hard it was to give them any personality. I preferred the charm of my 1920s-era apartment.

"Wait in the car for me," I said. "I'll just be a minute."

"Oh, Geri," Pepe said, "please just let me out. I have to pee."

"OK, but not on my sister's lawn!" But it was too late. He jumped out the open door, ran across the tiny lawn, and lifted his leg on the rhododendron closest to the front door. At least they were acid-loving plants.

Naturally, at that moment, my sister opened the door to see who had driven into her driveway. She has one of those alarms that sounds a beep inside the house when anyone crosses her property line.

"Good afternoon, Geri's sister," said Pepe, running up to her, his little tail wagging. "Are you going to feed us? Please say yes."

"Shoo!" said my sister, flapping her hands at him. She had an apron tied around her waist. We had obviously interrupted her in the middle of preparing dinner. "Get out of here! Or I'll call Animal Control."

"Wait a minute, Cheryl," I said. "That's my dog!"

Cheryl frowned at me. "Since when do you have a dog?"

"I adopted him two days ago," I said. It was hard to believe I had only known Pepe for two days.

"Well, he can't come in. It's unsanitary," she said.

"Yum! I smell roast beef!" said Pepe, running into the house.

"Now where has he gone?" asked Cheryl, hurrying after him. "You know, we can't have a dog in the house."

I hurried after her. She was peering around the living room, which was crammed with the most hideous modern furniture, things she bought at a store named Furniture for Less. It was dim because she always keeps the blinds drawn ("for privacy"). You need privacy when your neighbors' windows are only one foot from yours.

"Where did he go?" asked Cheryl.

"Probably the kitchen," I said.

"Oh!" she said and hurried off in that direction. The kitchen was equally hideous (in my humble opinion). She had chosen a sunflower theme and everywhere you looked there were sunflowers—on the curtains, on the tiles, on the towels, even the plates. Pepe was standing in front of the oven, looking at it eagerly.

"Can I have some, please?" he asked.

I snatched him up. "I guess he's hungry," I said.

"Leave it to you to get a new mouth to feed when you can't even feed yourself," my sister said. "I suppose you're here to borrow more money."

"Not at all," I said. "I'm here to pay you back." I tucked Pepe under my arm while I pulled some bills out my purse. I counted out three one-hundred-dollar bills. Cheryl's jaw dropped.

"Where did you get this?" she asked.

"I have a new job," I said.

"What is it?"

"It's totally legitimate," I said

"So why aren't you telling me what it is?"

"OK," I said. "I'm working as a private investigator."

"Oh, Geri!" said my sister. "When will you get a real job?"

This was my sister's constant complaint. I never did anything right as far as she was concerned.

"It is a real job," I said. "I earned this money on my first day of work. And I just stopped by to give it to you. I should go now."

"Fine," said Cheryl, "but I hope you remember that I'm expecting you for dinner on Sunday."

"What?"

"It's Easter. Have you forgotten that as well?" Her tone was sharp. Cheryl still went to Mass every Sunday. She knew I had stopped going years before.

"Oh, yes. It's on my calendar," I said. It was. I just never checked my calendar any more since there was rarely any reason to do so.

"You could have brought the money then," she said. "It would have been more efficient."

"Yes, I should have," I agreed. It was always easier to agree with Cheryl than to argue with her. "Where are the kids?" I asked.

My sister had studied to be a dental hygienist but ended up never working in the field because she married a dental student she met while doing her training at the University of Washington's dental clinic. She got pregnant almost immediately (or perhaps slightly before the engagement—the timing was a little suspicious) and had been a stay-at-home mom ever since.

"Oh, the nanny took them to the park." Cheryl always has a college girl as a nanny; she rotates through them at the rate of one every few months. I wasn't sure who was harder on the nannies: Cheryl, who used them to do laundry as well as cleaning, shopping, and child care, or the kids, who could be holy terrors.

"Well, I'll see you on Sunday," I said, heading towards the door with Pepe in my arms. "Do you want me to bring anything?"

"Um, Geri, I have something I should tell you," Cheryl said, as I opened the front door.

"What's that?" I asked.

"I invited Jeff as well."

"You did what?" Jeff was my ex-husband. He was also Cheryl's husband's best friend. I had met him at their wedding. He was the best man and I was the maid of honor. It seemed like a match made in heaven.

"I invited Jeff," she repeated. She had the grace to look embarrassed. "And Amber." Amber was his fiancée.

"Great!" I said. "Just great."

"I told him you were coming and asked him if he had a problem with that and he said no," she said. "So I don't see why you should have a problem with it."

"Because he dumped me!" I said. "For his secretary. After I put him through business school. By working as a secretary. At a waste disposal plant!"

"That was two years ago, Geri," my sister said. "You've got to get over it. Move on. In fact, why don't you bring a date to the dinner?"

She knew I wasn't dating anybody. It was another way for her to nag me about my lack of romantic prospects.

"Sure, I'll do that!" I said and slammed the door in her face.

Chapter 13

My phone started ringing as I got on the highway headed west towards Seattle, but I ignored it. I had enough on my hands what with Pepe who was chattering away about what we should have for dinner and my angry thoughts about my sister's announcement. How dare she invite Jeff to Easter dinner without asking me?

I tried to think of the bright side, which is what my counselor would suggest. And that was the only bright side I could imagine: I would have plenty to talk about at my next appointment. Which triggered a new problem. What was I going to tell her about Pepe? If I told her my Chihuahua talked, she'd probably suggest voluntary commitment.

Suddenly Pepe went silent. I glanced over at Pepe and saw he was on his hind legs staring out the window.

"What is it, Pepe?" I asked.

"Geri," he said, turning towards me, his little

dark eyes shining, "this place is *muy bonita*. Now I see why you live here!"

I looked out the window and saw what he was seeing. We were in the middle of the bridge, which appears to float on the waters of Lake Washington. On one side of the highway, the water was choppy, the top of the waves flecked with foam. On the sheltered side, the lake's surface was a shimmering pool of silver. Meanwhile the setting sun was breaking through the heavy gray clouds in the west, piercing the landscape with shafts of golden light. Ahead of us were the dark hills and twinkling lights of Seattle.

I sighed. Now I knew why I had adopted this dog. He was going to make my life better.

"It is *muy bonita*, Pepe," I said. "And so are you."

"*Suave*," he said.

"*Suave?*"

"*Sí*, I am *muy suave*."

We cruised by the Tyler residence on our way home but there were still police cars in the drive and crime-scene tape on the porch, so we didn't stop. Instead, I headed over to my best friend's shop, only a few blocks from where I live. I needed a hug and some sympathy. Plus I was overdue on my promise to introduce Brad to my dog.

Brad was one of the people who encouraged me to adopt a pet (my counselor was the other). He thought adopting a dog would encourage me to get out more. Plus I think he was hoping to be a surrogate dog owner. He imagined a dog frisking around the shop while we worked.

Brad and I met in the interior design program at Bellevue Community College. We were the oddballs in our class. Most of the career opportunities were in the field of office design or as sales reps for furniture companies, and so that's what our teachers emphasized. But both Brad and I wanted to design living spaces, and we both had very distinctive tastes, as evidenced by the décor of Brad's shop.

He rents a little storefront at the edge of Eastlake, by the approach to the University Bridge, one of our many drawbridges in Seattle, and just under the high I-5 Freeway Bridge. Cars thunder by practically overhead (the freeway is double-decker here, thanks to the Express Lanes). The store is in an old one-story wooden building, the shape of a shoebox, and just as wide as the front window and door.

In the front of his shop, Brad displays his wares— black lacquered Chinese chairs; a dark-green on pale-green striped Victorian sofa, dotted with needle-worked pillows; a larger-than-life parrot sculpture; a brass hookah; a tall blue and white Chinese vase.

The front of the shop is small and shallow, but the back room is a dim cavern. It functions as both a work room and a storage room, lit by flickering fluorescent lights. Rolls of upholstery fabric lean against the walls. Scattered here and there are chairs, sofas, and end tables in various stages of restoration. Most of them are mine—I have a weakness for rescuing the scarred chests of drawers and ratty chairs that people leave out on the sidewalk. Brad generously allows me to store them while I work on them. He also lends me a lot of the furniture and accessories I need when staging homes for sale. Not that I had done any of that lately.

Brad and I both love fantasy in design. But whereas I tend towards Americana from the thirties through the fifties, Brad prefers the British style of the nineteenth century. Brad and his partner live in an old Victorian mansion on Queen Anne Hill. It's full of antiques—feather fans, gold-tasseled red velvet curtains, gilded chairs covered in toile, porcelain figurines of birds. Brad's partner, Jay, has a thing for birds. He owns a bad-tempered Quaker gray parrot that always tries to bite me when I get near it. That's why Brad can't have a dog.

Brad's personal style is similarly rococo. Today he was wearing a red velvet smoking jacket over a pair of loose-fitting black canvas pants.

"Geri!" he said, when I came walking in the front door. I had stuffed Pepe back in my purse. I wanted to surprise him. "Darling, I've been trying to call you for days! What's going on? Are you avoiding me?"

"Of course not, sweetie," I said, giving him a quick kiss on the cheek, our usual greeting. "I've just been busy. I've got great news!"

Brad put down the pillow he was holding. "You got a dog!"

"Better than that!" I said.

I could hear Pepe inside my purse. "Nothing could be better than that."

"You didn't get a dog?"

"How could that be good news?" Pepe asked.

"I did get the dog," I said. "Here is he!" I opened the flap of my purse.

Pepe stuck his head out and looked around. I think he was a little confused by the sight of the stuffed bobcat mounted on a tree branch that protruded from the wall. Brad loves taxidermy animals. He has a whole collection of them including a group of dancing hamsters. He keeps them in the back because they freak out most people. Like this one was freaking out Pepe.

Pepe growled. For a dog so small and a sound so tiny, it still managed to make the hairs curl up on the back of my neck.

"Oh, it's so cute! It sounds so ferocious!" said Brad, lifting Pepe out of my bag and looking him over. "He is so precious! What have you named him?"

"Actually, he named himself. His name is Pepe!"

Brad frowned. "Isn't that a bit too obvious, Geri?"

"I suppose *you* have a better idea," Pepe said.

"You should call him Angelo! Then you could dress him up in wings and a halo."

"No way, José!" Pepe said.

"He doesn't really like to be dressed up," I told Brad.

Brad looked hurt. "But all those designs we sketched . . ." One rainy afternoon we had amused ourselves by drawing pictures of dogs in disco togs and pirate costumes.

"He seems to have strong opinions of his own," I

said. "We can talk about it later." I didn't really want to discuss this subject in front of Pepe.

"Once he sees what we have envisioned, he will come around," said Brad, setting Pepe down on the floor. Pepe sniffed around the legs of the sofa and behind the oil paintings stacked against the wall.

"No marking your territory in here!" I told him.

Brad looked concerned. "I hope he understands English!"

"Actually he speaks Spanish," I said.

"Oh, well, then tell him not to pee in Spanish," Brad said.

"I don't really know how to say that in Spanish," I said. "It hasn't come up before."

"Well, he's adorable," Brad said. "I'm so glad you brought him over to show me. I was just closing the shop and heading home so your timing is impeccable. Jay has some big event at the Seattle Art Museum he's catering tonight, and he wants me to do the table designs."

I was disappointed. Brad and I usually hang out together after work. Often we go to a nearby restaurant for cocktails and dinner. Since Jay runs a catering business, he is usually gone until late in the evening and Brad is often on his own, like me. I wanted to complain to him about Cheryl's cruel invitation and also tell him about my new job.

"You didn't even hear my biggest news!" I said.

"What is it, if not me?" asked Pepe, emerging from behind the Victorian sofa.

Brad raised his eyebrows.

"I got a job! I'm working as a private investigator."

Brad's eyebrows fell. "Darling, that just doesn't sound like you!"

"Actually I'm well suited to the job," I said. I laid out all the talking points I had rehearsed for my interview. "When I worked at the sewage treatment plant, I learned how to do research and write reports. That will come in handy for writing up my cases! And, you know, we learned a lot about interviewing and working with clients in the interior design program. Plus as a stager, I'm used to reading all the clues in an environment."

"If you say so," said Brad. He sounded dubious.

"And my boss is the most eccentric character! You'll have to meet him. He totally thinks he's living in the fifties. Or maybe the forties. He calls me 'doll!' Can you believe it?"

"I'll call you doll, if it pleases you so much," said Brad. "I just don't know about this, Geri. It sounds like it could be dangerous."

"It is *muy* dangerous," said Pepe, "but luckily she has me as a partner."

"You're so right!" I said. "On my first assignment, Pepe and I actually found a dead body."

"No!" said Brad, falling back in feigned horror, rattling all the crystal in the china hutch.

"Seriously! We got sent on an assignment—"

"You think of your dog as your partner?"

"I am her partner!"

"He *is* my partner!"

"I thought I was your partner!"

"No, I am," said Pepe.

"You're my business partner," I said. I could see

that even though Brad was joking, he was a little jealous at being left out of my new life. "And Pepe is my detecting partner. Anyway, we went to interview a woman whose husband was missing and found him dead on the living room carpet. In the middle of the most god-awful white on white decorating scheme you've ever seen!"

"Melissa did that home," Brad said. Melissa was one of the other students in the interior design program and our nemesis. We hated her work, which managed to be both opulent and trite.

"Oh, that explains it," I said. "But how do you know that?"

"It was David Tyler. Right?"

"Yes."

"It was all over the news last night. Microsoft millionaire slain in his home! Did you know that Jay did a party for them last Christmas?" Brad didn't wait for me to answer but just kept on going. "Jay couldn't stand the wife. Said she was a total bitch. Jay said they'd probably find out it was suicide. The poor guy no doubt killed himself because it was the only way he could get away from her nagging."

Chapter 14

When we got home, Pepe went straight to his food dish. But he cleared out of the kitchen fast when Albert came wandering in looking for his own dinner. Pepe headed for the living room and in a few minutes, I heard the click of the TV.

After pouring myself a glass of Chardonnay, I drifted into the living room to see what he was watching. He was channel surfing, clicking through all the channels.

"There is nothing on TV on Friday night," he complained.

"Just don't watch anything On Demand," I told him. "I'm not going to pay for it."

I checked my home phone, hoping for a message from my sister, apologizing for inviting Jeff without telling me. But she hadn't called. I did have two messages.

One was from Sherman Foot. He sounded annoyed. He wanted to know why I hadn't called him.

"It's urgent that I speak to you, Miss Sullivan," he said. "Contact me as soon as you receive this message."

I didn't think Foot would answer his phone on a Friday night but I tried the number anyway. I got voice mail and left a message.

The second call was from Felix. He said he had enjoyed meeting me and my dog, although he was sorry about the circumstances, and he hoped I would call him. I thought about it. He had a nice rich baritone voice, and it sounded soothing. I imagined that calm, confident tone really worked on dogs, but the last thing I needed was an attractive man in my life.

As I was considering this, the phone in my hand rang, shaking me out of my reverie. My caller ID said the caller was F. Navarro. Well, if he was going to be persistent, I might as well end it quickly.

"Hello?"

"Hello. Is this Geri Sullivan?"

"Yes. Who is this?"

"Don't you have caller ID?" he asked.

"Oh!" How did he know that? I have to admit, I'm not a very good liar. It might be a problem in my new career. I imagined there were plenty of circumstances when lying would be a great way to get information. "Yes, I do," I said.

"So you know it's me, Felix," he said.

"Yes, otherwise I wouldn't have answered." I wasn't sure if I should have said that. But he laughed.

"Well, I'm glad you did," he said.

"Oh really? Why?"

"I felt terrible all day because of what happened. I want to make it up to you. Can you get an estimate and let me know how much it will cost to fix your car?"

"Felix," I said, "it would cost a lot to fix my car. Didn't you notice the moss growing on the rubber?"

"Well, yes, I did," he said. "I thought it was rather charming."

He must be kidding. Guys never thought my neglect of my car was charming.

"Really, the car is a hand-me-down from my sister, and I'm trying to drive it into the ground. I don't plan to have any work done on it."

"How about if I pay for the cost of the repairs, even if you don't intend to do them?"

"I couldn't accept any money from you under those circumstances," I said.

"Well, it doesn't seem right," he said. "Can I make it up to you in some other way? Dinner? Or a free training session for your dog?"

"Pepe could certainly use some training," I said.

Pepe said "Hey! I heard that!"

I noticed the way Felix had slipped in the dinner invitation. Was he asking me out? It had been so long since I had been asked out, I wasn't really sure.

"Can I think about it and call you back?" I asked.

"Sure, I'll be looking forward to that," he said. He repeated his number and then said good-bye. I stood there looking at the phone.

"Who was that?" Pepe wanted to know. "The guy with the rude dog?"

"Yes, it was," I said.

"He is trying to get closer to you by using me," Pepe said. "That is a clever strategy. I have used it myself to good effect."

"I'd actually like to see him train you," I said to Pepe.

"What would you like to see me do?" Pepe asked. "I can already jump through a ring of fire." He looked around the living room. "But you do not appear to have one nearby."

"When did you learn to jump through a ring of fire?" I asked.

"When I performed in the circus," Pepe said, with great dignity. "A Mexican circus. The very best kind."

I needed to go to Pete's Market to get ingredients for dinner. I was hoping Pepe would insist on going along, but he had gotten really involved in an old episode of *Law and Order*. He told me he wanted to pick up some pointers on interrogation techniques.

"Do not forget we are out of bacon," he said, as I headed out the door.

It was still raining, and I got soaked, though the market is only a few blocks from my home. I picked up ingredients for nachos, thinking Pepe might enjoy it, but he just turned up his nose.

"Beans give me gas," he said.

Luckily I'd also purchased some fancy dog food that looked like stew. Pepe seemed to approve of this. He danced around as I was spooning it onto a saucer and polished it off within a minute.

I'd picked up some books from the library between Brad's shop and home, so I opened up *The Idiot's Guide to Being a Private Investigator* while I was eating. It was very informative. I learned that careful note-taking was the most imperative task so I got a blank notebook out of my desk drawer and labeled it CASEBOOK NUMBER 1.

I started recording all that had happened since I first went to meet Rebecca Tyler. While I was writing, a commercial came on and Pepe strolled over to see what I was doing.

"Geri, how long have you been a PI?" he asked.

"Not long," I said.

"That's obvious," Pepe said. "What did you do before?"

"I was a stager."

"Is that like an actress?"

"No, a stager decorates houses that are for sale to help attract customers."

"So you create a false appearance to produce a positive impression," said Pepe thoughtfully.

"I guess you could say that. But I don't really think of it that way."

"How do you think of it?" Pepe asked.

"I think of it as bringing out the inherent personality of the place so people will see its possibilities."

Pepe seemed perturbed. "I do not see how that will be of benefit in our current case."

"I suppose I might notice something that seems out of place that other people might not notice."

"Did you notice anything at the Tyler residence that was out of place?"

"Come to think of it, yes! I did think it was odd that David Tyler was in the living room. It didn't seem like the sort of room where someone would be sitting and relaxing. I would expect him to be in his office or bedroom or even the kitchen."

"Yes, but what if he surprised an intruder?" Pepe asked.

I nodded. "A possibility. But why would an intruder stand in the middle of the room? One would expect he would be looking for something to steal. There was nothing of value nearby."

"Unless something was taken that we do not know about!"

"Very nice, Pepe. I'll put that in the casebook as one of the questions we should try to answer tomorrow."

Chapter 15

It was shortly after noon when we got to the Tyler residence. I drove by it slowly, scanning to see if there was any police activity around it. Seeing none, I found a parking spot up the street.

"Do you see any *policía* at the Tyler *casa*?" Pepe asked, as I parallel parked.

"How do you know where we are?" I asked. He was curled up in the passenger seat and had barely lifted his head. "You can't possibly see out the window."

"We dogs have the uncanny ability to know where we are at all times," he told me. "It is a vestige of our survival skills from ancient times."

"Oh, come on," I said.

"If that's true, tell me *exactly* where we are right now."

"We are at 648 Fourteenth Avenue East."

"Ha! Gotcha!" I wagged a finger at him. "That's not the Tyler address."

"I did not say it was. You asked me to tell you *exactly* where we are, and I have done so. Specifically, we are four houses north of the Tyler casa, thus the address of the house we are parked in front of is 648 Fourteenth Avenue East."

I looked out Pepe's passenger side window. He was right. The number set in tile on the stone pillar of the large Tudor mansion read *648*.

"How did you know that?" I asked.

He stood up and took a stretch. He put his little paws down and stretched his butt and tail up so that he looked like a comma. "Geri, what if I were to tell you that, even lying down, I could see the address in big bold letters on the front gate of the house on *your* side of the car—"

I swiveled around in my seat. It was true: the house on the other side of the street was elevated from the sidewalk, and the address was plainly visible.

Pepe continued, "And that I knew that the casa on *my* side of the car would be the even number, 648, which I remember is four houses north of the Tyler residence. Would that not have spoiled your sense of wonder and amazement at my uncanny abilities?"

"Oh, good grief."

"Just as I thought," he said, looking smug. "Now, I ask you again—do you see any signs of *policía* at the Tyler residence?"

"No, no, there aren't any cops around."

"Ah, *muy bien*."

Regaining my composure, I said, "I don't see any cars in the driveway either, so let's hope Rebecca Tyler's not home." I reached over, rolled his window up and grabbed my purse.

"Let's go and see if we can find any clues, Pepe."

I managed to get a leash on Pepe by persuading him that we had to pose as a dog owner and pet out for a walk. The Tylers lived just a few blocks from Volunteer Park, the oldest Seattle park, a spacious green landscape of sweeping lawns and tall trees designed by the famous Olmstead brothers. There were plenty of other dogs and their owners heading towards the park or coming home. Pepe growled at every one he saw, and I had to scoop him up and tuck him under my arm to keep him from lunging at the other pets. The other dog owners gave me sour looks. Apparently they didn't find Pepe as amusing as I did.

"Now here's our plan," I said to him, as we got close to the driveway of the Tyler residence. "I'm going to set you down on the ground. I have surreptitiously unhooked your leash. You're going to pretend to run away from me and dash into the Tyler yard. I'll chase after you and that way we'll be able to look for clues."

Pepe regarded me with amazement in his dark eyes. "Geri, that is a very good plan," he said. "You are turning out to be more devious than I thought."

"Thank you," I said, though I wasn't sure that was a compliment.

"It is a very good trait for a private detective," he said, as I plunked him down on the ground. "Luckily, I have a talent for it myself." He shook himself, then took off running up the Tyler driveway.

I wasn't sure whether to call his name or not, to establish our pretext, but decided against it and followed him, trying to look harried and worried. That was easy.

The house seemed to be closed up. Blinds were drawn in the windows facing the front.

Pepe dashed across the lawn, rounded a big rhododendron at the corner of the house and headed towards the back yard. I followed reluctantly. A yew hedge shielded us from view on one side but I crept along cautiously, afraid someone inside the house would notice me passing by.

Pepe headed straight for an azalea bush, bright with red blooms, and dug into the earth. But he ran back quickly, squeaking, "Ow! Ow! Ow!" He was jumping up and down and circling around, trying to rub his nose against the ground.

"What is it, Pepe?" I whispered.

"Someone has done a very bad thing!" he said. "Ow! My nose! Ow!"

"Hold still, Pepe," I said, kneeling down to see what was wrong. He squirmed under my hand but eventually I saw tiny splinters of redwood bark in his nose. I set him on my lap and took out my tweezers from my purse and extracted them one by one. He made a lot of noise during this process, but luckily no one seemed to hear him.

When I was done, I patted his nose with a Kleenex.

There were tiny spots of red on the Kleenex as I folded it back up.

"Blood!" he said and seemed to sway on his feet.

"It's OK, Pepe, you're fine," I said. "But don't go back under there."

"It's *muy malo*," said Pepe. "Someone has put this nasty stuff everywhere under the bushes to prevent us from looking for clues." I saw that fresh redwood mulch had been heaped at the bases of all the trees in the back yard, and all the rhododendrons and azaleas which edged the house. The smell was overpowering, even for my human nose.

"It looks like it was done recently," I said.

"Today," he insisted. "It was not there two days ago. This is where I smelled the bad smell, but it is buried under this stuff. Luckily I can track it away from here."

He put his nose to the ground and sniffed the grass.

"Do you not see?" he said. "Right here—the faint outline and depression made by a pair of shoes."

I squatted down and gave the area a close inspection. "Well, maybe I can see what you're talking about. Are you sure?"

"Of course I am sure. I can smell the leather. Italian, I believe."

"Can you tell the shoe size?"

"I am not a shoe salesman." He put his nose to the grass and headed towards the back of the house. "Come along, Geri," he said.

I followed reluctantly.

"Over here," called Pepe, his voice growing faint.

He was digging again, this time in the back yard under the base of an ornamental cherry tree with long weeping branches, laden with fat, pink petals. As I reached his side, I heard voices coming from the back of the house.

"All right, go on," said a male voice. "You wanted out, so go out already."

"Luis," said a woman, "Mrs. Tyler doesn't like it when—"

"I don't care. It's a dog, not a piece of Waterford crystal. Besides, she drives me crazy when she wants out."

"But—"

"She always comes back. Don't worry. There you go, girl, have some fun."

I scooped Pepe up and ducked behind a topiary boxwood, shaped like a giant urn. "*Shhhh!*" I told him.

A reddish-gold Pomeranian came prancing out into the yard. She was an exquisite little creature, a puffball of long, fluffy fur.

Pepe craned forward in my arms.

"Oh," he sighed. "It is the bitch. She is so lovely. I am smitten!"

"Hold still," I said while he was squirming in my arms.

The Pomeranian sniffed the air. I was afraid she would catch our scent and begin barking. But instead, she headed straight over to the base of the tree where Pepe had been digging and began digging herself.

"She is going to steal our clue!" said Pepe, wriggling out of my arms, and dashing towards her.

I took off after him. Sure enough, by the time I arrived, the Pomeranian had unearthed something. It was a soggy piece of plastic, covered with dirt. It took a minute for me to realize it was a latex glove. Possibly worn by the murderer! And buried here after the deed! The police hadn't found it. I needed to get that clue before the dogs destroyed it.

The little Pom had her teeth on one end of it and Pepe had his teeth on the other end. They were both growling and pulling it back and forth.

"Give it to me," said Pepe. "It is mine. I found it first."

The Pomeranian growled.

"Stop it, both of you!" I said, perhaps a bit too loud. For the next moment, I heard a man's voice behind me.

"What's going on here?"

Chapter 16

I turned and saw a young man in khaki pants and a white T-shirt coming toward me. He had the browned skin of someone who works in the sun and the broad shoulders and strong biceps of someone who works with his hands. Behind him was an older woman with dark hair pulled back into a bun at the nape of her neck. She wore magenta polyester pants and a matching tunic top. Both had a look of concern, especially the woman.

I was concerned myself. The glove was a clue I couldn't afford to lose. I knelt down and grabbed at it. We had a three-way tug-of-war until I pulled up on the glove, almost lifting both dogs off the ground. They finally released their hold. I shoved the glove into my coat pocket. Then I stood and turned to face the man and woman.

"Oh, hello," I said. "I'm sorry for coming onto your property. I was just passing by, and my dog saw your dog and got off his leash. It is your dog, isn't it? This cute little Pomeranian?"

"She isn't ours," said the man, approaching me. The Pomeranian was dancing around me with her dark eyes focused on my pocket. Pepe was following close behind her. "She belongs to Mrs. Tyler. We work for her."

"Luis, *que pasa?*" the woman asked, giving him a light poke in the arm. "Who is this lady?" she continued in Spanish. "What's she doing here?"

"No problem," Luis told her in Spanish. "Her dog just got off the leash."

"I'm Geri Sullivan," I said, introducing myself.

"Luis Vasquez," he told me. "And this is my mother, Rosa. I'm sorry, she doesn't speak any English."

Just then, the Pomeranian jumped up, her eyes still focused on my coat pocket. She repeated the move as effortlessly as an acrobat—*boing-boing-boing*—like a furry bouncing ball.

"Siren Song, *down*," commanded Luis. "What's gotten into you?"

"It's OK," I said. "She probably smells the beef jerky in my pocket." I pulled the half full packet out.

"Hey," Pepe complained, putting his nose right up to the plastic pack, as did the other dog. "You said we were out of beef jerky," he accused. "You held out on me."

"You were eating it all," I told him.

"What did you say?" asked Luis.

"Nothing," I told him. "Your dog was working so hard for this beef jerky, I thought she should have some of it. Do you mind?"

Luis looked at Rosa. She shook her head, but he shrugged. "She can have a treat."

I gave a few pieces to the Pomeranian, who wolfed it down.

"No more for her," Rosa told Luis. "Siren Song will get fat."

"She's got too much energy to get fat," said Luis. "She can have some more."

I broke off a small bit for Pepe and gave the rest to Siren Song. She gobbled it right up, but Pepe took his piece gently in his mouth, then carried it over to Siren Song and laid it down on the grass in front of her. She gave him what I can only describe as a surprised look, then scooped it up, swallowed it, and licked her lips.

"Hey baby, *que pasa*?" Pepe said to her.

"Hey baby, *que pasa*?" I repeated.

Luis must have thought I was speaking to him. He rattled off a string of rapid Spanish. About all I could figure was that he thought I was fluent in Spanish, too.

"*No hablo Español*," I said in my high school Spanish. "I was talking to my dog."

"Your dog speaks Spanish?" Luis asked.

"Well, actually, I think it's more like Spanglish." Thinking it best to change the subject, I asked Luis, "I saw the police were here yesterday. What happened?"

"Mr. Tyler was found dead," he said. "The police think he was murdered."

"That's terrible. I take it you and your mother weren't here when it happened?"

"No. We had the week off. Mrs. Tyler was in L.A., and Mr. Tyler was at their cabin in Aspen."

"Luis!" his mother yelled. She pointed toward the dogs. "Do you see what that Chihuahua is doing?"

"But she is spayed," Luis told her. "They cannot do anything. They are just smelling each other."

And so they were. They had been circling round each other the way dogs do but eventually they had stopped, side by side, head to tail, and were sniffing each other's butts. Pepe looked at me, his dark eyes dreamy, and said, "A rose by any other name would smell as sweet."

"Shakespeare again," I mused, thinking how odd it was to hear my dog quoting from *Romeo and Juliet*. Then I remembered what I was supposed to be doing.

"So what happened?" I asked, deciding to play the role of a concerned neighbor. "Was it a burglary?"

Luis shrugged. "We don't know. Mrs. Tyler called us last night and asked us to come over. The police wanted to question us. To see if we had noticed anything out of place."

"And had you?"

"I didn't work that week since there was no need to water. Because of the rain. And my mother was supposed to come that day to open up the house for Mrs. Tyler, but then Mrs. Tyler called her and told her not to come."

"Why?"

Luis looked at his mother, but she wasn't paying

attention. All of her attention was focused on Siren Song. The Pomeranian was standing up on her back legs, with her paws held in front of her, and turning in circles. She could have been a ballerina doing pirouettes. She was that graceful.

"Wow!" I said. Pepe seemed equally impressed. He tried to get up on his hind legs and imitate her actions, but he could only stay upright for a moment.

"The dog dances," said Luis.

"Yes, it certainly looks like she's dancing," I said.

"No, really," he said. "Mrs. Tyler has trained her to dance. That is her hobby. She takes her dog to shows where dogs dance."

Siren Song backed up, still standing on her hind legs. Then she moved forward again.

"It looks like she's doing a cha-cha," I said.

"Probably she is," Luis said. "She's a very talented dog. She has won many prizes."

Rosa walked towards the dogs, clapping her hands. At first, I thought she was applauding Siren Song's performance, but then I realized she was trying to shoo Pepe away.

"So your mother was lucky," I said.

"What?"

"If she had come that morning, she would have found the body," I said. I didn't mention that I had been the one to find it instead.

"Yes, we were just talking about that," said Luis. "It would have been a terrible shock. My mother has worked for the Tylers for twenty years. I've been coming along with her since I was eight. In fact, Mr. Tyler was my *patrón*."

Rosa picked up Siren Song, tucked her under her arm and headed back to the house. Pepe followed at her heels, his nose practically touching her ankles.

"*Patrón?*" I asked.

"It means godfather," Pepe said, as he trotted by me. I picked him up as well. He struggled to get down but I told him, "Hush, I need you to translate."

Just then, Rosa rattled off a string of Spanish at Luis. I caught a word here and there but the gist of it was that she wanted him to get back to work and stop talking to snoopy strangers.

"She wants him to go back to work and stop talking to snoopy strangers," Pepe said. "Now will you put me down?"

"No," I said. "That dog is way out of your league. No way are you getting anywhere with her."

"I am insulted," Pepe said, and he hung his little head over my arm in the most dejected position possible.

"He definitely seems to understand English," Luis said. His mother was already back in the house with Siren Song. Pepe let out a pathetic whimper.

"My mother wants me to get back to work," Luis said. He very kindly left off the phrase about talking to snoopy strangers.

I cast about for some further topic of conversation, and my eye fell on the wheelbarrow full of mulch on the driveway behind him.

"Oh, I see you're mulching all of your plants," I said. "Is this the time of the year to do that?"

Luis shrugged. "You can do it any time of year but since it's spring, the weeds grow rapidly. I try to keep up with them but it offends Mrs. Tyler if she sees just one. So she told me to apply the mulch." He turned away.

"But why today?" I asked. "What if it covered evidence needed to solve the crime?"

"Oh, the police told us they were done. And Mrs. Tyler insisted we stay on schedule. She has her calendar laid out with things to do each day."

I heard the sound of car tires coming up the driveway. A dark black Town Car pulled into view—just the nose of it since the wheelbarrow blocked the drive.

"Well, it was lovely talking to you," I said. "Thanks for letting my dog play with yours."

I spun around, planning to make a quick escape along the side of the house. But I was too slow.

"Hey!" Rebecca Tyler jumped out of the car. She was dressed in black today—a long black wool coat over black leggings and black high heels.

"What's going on here?" That was addressed to Luis. I put Pepe down, thinking we could make our getaway faster.

"You! Stop!" she said. Her voice was so commanding I did as she said. So did Pepe.

"I was just talking to this lady," Luis said, holding out his hands in supplication. "She's a neighbor whose dog got loose and came into our yard."

"That's no neighbor!" said Rebecca. "She's the one who murdered my husband!"

Chapter 17

"I most certainly did not murder your husband," I said.

"Luis, restrain her," said Rebecca. "I'm calling the police."

Luis looked uncertain. "What am I supposed to do?" he asked.

"Hold onto her," said Rebecca, pulling her cell phone out of her purse.

Luis looked apologetic but reached out and put his arms around my waist from behind. I struggled to get free, squirming this way and that. Pepe circled Luis, nipping at his heels and barking. I could hear Pepe muttering under his breath. "Unhand her, you brute."

"Do you get all your lines from Mexican soap operas?" I asked.

"Huh?" said Luis.

"Never mind," I said.

Meanwhile, Rebecca was on her cell phone.

"Hello," she said. "I need a squad car here immediately. I caught a suspect in a murder investigation."

"That's totally untrue," I said.

I quickly realized there were some advantages to being so close to Luis. He smelled delicious: a mixture of hot sun and clean skin and spicy cologne. Plus my struggles to get free put me in contact with every muscle in his body, and I do mean, every muscle.

Luis must have realized this too for he suddenly took a step back and collided with Pepe.

"Hey, your dog bit me!" he said, letting go of me.

"Ow!" said Pepe. "He kicked me in the teeth!"

I fell to my knees to check Pepe out. He seemed to be all right. He wasn't bleeding anywhere. I couldn't say the same for Luis, who had a few tiny puncture wounds in the back of his ankles.

"Now's your chance, Geri," Pepe said. "Make a run for it. I'll distract them!"

"No, Pepe," I said, "I'm OK. I'm not in trouble here. You are!"

"I did not bite him," Pepe said indignantly. "I was just standing still, and he ran into my teeth."

Rebecca gave her address to the police, then snapped her phone shut. "They're on their way," she said looking straight at me.

"Why would I be here if I murdered your husband?" I asked.

"Everyone knows that criminals return to the scene of the crime," she said.

"But I couldn't have murdered him. He was dead long before I arrived."

Rebecca looked confused now. "How do you know that?" she asked.

"Didn't the police tell you? Your husband had been dead for at least . . ." I looked at Pepe.

"A day," he said. "More or less."

"At least twenty-four hours," I said. "The police didn't mention that?"

"Oh," she said, "that explains why they kept asking me when I started calling him." She gave a little gulp and her eyes softened. "But then why didn't he answer the phone the day before? And why did he come home early from Aspen?" She dabbed at her eyes with a knuckle. "I thought maybe he was having an affair."

She narrowed her eyes and looked at me again.

"Not with me!" I said.

"No," she gave me the once-over. "David wouldn't be interested in someone like you."

"Hey!" I said.

"Pay her no mind, Geri," Pepe told me. "Tell her *she is* the most likely suspect. It is the spouse in 80 percent of all homicides."

"You're a more likely suspect than I am, Mrs. Tyler. The police always suspect the spouse in these cases."

"But I would never kill David," she wailed. "Especially not now."

"Why not now?" I asked.

"He was financing my show," she said.

"Oh? What show is that?"

"*Dancing with Dogs*," she said, a wistful smile crossing her face as she described it to me. "It's a reality show—rather like *Dancing with the Stars*, but with dogs and their owners dancing together. Siren Song, naturally, would be a star performer."

"No kidding?"

"It would be such a hit. I just know it," she said. "That's why I was trying to reach my husband. We'd wrapped up all the preproduction work in L.A. The producers were waiting for David to wire the money to film the pilot. But it never came. And without it, they said they would have to cancel."

"That gives you all the more reason to kill him," I said. It really didn't occur to me until later that it wasn't a good idea to accuse a murderer of murder.

"That shows what you know," she said. "The estate will be tied up for months, maybe a year. My show will be canned long before that. I've already talked to Sherman about it and he says there's nothing I can do."

"Sherman Foot?"

"Yes, my lawyer."

"He's my lawyer, too," I said.

"How could you get Sherman as a lawyer?" she asked. She really didn't have a very high opinion of me. Not good enough for her husband or her lawyer. I didn't think I looked *that* low-class.

"I work for the Gerrard Agency," I said.

"Oh, that makes sense."

"Really? Why?"

"Stewart and David and Sherman were all in the

same fraternity at the U Dub. Delta Alpha Gamma. They keep in touch. Old boy network and all that."

I figured I wouldn't mention that I worked for Jimmy Gerrard, not Stewart Gerrard. After all, I had finally gotten her to believe that I did work for the Gerrard Agency.

"Ask her about the dancing," said Pepe. "I want to dance. With Siren Song."

"Not now, Pepe," I said.

"Geri, do not argue with me. The dancing is *muy importante*," he said.

"Oh, all right," I said.

"What?" asked Rebecca.

"My dog wants to dance," I said, warming to the subject. "Like Siren Song. She looks so cute when she dances. I think my dog would be a good dancer, too." I could see this topic was having the desired effect. Rebecca relaxed and looked Pepe over thoughtfully.

"It's possible," she said. "People do seem to find Chihuahuas appealing."

"How do you do it?" I asked, seeing that the subject had softened her up. Maybe she'd even call the police back and tell them not to come. "How do you teach a dog to dance?"

"I'll show you," she said, shooing away Luis who was still hanging around, rubbing his ankles.

"Come inside," Rebecca said. "Let's go into my dog-training lounge."

And that's where we were when the police arrived.

Chapter 18

The training lounge was in the basement of the mansion. Its floor was completely covered with black rubber. I assume that made it easier for the dogs to get traction and also meant their falls were cushioned. One wall was covered floor to ceiling with mirrors, as in a ballet studio. There was even a little dressing area in the corner, containing a rack of tiny sparkly outfits. A big-screen TV took up most of another wall and on that screen Rebecca and Siren Song were waltzing to "The Blue Danube" in matching outfits made of blue chiffon and rhinestones.

At the moment, the little star was acting more like a dog. She and Pepe were frolicking around the basement. She would dash at Pepe, then scamper away when he darted towards her. His tail was wagging like crazy.

"That's fascinating," I said, watching the video. "But how do you teach her to do that?"

"Here—I'll demonstrate." She used a remote

control to turn down the volume of the music and then she snapped her fingers. In an instant, Siren Song was sitting at her feet.

"The first command is a gentle uplifting of your palm," Rebecca told me. "Thus," she said, ever so lightly raising the palm of her right hand.

The little Pomeranian stood effortlessly on her hind legs.

"If I move my hand in a circular motion, then she'll turn!" Rebecca demonstrated and Siren Song turned in slow pirouettes. "I can make her go faster, too. Of course, when she's learning a new move, I reward her with treats." She nodded at a small refrigerator standing against the wall. "She likes cheese. And turkey breast."

"I want to try that," said Pepe, frisking around me.

"You just want the treats," I suggested.

"Your dog seems excited," said Rebecca. "What—"

"I think he wants to try dancing," I told her.

Pepe stood on his hind legs. He wobbled a little from side to side, staggering back and forth across the room, zigzagging closer to Siren Song.

"Look at that!" said Rebecca. "He did it without a command."

"He's a very smart dog," I said.

"Look at me, Geri! I am dancing!" Pepe called out. He turned in circles, too.

"Wow!" Rebecca said. "He's a natural!"

Pepe tottered over to Siren Song and put out one paw to touch hers.

"Oh, look!" said Rebecca. "That's so darling! It looks like they are dancing together." She turned to me, all enmity forgotten. "I would love to train him for you. Perhaps he could be on the show as Siren Song's partner."

"Oh, yes, Geri," said Pepe. "I would love that."

Rosa appeared in the doorway and announced, "Mrs. Tyler, the police are here."

"*Policía!*" said Pepe and scampered off toward the dressing area where he hid behind a rack of sequin-studded tutus.

"Oh, tell them I don't need them anymore," Rebecca said, with a wave of her hand.

"I'm afraid that won't be possible, ma'am," said a burly uniformed cop, pushing into the room past Rosa. His blue uniform was almost hidden beneath layers of equipment, including a squawking radio and a baton. My heart sank when I recognized him. He was one of the patrol cops who had caught me with the gun in my hand the day before. "Detective Sanders wants us to bring her down to the station for questioning."

I started to protest, but then realized this would give me an opportunity to turn the glove over to the police. "I'll go," I said, "but this time I'm taking my dog."

"What dog?" asked the policeman.

Oh, yes, where was he? I looked around the room for Pepe. Where had he hidden?

I found him under the wardrobe rack of little outfits and pulled him out. He had put his head through one of Siren Song's pink skirts and he looked ridiculous. He took one look at the policeman and shivered.

"Why don't you just leave him with me?" Rebecca suggested, taking in his forlorn expression. "I can try training him while you're gone."

"Oh, yes, Geri, that is a good idea," said Pepe. "I can do some investigating here while you are talking to the *policía*."

"OK." I handed him over to Rebecca. I have to admit I was disappointed Pepe would rather stay with Rebecca and Siren Song than come along to protect me from the police.

They put me in the same interrogation room I had been in the day before and made me wait. There was a camera mounted on the wall and a big window through which I assumed they were watching me. I tried not to do anything suspicious.

After a while, Detective Sanders, the young black detective, came into the room. He said his partner, Detective Larson, was out.

"Looking for doughnuts?" I suggested.

Sanders did not laugh at my joke. Then again, most people don't laugh at my jokes. "No," he said curtly. "Another homicide investigation. Yours is not the only case we are working on."

"Do I need my lawyer?" I asked.

"Do you?" Sanders asked. He crossed his arms and tried to look nonchalant. I thought about calling Sherman Foot and hesitated. I knew enough to realize that Foot had a conflict of interest. And I didn't think he'd side with me if he had to choose between me and Rebecca.

"I really came along because I wanted to give you this," I said, pulling the dirty plastic glove out of my pocket.

"What's that?" Sanders frowned.

"It's a glove. My dog dug it up. It was buried under a tree in the Tyler backyard. I think it's a clue. The murderer may have worn it."

"Well, it might be a clue . . ." said Sanders, indicating that I should drop it on the table. He poked at it with a ballpoint pen. "But it's been contaminated. You say your dog touched it. And then you touched it. The chain of evidence has been broken."

"But maybe there's DNA evidence *inside* the glove," I suggested.

He frowned. "It's possible."

"If you swab the inside of the glove and isolate the DNA, you can run it through your database and identify the murderer," I suggested. "Or at least identify the person who was last wearing the glove." He was looking at me like I was crazy. "That's how they do it on TV," I said, trying to be helpful.

"This is real life," he said. "The state lab is backed up. Even if we could get any DNA out of the glove, we'd be lucky to get the results in a month."

Chapter 19

He pulled out his folder. "Now let me ask you a few questions. When did you get the call from the Gerrard Agency?"

"Well, I'd just picked up my new dog. My appointment was for 2 PM but I was a little bit late because I had to run by the store for some dog food—"

"I just need the time you got the call." His voice was weary.

"It was 3:30. I remember that because I only had a half hour to get to Mrs. Tyler's house."

He nodded. "That checks out."

"You have phone records?"

"That's how we check alibis." He scribbled something on the page. "And you say Mrs. Tyler called you?"

"No, I never said that."

He looked at me with narrowed eyes.

"I assume she called the agency."

"Hmmm," he murmured and made another note on his piece of paper.

"Did you talk to the housekeeper, Rosa?" I suggested. "She said Mrs. Tyler called her and told her not to come in that morning."

Detective Sanders looked interested. "We'll check that out," he said, scribbling.

"Doesn't that seem suspicious?" I asked.

"Lots of things seem suspicious," he said. "For instance, what were you doing there today?"

"I was just walking by with my dog."

He flipped over a few pages, then fixed me with his dark eyes. "You don't live in that neighborhood."

"I was taking him to Volunteer Park."

"No reason to park near the Tyler house. There's plenty of parking available at the park."

How could I explain that my dog wanted me to investigate? I had to think of a good story. "I thought I saw someone out the window when I found the body and I wanted to see if there was any evidence there."

"Interesting!" Now I had his attention. "Which window?"

"The corner window in the living room. North side of the house, closest to the street."

He was nodding even more now.

"We did get a shoe print from underneath that window. It was a woman's shoe, with a distinct heel. Size 8. What size do you wear?"

For once, I was grateful for my big feet. "Size 10!" I said eagerly, sticking out one foot in front of me, to demonstrate. I was wearing my black cowboy boots. I thought they looked stylish when worn with black tights and one of my favorite vintage dresses: gray cotton with little cherry pies all over it.

"Are these the shoes you were wearing on the day you found the body?" he asked.

I hated to admit it. "As a matter of fact, they are."

"We're going to need them," he said. "Can you take them off?"

"What am I supposed to do for shoes?" I asked, as I struggled to yank them off. You'd think he would have offered to help but he just watched with an amused grin as I wriggled back and forth.

"We can give you a pair of slippers," he said. He gestured at a pile of pink rubber sandals in the corner. "Those are the sandals we issue to prisoners in the jail."

"No thanks," I said, thinking how they would clash with my outfit. "Did you ever find the murder weapon?"

"Yes, as a matter of fact, we did. With your finger-prints all over it!"

"Oh, that's right! I'm really sorry about that. My dog warned me not to touch it."

Sanders fixed me with his dark eyes, then shook his head like a dog shakes off water. "It's OK. It probably didn't make much of a difference. The murderer had wiped it down with something like rubbing alcohol, which effectively eliminated any prints. Which tells us that even though it might have been a crime of passion, the murderer took great pains to clean up the scene afterwards."

"Why not just take the gun away?"

"Yes, that would be the most logical thing to do. Perhaps it was because the gun wouldn't really lead us anywhere."

"Why is that?"

"It was Mrs. Tyler's gun. Apparently she kept it in her bedside table."

"Isn't that suspicious?"

"Well, not necessarily. Almost everyone in that household would have known that. Especially Mr. Tyler. It's possible he got the gun because he heard a noise and then confronted a burglar."

"So you think it was a botched robbery?"

"No, there's no evidence anything was taken except a few sentimental objects that Mrs. Tyler had given Mr. Tyler."

"Again, doesn't that tell you something?"

"Not really."

"Did you check Mrs. Tyler's alibi?" I asked.

"We're still working on that," he said.

"But it must be fairly simple," I said. "Either she was on a plane from L.A. or she wasn't."

"Seems like it would be simple, doesn't it?" he observed.

"Do you mean she wasn't on that plane?"

"Let's just say we're still confirming her alibi."

That made me nervous. I had left my dog with this woman.

"Do you think she murdered her husband?"

"We haven't ruled out anyone." He looked me over. "You're still a suspect as well."

I sighed. "What do I have to do to prove I'm innocent?"

"We're going to need the clothes you were wearing that morning, too." He shook his head. "I can't believe no one asked you for those on Thursday. Can you bring them in?"

"Sure."

I had to get back to Pepe, and I was willing to agree to almost anything to get out of there.

"And what about your dog?"

"What about him?"

"Did you ever find him?"

It was the first sign of any human compassion I had seen from him. I was almost touched. "Yes," I said, then faltered to a stop not sure how to explain how Pepe had found his way to my door.

"Well, we still need to process him," he said, snapping shut his folder. "See if he has any evidence."

"He was out in the rain all night," I said. "Any evidence that was on him got washed off."

"Nevertheless, we have to be thorough. Please bring him in when you drop off your clothes."

Chapter 20

I had to wait in the lobby for a ride back to the Tyler residence. It was completely empty and quiet—a big, Y-shaped room, with a gray tiled floor and big glass windows on either side, looking out over the busy intersection of Twelfth and Pine. A female police officer in a blue uniform stood behind a glass-partitioned information counter in the middle of the room. She seemed to keep busy checking computer screens in front of her but occasionally she had to deal with people who wandered in. A black woman wearing a tin-foil hat who complained about the radio transmissions blocking her thoughts. A tattooed young man with a safety pin stuck through his eyebrow who wanted to report the theft of his skateboard. She handled them both with aplomb and courtesy.

I spent my waiting time updating my notes in my casebook. I had learned a lot from talking to Detective Sanders, but everything he told me made me more nervous. Rebecca was the spouse of the murdered man, she thought he was having an affair, and she was trying to get her hands on a large sum of money. Plus she had asked her gardener to cover up possible evidence on her property, she had told her housekeeper not to come in that morning, and it seemed like her alibi might not be checking out. And I had left my dog in this woman's care! Finally, one of the parking enforcement officials gave me a ride back up the hill in one of their golf-cart-type vehicles.

I felt like a fool standing on the doorstep of the Tyler residence in my stocking feet. At least, it wasn't raining. But the bricks were cold and damp. Rosa answered the door. I couldn't resist looking down at her shoes. They did look about size 8, but they weren't high heels—she was wearing scuffed white sneakers. She caught me looking and frowned.

"Nice shoes!" I said. "What size do you wear?"

She must have thought I wanted her shoes. She just kept shaking her head and saying, "No! No!"

"*Dónde está mi perro?*" I asked. "*Perro? Perrito blanco?*"

My pronunciation must have been pretty bad because it took a while before she understood. Then she motioned that I should follow her. We went through the foyer.

The door to the living room was open, and I looked in. The sofa and table had been removed but the carpet gleamed white again with no trace of blood. I shuddered. Surely Rebecca should have closed the door to block out the memory of her husband's corpse rather than restore the room to its icy splendor.

As I descended the stairs to the basement, I could hear the music swelling. It was a swing song from an old Fred Astaire and Ginger Rogers movie. And when I walked through the door, there was Pepe in a little tuxedo jacket trotting next to Siren Song, who was wearing a slinky black satin skirt.

Rebecca spotted me and came rushing over. "Look at them! They are perfect for each other," she said.

She looked down at my stocking feet. "What happened to your shoes?" she asked.

"The police wanted them," I said. I looked at her feet. She was wearing fancy black sneakers. It looked like she wore a size 8.

"What size are your feet?" I blurted out.

"Why?"

"Just hoping I could borrow a pair," I said.

"I don't think we wear the same size at all," she said. "What size do you wear?"

"Ten."

"Oh, no, mine are much smaller." She had managed to evade my question. Was that on purpose?

Meanwhile Pepe spotted me and came running up. "Geri! Geri!" he said. I had never seen him so excited. He was practically jumping into the air to try to get into my arms. "Get me out of this jacket!"

"OK, Pepe!" I picked him up and peeled off his jacket.

"Thanks for training my dog," I said to Rebecca. "I think we should be going now."

"Oh, but you can't leave!" Rebecca said. I looked back at the door to see if it had been locked behind me. Rosa was standing in the shadows, a magenta wraith, watching me. Was I in trouble? Did Rebecca know I suspected her? Could I get out alive? With Pepe?

"But I have to—" I started to babble.

"I'm just making progress with them. They're brilliant together," Rebecca said. "Your dog is a major talent."

"Did you hear that, Geri?" Pepe asked.

"I think I can make him a star," Rebecca said.

"Yes, Geri, I want to be a star," Pepe said.

"Well, I'm sure he would love that," I said, tucking him under my arm, like a clutch purse. "We can talk about it later." I backed toward the door. Siren Song was bouncing up and down like a golden ball of fluffy fur. No treats in my pocket so she must be trying to get to Pepe.

"He's worth a fortune," Rebecca said.

That stopped me. "Really?"

"Oh, yes. He could easily bring in fifty thousand dollars a year, and that's not counting residuals every time the show is shown. Plus endorsements. He would be a great spokesdog."

"That would show Caprice!" said Pepe.

"Pepe, you don't have to prove anything."

"*Sí*, Geri, but I could earn *mucho dinero* for me and you! You could live a life of luxury. No more slaving away at staging and spying. Would you not enjoy that?"

"Of course, I'd enjoy that," I said.

"I'll have Sherman draw up a contract," Rebecca

said. "But there is one problem." The edges of her lips lifted but the smile did not reach her eyes.

"What's that?" I asked, still backing towards the door.

"Well, you would need to dance with him," she said. "That's the whole premise of the show—owners dance with their dogs."

"I thought you didn't have the money to do the show," I said.

"I'm not giving up," she said firmly. "I'll figure out a way to get some of it down to the producers. I just hope they give me the time I need."

I couldn't help but think this woman was the sort of ruthless person who would kill her husband. It seemed she wouldn't let anything get in her way when she wanted something. And now she wanted Pepe.

"So, will you do it?" she asked. "We can start training on Monday."

"I have a job," I said. I didn't want to tell her what was really bothering me, which is that I can't dance. Not at all. No rhythm. "I'm working as a private investigator now. Remember?"

Rebecca thought about that.

"Even better," she said. "I can train you and your dog, and you can help me sort through David's papers and track down the funds I need."

Pepe piped in. "Geri, if we are here in the house, we can do some investigating of our own. Then you can clear your name. And mine."

"I'll pay you an hourly rate. Whatever you get for your detective work," Rebecca said. "It might take a while since David has a lot of papers. And then we'll come up with a list of people you can interview. It will be better if you do the interviews than me. Makes me look suspicious."

"Yes, it does," I said.

"Say yes, we want to do it," said Pepe.

"I don't know," I said to Rebecca. "I just don't get your attitude. I mean your husband was murdered, and all you're thinking about is the money for your show."

Rebecca looked offended. "Well, I'm sorry I'm not grieving the way you think I should." She crossed her hands over her chest. "Do you have any idea what it's like to have people telling you how you should behave at a time like this?"

"Well, yes I do," I said. "My parents were killed in an automobile accident when I was sixteen."

"Oh, I'm so sorry," said Rebecca. Her blue eyes filled with sympathy. "That must have been dreadful."

"*Pobrecita*," said Pepe. He stuck out his long pink tongue and licked my cheek.

"I do understand that everyone grieves in their own way," I said. Everyone kept encouraging me to cry after my parents died, but I didn't shed a tear for over a year.

"I need to stay busy," said Rebecca, clenching and unclenching her hands. "I just can't afford to think about what happened to David. Not for one moment." Her voice caught, then she went on. "I have to be proactive. David encouraged me to pursue this passion of mine, and I can't help but think he wouldn't want me to give it up, despite the circumstances. You might say I'm doing it for him." She shook tension out of her hands with an impatient gesture. "Will you help me?"

"Geri, this will be good for us," said Pepe. "It will make our reputation."

"Please," said Rebecca.

"OK," I said. "Yes, I'll help you." But I wasn't planning to dance.

"Great! Be here at 1 PM on Monday."

Chapter 21

"What was that all about?" I mused as I drove away from Rebecca's house. It had started raining again. By the time I reached my car, my socks were soaked. I peeled them off and tossed them into the back seat.

"Can you turn up the heat please?" Pepe asked, shaking the water off his fur.

"It takes a while," I said, trying to peer out past the windshield wipers. "The car has to warm up first."

Pepe made a disapproving sound.

"What did you find out when you investigated?" I asked him.

"Geri, that woman is *muy loca*," said Pepe. "I could not leave the room. She kept me trapped down there."

"Is she so *muy loca* she would kill her husband?"

"She is capable of anything," said Pepe, shuddering. "When Siren Song did not move fast enough for her, she hit her on the nose!"

"Perhaps that's a common training technique," I observed. "Perhaps I should use it on you."

"That is dog abuse, Geri!" Pepe was indignant. "Someone should report her to the authorities."

"Then why did you want me to work for her?" I asked.

"Is it not clear?" Pepe asked. "I must rescue Siren Song. Like in the soap operas. And the best defense is a good offense. Now we have access to the house. We can scope out the situation and plan our next move."

I went home to get some shoes—my Dansko Mary Janes—then took Pepe with me and headed over to Brad's shop. Brad stuck his head out of the back room when he heard the bell ring that was attached to the front door.

"Geraldine!" he sang out.

"You know that's not my name!" I said crossly. He knows I hate it. Besides my parents did not name me Geraldine. They named me Geri.

"And the Pepperoni!" he said, spotting Pepe at my feet.

"Hey, that is not my name, mister!" said Pepe.

"Call him Bradley," I suggested to Pepe. "He hates that!"

"*Ola*, Bradley," said Pepe.

"Isn't he cute!" said Brad. "It's almost like he's talking."

"You can hear that, too?"

"What? His cute little barking? Of course, it's adorable."

"Sometimes I think he really is talking to me," I confessed.

Brad got a worried look on his face. "Is this after you've had a glass or two of wine?"

"No! I mean, yes! Sometimes. But I hear him talking all the time."

Brad shook his head. "I think you might want to talk to your counselor. She might need to up your meds."

"Brad, you know I'm not taking any meds."

"Well, maybe you need to. They've done wonders for me!"

"What are you working on?" I asked.

"Come with me. I'll show you."

We followed him into the back room, Pepe giving the stuffed bobcat a wide berth.

"Voilà!" said Brad, gesturing at his work table in the center of the room. "What do you think?"

I couldn't believe my eyes. Pepe took one look and dashed under a sofa.

Arranged on the table was a tableau of stuffed hamsters, all dressed in sixteenth-century garb. They wore various shades of silk and satin costumes, and all wore stylized masks. Center stage was a larger, stuffed guinea pig, arms outstretched, holding a tiny knife in his right hand. He was dressed all in white, with big, puffy black buttons down his flowing shirt, like an Italian commedia dell'arte clown. At his feet was a prone hamster wearing a flowing gown. There was something very familiar about the tableau.

"For heaven's sake," I said. "This is from the opera *Pagliacci!*"

"Yes," Brad said proudly. "I knew you'd recognize it." We had seen it together the previous season at the Seattle Opera.

Pepe looked up at me and asked, "All these small rodents gave their lives for *this?*"

"It's the penultimate moment of the opera," Brad continued. "Canio has just killed his unfaithful wife."

I stared. Everything was right, from the poses to the costuming to the staging, even though I'd never seen *Pagliacci* done with stuffed hamsters and a guinea pig before.

"It's a bit weird, but it does have a strange fascination," I said. "What made you think of it, Brad?"

"Well, you know Mrs. Fairchild." She was one of Brad's regular customers. "Her guinea pig died. And she wanted him stuffed. Since she's quite the opera buff, she had named him Pagliacci, so I promised to dress him in a little clown costume." He carefully readjusted one of the hamster figures. "You know me. I had a bunch of extra stuffed hamsters, and got carried away and created the whole scene. Do you think she'll like it?"

"I do not think so," said Pepe, with a shudder.

"I bet she'll be delighted," I said.

"Good," said Brad. "I'm almost done. Let me clean up and we can go out and get something to eat. I've got some gossip for you."

We headed over to an Italian restaurant where Brad knew the owner. They let us bring Pepe in, as long as he stayed under the table and under the tablecloth. Pepe was having none of that but I found if I put him on my lap, I could conceal his presence.

I ordered the spaghetti with butter and garlic sauce, and a side of meatballs for Pepe. Brad went with the clam linguini and chose a decent bottle of Chianti for us to share.

"I wish Siren Song was here with me," said Pepe. "I would share a plate of spaghetti and meatballs with her like in the Disney movie about the two *perros* in love."

"You're talking about *Lady and the Tramp*?" I was amazed.

"*Sí*, it is one of my favorite movies."

"Yes, it does remind me of *Lady and the Tramp*," Brad said, waving his hand at the plastic grape clusters hanging down from the restaurant's latticed ceiling. The tables were covered with red-and-white-checkered tablecloths and decorated with wax-covered wine bottles with candles stuck in them. "Just look at the decor. It's just so—"

"Retro," I said. "There's not another place like it in town."

"I know, but—

"Enough of this bickering," said Pepe. "I want my meatballs."

"Anyway, Brad, are you doing anything for Easter?"

"No," he said taking a sip of his wine. "We never do anything for Easter. It's just not a holiday we celebrate and, God knows, we celebrate as much as we can. Why? Are you inviting me to Easter dinner?"

"Yes," I said. "At my sister's house."

"Oh, nooooo," he said, elongating the *no* for emphasis. "Not with *her*. Fate worse than death."

"You're right—that's why I don't want to go alone."

"Once was more than enough. There is nothing that could induce me to accompany you to that house of horrors. And endure the ravages wrought by those two rug rats. Or the inane patter of the dental husband."

"I know they're boring, Brad. But she's family!"

"It's hard for me to believe you are related," Brad said. "You must know someone else you can inflict your sister on. Some gullible innocent who has no idea what's in store for them."

"Perhaps that man you just met," Pepe said. "You could inflict your sister on him!"

Chapter 22

"No, I couldn't invite Felix!" I said.

"Who's this Felix?" Brad asked, pausing with his wine glass half raised. "Are you holding out on me?"

"Just a man I met while walking my dog," I said.

"I told you it would work!" crowed Brad. It had been his theory that if I had a dog I would meet other dog owners at parks and on walks and at doggie day care, and some of them would be single men. "What's his name? Tell me all about him."

"Well," I was blushing, "his name is Felix Navarro, and he's really good looking. Olive skin, dark hair, dark eyes, tall, well-built."

"Sounds delicious!" said Brad with a dreamy look in his eyes.

"I hardly know him!" I said. "I certainly wouldn't inflict my sister and her family on him. That would be cruel and unusual punishment."

Luckily, our meals were served at just that moment.

"Ah, there is a meatball with my name on it," said Pepe, his nose snuffling as he licked his lips.

I put one on the napkin on my lap for Pepe to eat.

"Yum!" he said. "This meatball is preferable to Felix Navarro any day of the week."

"So, what's the gossip?" I asked Brad, hoping to change the subject.

"I told Jay you were mixed up in the Tyler murder, and he gave me the scoop on Rebecca Tyler."

"Yes, and—"

"Well, did you know she's been married three times?"

"So David Tyler was her third husband?"

"Yes. She's been sleeping—or I should say marrying—her way up the social ladder. Her first husband was a construction worker. He died in an accident on the job site, and she married his boss, a real estate developer. Husband number two died of a heart attack. Shortly afterwards she met David Tyler at a charity fundraiser. She hit the big time with him. Retired at age forty. A Microsoft millionaire. He was looking for ways to invest his money, and she was looking for someone to invest in her."

Brad paused to take another sip of his wine.

"So she's sort of a black widow."

"I would say so. Those first two deaths could be considered suspicious. And now a third! And get this! Except for her first husband, all the guys were married when she met them. She actually convinced them to divorce their wives and marry her. Yet Jay says she's incredibly jealous. She always thinks that other women are trying to steal her man."

"It takes one to know one," said Pepe.

"The party he did at her house? She accused the beverage manager of having sex with David Tyler in the basement! Threw the woman out! Jay said David was just showing her where the extra refrigerator was located."

"These could be important clues, Geri," said Pepe.

"I had no idea," I said to Brad.

"Let's just say, I'd watch out for her, honey. She's dangerous."

"Well, I think I'm pretty safe. After all, I'm not after her husband."

The phone was ringing when I walked in the door. If I hadn't had three glasses of wine, I probably wouldn't have picked it up. But I was feeling a bit frisky. I could see the caller was F. NAVARRO and I was surprised that he was calling again. On a Saturday night, no less.

"Hello, Geri, it's Felix Navarro. The guy with the dog who damaged your car the other day."

"Sure, I remember you." He was sort of hard to forget.

"Did you have a chance to think about my offer?"

"Actually, I did," I said. I had been thinking over Pepe's suggestion.

"And?"

"Well, I'll let you off the hook, in terms of paying for my car, if you agree to go with me to my sister's house for Easter dinner."

There was a long silence. I started to get nervous.

"OK, I was just kidding," I said. "I know that's ridiculous. I don't even know you."

"No, actually I'd be happy to do that. It sounds like fun."

"Believe me, Felix, this will not be fun." I told him a little about my relationship with my sister. And how she had invited my ex-husband. And his new fiancée. "So you see, it's going to be very awkward."

"That's perfect," he said, "I'll use it for research."

"Research on what?"

"I'm writing on a book about how to apply the training techniques I use for dogs on people. It sounds like this dinner might offer some opportunities to apply my techniques and see how they work."

I had to laugh at that. I couldn't help thinking about how shocked my sister would be if I showed up with a date. Especially a date who looked like Felix Navarro. I thought again of his honeyed skin, muscular form, and prominent cheekbones.

"OK," I said. "Let's do it."

"Great. Tell me where you live and what time to pick you up."

When I hung up the phone, Pepe was shaking his head. "Who was that, Geri?" he asked. "Was it that guy with the rude dog?"

"My date for Easter dinner," I said.

"I thought I was your date for Easter dinner," Pepe said.

"No, you're my dog, and dogs don't get invited to Easter dinner," I said.

"That is not true, Geri," Pepe said. "When I was

working at the tamale factory, I was an honored guest at the Easter table. They said I brought them good luck."

"Good grief, Pepe," I said. "Not another preposterous story about your past life."

"Very well, Geri. I suppose you would rather go and listen to *el Gato*. He must have some pretty stories to tell."

"Actually Albert has never learned to speak English," I said. Which raised a new question. "How do you do it, Pepe?"

"I am a student of languages," he said, with a mighty sniff. "Every place I go, I make a great effort to learn the language of the locals. What is so odd is that they never seem to understand me." And he hung his head and looked sideways at me out of his big brown eyes. Nothing looks as sad as a sad Chihuahua.

"Oh, Pepe!" I said. "That must be terrible! Do you mean to say that I'm the only person who's ever understood what you're saying?"

"*Sí!*" he said, his ears perking up. "So you see why you are so important to me, and why I must insist on going to the Easter dinner with you."

I sighed. "Very well. You can go to Easter dinner with me."

Chapter 23

I woke up on Easter morning feeling blue. Even though I had stopped going to church back when I was in college, I still missed the ritual of worship. It was especially true at Easter. I loved seeing all the women and girls in their brightly colored dresses, listening to the exuberant singing of the choir, hearing the message of hope and resurrection.

My morning was quite different. After a quick breakfast of scrambled eggs and toast, I headed back to Mrs. Snelson's with Pepe. With any luck, Bruiser would transgress again. I would get my photo of him and be able to salvage my reputation as a detective.

At the Gladstone, I found a parking place with a good view of both Bruiser's home and Mrs. Snelson's flower beds. There was a bunch of little kids, all dressed up in fancy clothes and clutching baskets, on the lawn in front of the building. It looked like an Easter egg hunt.

I thought about the Easters of my childhood,

how we used to hunt for Easter Eggs inside the living room. My mother never remembered how many eggs she had hidden and so, inevitably, one was missed and only found a month later, when it began to emit an awful stench.

The kids at the Gladstone were all lined up on the patio. Someone gave a signal and they ran down the hill, shrieking with delight and poking around in the bushes. One of the residents, or perhaps the management, must have hidden candy or eggs for the kids to find. Every once in a while, one of the kids would shout and hold up an object that glittered in the sun.

"This Easter business is always confusing to me," said Pepe, watching this activity.

"How so?" I asked.

"Well," he said, giving his ear a quick scratch with a hind paw. "It is the Easter Bunny. Even I know that rabbits do not lay eggs."

I had to chuckle. "Pepe, the rabbit is a symbol of—"

"Let alone colored eggs," he continued.

"Well, the eggs are also symbols—"

"And put them into decorative baskets," he said. "Where would rabbits get baskets?"

"Pepe, the rabbits don't have anything to do with the baskets—"

"It would be most difficult for rabbits to fit into those baskets to hatch colored eggs, if, indeed, they did lay colored eggs, would it not?"

I gave up. I couldn't figure out how to explain the real meaning of Easter to him. Actually, I was marveling at even being in the position of trying to explain Easter to a dog.

"And the candy," said Pepe. "What has candy got to do with it?"

That was a good question. I wasn't really sure I knew the answer to that.

"And chocolate bunnies," he said, "they are the worst. I ate one once and was sick for days."

"That's because dogs aren't supposed to eat chocolate, Pepe."

"Those marshmallow things, though," he said, his tone brightening. "The yellow ones like little birds. How are they called?"

"You mean Peeps?"

"*Sí.* Peeps. They are *muy divertida!*" His small body quivered with pleasure at what was obviously a good memory. "Caprice gave me some last Easter. She lined them up so I could pretend I was hunting. I would catch their scent, stalk them most silently, and then pounce! The flock would scatter but I always caught them all. I tell you, Geri, if we ever go hungry and there are any little yellow birds around, we will not be hungry for long."

"I'll remember that," I said.

"Speaking of that," he said, "I am hungry now. Where are our supplies?"

"I'm sorry, Pepe," I said, "but I don't think we have time to go to the store. Bruiser could show up at any moment, and I need to be ready to take his picture."

"That is OK," he said. "I always hide some food, just in case."

"What do you mean?" I asked.

"Turn your head, Geri," he said. "I cannot reveal my hiding places."

I pretended to turn my head, watching the kids on the hill, but I actually could see him, out of the corner of my eye, digging in the crack between the back and the seat on the passenger side. He worked away at the fabric with his little paws, and finally came up with a piece of beef jerky in his teeth. He hopped over onto my lap and dropped it.

"For you, Geri," he said.

What could I do but say thanks? I thanked him and then offered it right back to him. He seemed so proud of himself. He quickly devoured it.

"Do you have more food hidden in my car?" I asked. I really didn't like the idea, especially since some of the food we had eaten the day before was perishable.

"*Sí*," he said with great pride. "I have many other caches in the car. They will serve us in good stead on future expeditions."

I turned and saw Bruiser crossing the street and heading up the hill. In a minute, he would be right in the middle of the Easter egg hunt.

"Oh, no!" I said. "Bruiser's on the move. And I don't trust him around those kids. We've got to get him out of there."

I opened the car door and hopped out. Pepe was right behind me. I hurried up the hill, flapping my hands, and shouting Bruiser's name. He kept dodging away from me, almost knocking over a little girl in the process, then rooting around in the child's abandoned basket. The little girl tried to pull her basket away from him, and he snarled at her.

"Is this your dog?" demanded her mother, coming up and pulling her crying child away. "Why are you letting him run around loose?"

"No, that's not my dog!" I tried to explain. "My dog is the little white one." I turned around to point at Pepe and saw that he was heading towards the terrace of the Gladstone, with a pack of little kids right behind him. He looked just like the Pied Piper of Hamlin, leading them away from the danger of Bruiser and towards the safety of the building.

Bruiser, having eaten his fill of the goodies he found in the basket, headed for Mrs. Snelson's flower beds and squatted to take a dump. I swore. I had left my phone in the car in my haste. I went sprinting down to the car to get it but by the time I returned, Bruiser was gone and all there was to show for his presence was a steaming pile of poop.

I figured I should at least get a picture of that and was poised phone in hand to take a photo, when Mrs. Snelson came out onto her patio.

"You!" she said. "What are you doing here?"

Then she spotted the pile of dog poop.

"Did you catch him in the act this time?" she asked.

"Well yes," I said. That was technically true.

"Maybe you are good for something," she said. "Send me a copy of the photo so I can send it to Animal Control, and I'll call your boss and tell him I'm willing to pay him after all."

"OK," I said.

She turned and went inside. I snapped a photo of the poop, then went looking for Pepe.

I found him in the foyer of the Gladstone. A little girl in a pink dress was cradling him close to her chest, while the other children surrounded her, each begging for a turn. Pepe was shaking.

"Geri, help!" he said.

His ears were down on top of his head and his tail was tucked between his legs.

"Sorry, it's time for him to go home," I said, gently prying him out of her hands.

"We want to hold him!" one little boy yelled.

"Yeah, it's my turn next," said another little girl.

"I'm sorry," I said, "but I think he's had enough excitement for one day." The kids set up an outcry. "He has to go home and take a nap," I added, trying to explain it in terms they would understand.

"Your dog was very brave," said one of the moms. "If he hadn't come along, the kids might have been hurt by that vicious dog. He deserves a medal."

To my surprise, Pepe didn't gloat at these words of praise. "I do not want a medal!" he said. He was shivering. "Take me home, Geri!"

As I carried him back down to the car, I told him how proud I was of him. "You saved those kids by leading them away from Bruiser. That was such a clever idea, Pepe. How did you think of it?"

"Geri," said Pepe, "I was not trying to lead them away. I was trying to run away, and they followed me."

"Why were you running away, Pepe?" I asked. "Does Bruiser scare you that much?"

"It wasn't Bruiser," he said, in a tiny voice, "it was those *niños*."

"No!" I said. "You're kidding me. You've fought in the bull ring, you've wrestled alligators, you've raced in the Iditarod, but you're afraid of kids."

"Geri," said Pepe solemnly, "there is nothing more dangerous to a Chihuahua than a child."

Chapter 24

Pepe napped on the way home and by the time we were back at the house, he seemed to have recovered. I gave him some more of the new dog food and went to check my phone for messages.

Sherman Foot had called again and left me another message. I called him back, and this time he answered the phone. I could hear voices in the background. It sounded like he was in a restaurant or a bar.

"I'm glad you called me, Miss Sullivan," he said. "I must let you know that I have been engaged by Mrs. Tyler to represent her, and, insofar as her interests might conflict with your own, I am obligated to let you know that I can no longer represent you."

"But what about Stewart?" I asked.

"I have already spoken to Mr. Gerrard and given him the names of several other attorneys I recommend. He indicated that was fine with him. Mrs. Tyler's interests must come first at this sad time."

"I totally understand," I said. Yes, I did. Money

talks. I hung up the phone feeling even more blue. Despite the fact that Sherman Foot had never represented me in any proceeding, I felt abandoned.

Pepe appeared in the hallway, licking his lips. "Let us go for a walk, Geri!" he said. "I have not yet fully marked my territory in your neighborhood. It is a task that cannot wait any longer."

"Very well," I said, thinking it would be a good distraction, "but you must be on a leash. It's a law in Seattle."

"Can we pretend I slipped out of it? Like we did at the Tyler residence?" Pepe asked.

I shook my head. "No!"

"But I am allergic to leashes," Pepe said. "They make me itch."

"Should I get you one lined with fur?" I asked. It was meant to be humorous but Pepe brightened.

"Yes. I had a mink collar when I lived with Caprice. It was very soft and comfortable."

I sighed. "Pepe, I doubt you'll be wearing a mink collar anytime soon."

I bent down to clip his red polyester collar around his neck.

Outside, Pepe bent his head to sniff the edge of the sidewalk. We proceeded down the street. Very slowly. Pepe had to stop every few inches to sniff the bushes and lift his leg. I could hear him muttering to himself.

The sky was covered with gray clouds but it was not raining. As we turned the corner, the view opened out over the gray waters of Lake Union. I love Lake Union. It's the most urban lake in Seattle, its banks lined with houseboats and marinas. Sea-planes launch from the southern end, heading to-wards Canada and the San Juan Islands, and splash down as they return from the north. Kayakers and scullers paddle along its edges. The lake reflects the sky, so it was gray. It usually is.

We headed down the hill towards the lake's edge. This section of the waterfront is lined with docks for houseboats. I've always had a fantasy about living on a houseboat. Jeff and I were going to buy one after he got his first job and we had the chance to save.

There's a little park where the lake meets the edge of the Montlake Cut, a man-made channel that leads to Lake Washington. I like to stand under the willow tree, whose branches dip into the water, and watch the boats passing by—barges, tugboats, sailboats.

"What is wrong?" Pepe asked, looking up from his inspection of the lower branches of a nearby bush.

"What do you mean?"

"You seem pensive," he said.

"I'm just trying to figure out how to get myself out of a tight situation," I said.

"The date with the dog trainer?" asked Pepe hopefully.

"No, that's a tight situation I would like to be in," I said.

"Then what?"

"Well, while you were inside the Gladstone with the kids—"

Pepe shuddered. "Do not remind me."

"—I sort of accidentally told Mrs. Snelson I got a picture of Bruiser in the act. But I didn't." I explained what had happened.

"*No problema*," he said.

"We have a photograph of that *perro*, right?"

"Well, yes, I took one of him in his yard. But not in her garden."

"Ah, but that is half the battle won. You also have a photograph of a pile of poop that he left behind in the garden. No?"

"Yes."

"Then all we need do is to put the two photos together."

"How on earth would we do that?" I asked.

"Photoshop," Pepe told me. "We combine the two photographs and give it to Mrs. Snelson. She is happy, the *perro* is disgraced, and Sullivan and Sullivan have solved another case!"

"It doesn't seem ethical," I said.

"The *perro* did poop in her garden, did he not?"

"Yes, he did."

"So we are just documenting it, but in a slightly different way than taking a photograph of him in the act."

"I don't have Photoshop on my computer," I said.

"They have the program on the computers at most large copy places—like Kim's Kopies," he said. "It will be nice and bright in one of those places, and we can bill the client for the expense."

He was right and there was a Kim's Kopies nearby in the University District.

"Well," I said, thinking that his crazy idea could be the answer to my prayers. "That might just work. Let's go!"

Usually I have a hard time finding parking in the U District, especially on University Way, which is commonly known as "The Ave." Just a few blocks west of the sprawling University of Washington campus, The Ave features the usual eclectic blend of small businesses that spring up near college campuses, including cheap ethnic restaurants, a sprinkling of coffee shops, a couple of new and used bookstores, a tiny crowded smoke shop, cheap clothing stores (the kind that feature clothes made in Third World countries or T-shirts with silk-screen slogans), a shoe store that sells Birkenstocks and Earth Shoes, and a bunch of inexpensive copy shops. Usually parking is a problem. But since it was Easter Sunday, The Ave was deserted.

Kim's Kopies appeared to be the only place open on the block.

I parked right in front and walked in with Pepe on his leash. The place had as much soul as your typical office building. Gray carpet. Blank beige display counters, loaded up with envelopes and reams of paper. Posters featuring smiling customers with slogans like YOUR OFFICE AWAY FROM HOME!

The young guy at the counter had spiky red hair, a small silver ring in his left nostril, and a tribal tattoo on the back of his left hand. He also wore a tomato-red polyester shirt with his name, Sean, embroidered in cursive on the pocket.

"Ma'am," he said. (I hate being called ma'am—I'm only thirty-two. But then again he was about eighteen, so maybe I seemed ancient to him.) "Dogs aren't allowed in here. You'll have to—"

"He's a therapy dog," I told him.

"A therapy dog?"

"Yes."

"I've never heard of a therapy dog."

"He's covered under the Americans with Disabilities Act."

"Oh," he said again. "In that case, just don't let him run around in the store, OK? How can I help you?"

"I need to use Photoshop," I said.

"We have that installed on most of our computers," he said. "Just use any of the first three in the line."

I headed over to the row of computers. No one was in the store. Who goes to a copy store on Easter?

It took me a while to remember how to use Photoshop. It was a new version and quite different from the one I used when I was in school. Pepe kept trying to tell me what to do, and that was really annoying. He was sitting beside me on one of the empty chairs.

"Hey," said Pepe. "That will not do. You have put the poop on his nose."

"Give me a second," I said. "I'll move it."

I tried again. But it still wasn't right.

"Now you have it right in front of him," Pepe pointed out. "It should really be behind him."

I tried to maneuver the poop to a different spot.

"Then again, we do tend to sniff our stuff after we are done . . . No, still it would be better behind."

"I know what I'm doing," I told him.

"Ma'am, do you need help?" It was Sean, at my shoulder. Probably he had heard me talking to myself and was getting worried.

"No, I'm fine," I said, turning around to give him a bright smile. In doing so, I gave him a clear view of the screen, which was currently zoomed in on a massive pile of poop. He examined it with a critical eye.

"Art project?" he asked.

"Why, yes," I said.

"I'm an artist, too," he said. "Have you ever heard of the Web site called Scat Shots?"

I couldn't say that I had, so I just looked interested.

"That's mine," Sean said with pride. "People send me photos of their poop and I post them. Turns out people get a lot of pleasure out of trying to read them, like semiotic texts, for meaning and significance. But what you're doing here is really unique. Dog turds, huh?"

"Yeah, that's my current project," I said.

"The perspective is slightly off," he said, looking at the screen. I could see what he meant. The light was hitting the pile of poop from a different angle than it was falling on the garden surrounding it.

"Here!" he grabbed an extra chair and pulled it up beside me. "You can manipulate the shadows with this tool!" In a few minutes, he had extended the shadows so you couldn't tell where the original photo began and ended. It would have taken me another hour to accomplish.

"Wow, thanks!" I said.

"Hey, we artists have to stick together," he said. His smile was genuine. "Let's print it out!" He hit the print button, then went over the printer and pulled a copy off. He came back and held it up for us to see.

"It is a masterpiece!" exclaimed Pepe.

"It is, isn't it?" I agreed. No one would have known the photo was staged. And really, I assured myself, it was totally fair. The dog had pooped in Mrs. Snelson's garden. Just not while my camera was ready.

"How much do I owe you?" I asked Sean.

"No charge," said Sean. "You made my day. But, if you don't mind, I'd love to have a copy for my Web site."

"Sure!" I said, as he hit the print button again. "My pleasure."

"Geri, we need some business cards," Pepe said, as we headed out of the store and passed a sign advertising a sale on business cards: 500 FOR $10.

"You're right," I said.

"Pretty cool!" said Sean, when he saw my business name—SULLIVAN AND SULLIVAN, PRIVATE INVESTIGATORS. "Another art project?"

"You could say so," I said.

I consulted with Sean briefly and picked out a good font—something with a bit of weight—and an icon to represent my profession. Sean suggested a magnifying glass.

"It's an old-fashioned symbol," he noted. "Yet it's still a signifier."

I also had to decide whether or not to use my cell phone or landline, but I finally decided it was best to use both. I didn't like giving out my cell phone number, but presumably a client might need to reach me at all hours of the day or night.

After the decisions were made, it was only a matter of minutes before Sean was handing us a box of brand new cards. As soon as we were in the car, I took one out and laid it in front of Pepe.

"What do you think?" I asked.

The card read: SULLIVAN AND SULLIVAN, PRIVATE INVESTIGATORS. There was a bright red magnifying glass in the upper right-hand corner.

"Very nice," Pepe said, "but I think you should have put a dog on the card. That is what truly makes our business unique. And the magnifying glass should be hot pink."

"We can redo them later. Maybe include a photo of the two of us together."

"I would like that very much, Geri."

I was feeling good about our partnership as I pulled out of my parking spot.

"Also you should have charged him for the photo," said Pepe, as we headed home. "You cannot call yourself an artist and give away your work for free."

Chapter 25

"What an old beater," said Pepe. "I have seen better looking cars in the Tijuana wrecking yards."

I came out of the bedroom, where I was getting dressed for my date with Felix.

"What are you talking about?" I asked, noticing that Pepe was standing on the back of the sofa. From that vantage point he could see out my front window.

"I am talking about this old Volvo wagon that is trying to park in the load zone in front of our *casa*," Pepe told me, a tone of disdain in his voice. "It looks so bad, I do not think we would have taken it at Hugo's. They would have had to go next door to Soledad's Auto Wrecking to get rid of it—and even then, they would have been lucky to get a few pesos."

"What do you know about wrecking yards in Tijuana?" I asked, walking over to the window to see what my dog was going on about. It was an old station wagon, with rust spots on some of the panels.

"It is where I worked as a junkyard dog," said Pepe. "At Hugo's, to be specific."

"*You?* A junkyard dog?"

"I know it is not glamorous, Geri, but you have to start somewhere."

"I don't believe it."

"*Sí.* It is true. I worked the night shift."

"No."

"As a matter of fact, it was the first time I wore a collar. It was black with spikes. I was very scary."

"That is ridiculous. Pepe."

"You doubt my veracity?" he said. "How else do you think I came to the attention of the *federales?* The rest, as they say, is history."

"And was that before or after you were a bull-fighter?" I asked, as sarcastically as possible.

"It was before," he said. "I was at the bullfights, working undercover, while doing surveillance on Joaquin, head of the Guacamole Cartel. Somehow my cover was blown. Joaquin ran and I gave chase. I was close to apprehending him, but I tripped over a tray of half-eaten tamales, and that is how I fell into the bull ring."

I laughed. "Pepe, I don't think I've ever heard anything so outlandish."

"It *was* a most interesting chain of events," he said, seeming utterly unfazed by my incredulity. He was about to go on, but the doorbell rang.

It was Felix. He looked very handsome in a crisp white cotton shirt, dark slacks, and a tie.

His eyes lit up when he saw me. "You look great!" he said.

I was wearing one of my favorite vintage dresses, navy blue with white polka dots. Combined with navy tights and navy high heels, I thought it made me look a bit like a thirties starlet. I did a quick turn, showing off the way the skirt twirled.

"Hey!" said Pepe. "Watch it!" He was right underfoot, and I had almost stepped on him.

"Oh, I'm sorry," I said, picking him up and giving him a kiss on the head. I left a little lipstick mark between his ears.

"What's his name again?' asked Felix, putting out a hand to pet him.

"Pepe," I said.

"Keep your hands off of her, buster!" said Pepe.

"Pepe!" I said again more sharply.

Pepe drew back his upper lip and growled. It was a small sound but plenty menacing.

Felix drew his hand back quickly. "These little dogs are very territorial," he said to me. "They were bred that way. To be loyal companions."

"Yes, he is," I said, putting him down.

"Are you ready to go?" Felix asked.

"What about me?" asked Pepe. "You forgot to mention I am going along, too!"

"Oh, that's true," I said. "Felix, is it OK if I bring him along?"

"Of course," said Felix. "He can ride in the back. I've got it all set up for the dogs I transport."

"I do not like that idea," said Pepe. "I do not want to ride in the back. I want to ride up front with you."

"Too bad," I said.

"Why is that bad?" asked Felix.

"Oh, I wasn't talking to you." I hastened to assure him. "I was talking to my dog. He wants to ride up front."

"That's really not safe," Felix said. "Especially for a little dog like this. If we were to come to a sudden stop, he could go flying right through the windshield."

"See, Pepe!" I said, turning to him. "He's only thinking of your well-being."

"I am not a little dog," said Pepe.

"He thinks he's not a little dog," I told Felix.

"That's so typical of this breed," he replied.

I saw that Pepe was about to protest. "Let me get my jacket," I said, "and we can go."

"Typical, schmypical," muttered Pepe, following me into the bedroom.

"Don't worry, Pepe," I said. "I know you are anything but typical."

I took my navy jacket out of the closet and held it in front of me. Then I looked over at Pepe. He shook his head no. "Too matchy," he said.

"How about this one?" I asked, pulling out my gray wool coat. "*Sí,*" he said. "Much better."

Felix was standing in the living room looking around when we came out of the bedroom. I tried to see the place as he might see it.

Everything was secondhand. I just can't pass up a bargain, plus I don't have a lot of money to spend and I like to rescue things, give them new life. My couch was from the forties, with big wide arms; I had reupholstered it in brown velvet. The dining room chairs did not match but they were all adorable. I liked to choose where to sit by how I felt each day. The draperies were vintage thirties prints, nubbly fabric splashed with tropical plants, all brown and moss green and peach pink. I had made a pillow out of a scrap of similar fabric and put it on the couch. I often found Pepe sleeping under it. The lamp on the end table was a favorite, a collectible from the seventies with an elongated neck made of swirls of pink and green glass.

I thought it looked stylish and quirky but maybe it just looked sad. I turned to him. "What do you think?"

"I really like your place," he said. "It seems like everything has a story."

"Yes," I looked over at Pepe. "You could say that's the story of my life."

Chapter 26

True to his word, Felix insisted on putting Pepe into the back of the Volvo, which was separated from the front of the car by a wire-mesh screen. Pepe made this as difficult as possible, scrambling to get away, then rushing for the door before Felix could slam it shut. Finally we got him in there but he set up a big ruckus. I don't know what it sounded like to Felix but to me it was a long monologue about the indignities of being treated like a mere dog and demanding his immediate release.

I tried to ignore him and talk to Felix, but it was difficult.

"How did you become a dog trainer?" I asked Felix.

"What are we having for Easter dinner?" asked Pepe.

"My family has been in the film business in L.A. for decades," Felix said. "My grandfather was a gaffer. My brother is a cameraman. My mother does hair and make-up. They assumed I would go into the industry, too, but my real passion is animals. So I decided to learn how to train animals for film and TV."

"You can make a career out of that?" I asked.

"Well, is it a secret?" asked Pepe, a little huffy.

"Yes, I made a good living at it for ten years," Felix said.

I pulled the sun visor down on my side of the car and looked in its small makeup mirror. I pretended to be checking myself out, but I was really using the mirror to keep my eye on Pepe. He had his nose pressed against the mesh screen.

"So how did you end up here?" I asked Felix.

"Well, I fell in love with Seattle when I was up here on a film shoot. And a few years later, when I needed to get out of L.A., it seemed like a natural place to come. I was in need of a change of scenery."

"I hope it is not chocolate bunny rabbits and colored eggs and candy. Some Peeps would be good, though." Pepe was still muttering about food.

"Why did you leave L.A.?" I asked.

"Oh, it's a long story," said Felix. He looked mournful. I was reminded of how Pepe looked when I asked him why he was no longer living with Caprice.

"What part of L.A. did he live in?" Pepe asked.

"Where did you live in L.A.?" I asked.

"Started out in the Valley," he said. "But I ended up in Venice." He looked over at me. "Does that mean anything to you?"

"Venice!" said Pepe with a little snort. "Not the best part of town. Now if he came from Palos Verdes

Estates or Bel Air or Beverly Hills. Even Encino. That would be different."

"I've never been to L.A.," I said. "I don't know why I asked." Though, of course, I did.

"Did you grow up in Seattle?"

"No!" I said. It was my turn to snort. "I grew up in a tiny town in eastern Washington. Half the town walked in the Fourth of July parade and the other half watched."

"Fourth of July," said Pepe. "Very scary! Bombs going off."

"You didn't march in the parade?"

"No, I wasn't into band or baton twirling or anything that would have earned me a place in it."

"So what were you passionate about when you were in high school?" Felix seemed genuinely interested in my life. That was new for me. I realized Pepe had never asked me anything about myself.

"I was an art nerd," I said. "Always doodling in my notebooks. My big claim to fame was winning an art contest when I was in eighth grade."

"It was *muy horrible*," said Pepe. "All around me explosions, like guns and bombs and bright lights and things bursting into fire."

Felix pulled off the freeway at the exit that led towards Issaquah. "Where do we go from here?" he asked.

"Take a left," I said.

"I'd love to see your art work some time," said Felix, as he turned and headed down the street.

"Oh sure," said Pepe. "That is the oldest line in the book. Do not fall for that, Geri!"

"I don't do art much anymore," I said. "But I suppose I can dig up something to show you."

"I think I am going to be sick," said Pepe.

"I'd like that," Felix said.

Then he looked in the rearview mirror. "Your dog seems upset."

"He really doesn't like it back there," I said.

"It stinks!" said Pepe.

"And he's very vocal about it," Felix said.

"Can you hear him?" I asked.

"Oh, yes, he's speaking quite clearly," Felix said.

"Really? What is he saying?"

"Well, his ears laid back tell me that he's angry and his tail down tells me that he's scared. And the fact that his nose is smashed against the screen tells me that he wants to be up here with us."

"He gets carsick," I said.

"He definitely doesn't look well." Felix took another look in the rearview mirror. "I think I'll pull over."

Felix brought the Volvo to a stop at a nearby gas station. We got out and went back to check on Pepe. As Felix lifted the station wagon's rear hatch, he said, "You don't like cars very much, do you, boy?"

"I like cars very much," said Pepe, "but not your stinky dogmobile!"

I picked him up and cradled him like a baby in one arm, stroking his tummy with the other. He wiggled his little feet in the air.

"He seems a little better now," Felix said. "Does he act like that when he rides in your car?"

"To tell you the truth, I always let him ride shotgun with me. And he's perfectly well behaved. Do you think it's OK if we try that?"

"Sure," said Felix. "But you know, I could also give you some tips to help him get used to traveling in the back of the car."

"Yeah, nice try!" said Pepe.

"Be quiet!" I told him.

"What?" said Felix.

"I'm sorry, I meant it would be great if he was more quiet," I explained. "If you can get him to do that, I would be *most* appreciative."

"Nice try, Geri!" said Pepe, as we got back in the car. "But is that what you really want? Do you want really me to be quieter? Because I can be."

"Sure," I said, "go right ahead."

Felix gave me another puzzled look.

"We're ready to go," I said, hoping that would explain my comment, as I settled back, trying to arrange my shoulder harness around Pepe as best as I could. He seemed content and curled up on my lap. But he was only quiet for about three minutes. Then he poked his head up and asked, "What do you suppose your sister is serving for dinner, Geri?"

"I hope you like ham," I said to Felix.

"*Sí*, ham! *Muy delicioso!*" said Pepe.

Chapter 27

I don't know what upset my sister the most, the sight of Felix or the sight of Pepe. She stood there in the front door, looking from one to the other without uttering a word. Her eyes were narrowed and her lips pursed. She wore a purple floral print dress but the effect was marred somewhat by the gaudy yellow sunflowers all over her apron.

Pepe greeted her with a happy "Hello, Geri's sister. What is for dinner?" then dashed by her feet and into the house while Felix gave her his name and extended his hand. She took it reluctantly and returned it quickly.

"Where did that dog go?" she asked, turning around.

"Probably the kitchen," I said.

"Oh!" She hurried away down the hall, leaving us to follow. Pepe was sitting in front of the oven, looking at it eagerly.

"You were right, Geri!" he said. "Ham. My favorite."

"Get him out of here," said Cheryl, flapping a towel at Pepe.

"Oh, you want to play tug of war," said Pepe. "A childish game but I accept the challenge." He grabbed the corner of the towel in his teeth and backed away, growling.

"He's ruining my towel!" said Cheryl. "Make him stop, Geri!"

"Drop it, Pepe!" I said. But my words had no effect.

I tried grabbing the towel myself but that only meant we were now engaged in a three-way tug-of-war.

"If you drop the towel, he'll stop," Felix observed in his quiet voice.

I let go first, then Cheryl. After a small triumphant toss of his head, Pepe released his hold as well. "I win!" he said.

"We let you win," I said.

"Nasty creature!" said Cheryl. "Now I'll have to wash it to get the germs off." She hurried into the adjacent laundry room and stuffed the towel into a basket.

"Where are the kids?" I asked her.

"In the backyard. Don hid eggs and they're trying to find them." She nodded towards the back door. "I thought they better get it over with before it starts raining again."

"Kids?" said Pepe in a meek voice.

"You insisted on coming!" I told him.

"Maybe there will be Peeps," he said.

We went out through the sliding glass door onto a small concrete patio. The yard was only slightly

larger than the patio, a little square of green lawn,
surrounded by gray concrete block walls. The land-
scaping consisted of two rows of purple pansies and
magenta petunias.

It was under these feeble flowers that Don had
hidden the eggs. The kids were out there with their
baskets in hand, lifting up the petals and leaves,
looking for their treats. Don tried to direct them
with hints of "warm" and "cold," just like our parents did when we were young. It made me feel a
little weepy.

Don is the perfect husband for my sister. He's one
of those perfectly normal, rather boring guys you
always see in the orbit of someone more dazzling. In
Don's case, that would be Jeff, my ex-husband. They
grew up together in a small town in central Washington, and have been best buddies ever since. Which is
why Don invited Jeff to be his best man at his wedding, where I met him, and the rest is history.

"Where's Jeff?" I asked Don.

"Oh, he called and said he and Amber were running late."

The kids, Danielle and D. J., are five and three.
Danielle was wearing a purple floral print dress that
matched her mother's. D. J. wore a little yellow
polo shirt like his dad's and forest green Gap Kids
corduroy pants. Should I mention how I feel about
parents who dress their children like miniature
versions of themselves? Perhaps it has something to
do with the trauma of being forced to wear matching outfits with my sisters for my entire childhood.

The kids were trying hard to keep their clothes

clean while searching for the eggs, but it wasn't working. Danielle had brown splotches on the knees of her white tights from kneeling in the dirt. And D. J. had found a snail and squished it against his shirt. Or else that was snot.

As soon as they saw me, they came running. "Auntie Geri! Auntie Geri! Look at my eggs!" said Danielle.

"I got eggs too!" said D. J.

"I got more!" said Danielle. She pushed him aside.

D. J. began crying. That was a familiar scenario to me, too. My sister always had to be the best at everything.

I thought I should distract them. "I want you to meet—" but when I turned around Pepe had disappeared and so had Felix. That was odd. I greeted Don and helped the kids find the remaining eggs until it began to rain and we went inside.

As we trooped through the kitchen, Cheryl scolded Don for letting the kids get dirty and sent him off to clean them up. Then she pulled me aside.

"Where did you find him?" she asked.

"At the shelter," I said.

"You picked up a shelter worker?"

"Oh, I thought you were talking about Pepe. No, actually I picked up Felix in a parking lot."

"Geri! You've got to really do something about your taste in men. You always go for—"

I interrupted her lecture. "Where did they go anyway?"

"I'm right here." It was Felix. He had come in behind me and put his hand on the small of my back.

I felt a little thrill run through my body. "Your dog was starting to shake—he looked scared—so I suggested we go back to the car and he seemed happy to comply."

"That doesn't sound like my dog," I said. "Are you sure?"

"Go and see for yourself!" he suggested.

"I think I will," I headed out to the car. Pepe was sitting curled up in the back with a bowl of water beside him. Felix had taken off his jacket and used it to make a sort of nest for Pepe. How thoughtful! He really seemed like a nice guy. The windows in the front of the car were rolled down about halfway so there was plenty of air circulation. And since the sun was hidden behind a bank of clouds, the temperature inside the car was cool.

"Are you OK?" I asked him.

Pepe lifted his head. "How could you not have warned me?" he asked.

"Warned you about what?

"Those *niños*!"

"Oh, sorry, Pepe, I forgot you hate kids."

"It is not that I hate *niños*," he said. "But that they like me too well. They grab me around the neck, they poke my eyes, they pull my delicate ears. It is not safe for me to be around *los niños*."

"So you're content to stay in the car?"

"*Sí!*" he said, "as long as you promise to bring me leftovers."

Just as I was about to return to the house, a red Ferrari pulled up. It was Jeff, with his petite blond fiancée, Amber. Pepe got up to check out the car.

188 *Waverly Curtis*

"¡Ay caramba!" Pepe said. "That is one hot ride, Geri."

"I never got to ride in it," I mumbled. "Jeff bought it after the divorce."

"He has good taste in cars," Pepe said. "I do not understand why you would dump this guy."

"I didn't dump him, Pepe!" I protested. "He dumped me!"

"Geri! Good to see you!" said Jeff, getting out of the car and heading my way. He looked as handsome as ever, which is pretty handsome. He has thick, dark hair, big brown eyes, and a square jaw. His body looked trim in a white polo shirt and tight jeans. He works out three times a week with a personal trainer. He gave me a quick hug, pressing close so I could feel what I had missed.

"Hi, Geri!" It was Amber, coming up on his flank. Her long blond hair had been carefully styled to fall in artless waves, and she wore a knit red dress that matched the color of the car. She gave me a hug, too, but hers was a mere gesture—a sort of cheek to cheek, pat on the back hug. There is no love lost between us. Amber knows she stole my diamond after I spent years polishing him. Suddenly she gave a squeal.

"What is it, honey?" asked Jeff.

"Oh look at that cute dog in Geri's car!" Amber said pointing at Pepe. "I want one just like that! Can I hold him?"

"Let me out, Geri!" said Pepe, his eyes bright. I was a little hurt that he was so eager to embrace my rival.

"OK," I said.

I opened the car door, planning to pick him up and hand him to her. But Pepe was faster than me. He jumped out, hurried over to Jeff, lifted his leg, and peed all over Jeff's loafers.

Chapter 28

"Pepe!" I yelled. "Why did you do that?"

"I want him to know who is top dog in your life!" Pepe said. "Thus I covered up his odor with my own." At least that's what I think he said. Jeff was shrieking in the background, while hopping up and down trying to remove his soiled socks and shoes.

"I'm sorry, Jeff," I said, hurrying to his aid. "I promise to replace them."

But I don't think Jeff heard me, so I repeated the offer once we were all sitting around the dining room table (Jeff in his bare feet). Don was bringing in the dishes from the kitchen. Jeff was at one end of the table, with Amber to his left, and Cheryl was at the other end, with an empty space for Don to her right. The two kids were beside their dad, and Felix and I were squeezed in between Amber and Cheryl.

"Just order a new pair, and I'll pay for them," I said.

"You couldn't possibly replace these," Jeff said. "They're authentic crocodile leather. We bought them while we were in Milan. They cost over four thousand dollars. You couldn't afford them!"

That's when Cheryl dropped the bomb and told everyone that I had a new job as a private investigator. Jeff started laughing, and Amber, after hesitating, joined him.

"No, really," said Cheryl, as she supervised Don's placement of the dishes on the table. "Put the Jell-O salad over by Geri and her friend." She had forgotten his name. "It's not a joke."

"I work for the Gerrard Agency," I said, as we began passing the dishes around.

"I think I've heard that name before," Jeff mused.

"How did you *ever* get hired?" Amber asked. There was a little too much emphasis on the word *ever* for me.

"The normal way," I said. "I saw an ad. I answered it. I went for an interview. I got hired." I wanted to add "not by being the daughter of the boss," but I restrained myself.

"Mommy, I don't like that!" Danielle was staring down at her broccoli. My sister is not a good cook. She takes after my mother. At least the food was familiar. It was what we had every year for Easter dinner—deviled eggs, a sliced ham, scalloped potato casserole, broccoli, and a green Jell-O salad with chunks of pineapple and cottage cheese floating in it.

"Just eat one bite of everything," Cheryl instructed. Don was feeding pieces of broccoli to D. J. who was strapped into a high chair to Don's right. Cheryl had overcooked it as usual. It was slimy and limp.

"The Gerrard Agency." Jeff paused with his wine-glass held high. He was twirling the stem in his fingers. An affectation I used to find charming. He's got a huge wine cellar and had brought several bottles as his contribution to the dinner. "Isn't that the guy who has an investment club?" Jeff directed that question at Don.

Don popped another piece of broccoli into D. J.'s open mouth and nodded. "I believe so."

"Really?" I asked. It was hard to imagine Jimmy G. running an investment fund. "Are you sure we're talking about the same guy? Jimmy Gerrard."

Jeff and Don looked at each other and shook their heads.

"No, never heard of Jimmy Gerrard. This guy's name is Stewart."

"Oh, you're talking about Stewart Gerrard," I said. "He's Jimmy G.'s brother."

"Yes, that's right," said Jeff. "I remember him now. We went to a presentation at his house."

"Whatever happened to the investment club?" I asked.

"Oh, it just didn't smell right to me," said Jeff. "I passed on it. Did you go in, Don?"

"Yes, as a matter of fact, we did," said Don, looking at my sister. "We're supposed to get our first dividends in June. According to the reports, the value of our investment has doubled."

"That seems impossible in this economy," said Jeff, with a frown.

"That's what we thought, but Stewart has a system. He buys high-yield securities in foreign currencies, and sells low-yield securities in U.S. dollars. Plus he takes out interest-free loans to protect the returns. It creates something he calls a mirror-image trading position."

"Well," said Jeff, shaking his head, "I'm sorry I passed on it."

"Yes," said Amber. Her voice was a little tight. "If you had invested, maybe we could afford to buy that vacation property in the San Juans."

"But you have to agree," Jeff said, with a chiding look at his fiancée, "that we already have everything we need right here. Family, friends, great wine, good food."

D. J. made a weird noise. His eyes got big and suddenly, as if someone had turned on a water fountain, green liquid gushed from his mouth. It burbled out, down his little yellow polo shirt and into the lap of his brand new Gap Kids corduroy jeans.

The sight of her baby brother throwing up had a contagious effect on Danielle. She gagged but was old enough to know to put her hand in front of her mouth. Cheryl whisked her away from the table.

"No causal connection with Jeff's comment," Felix whispered in my ear. I had to smile.

Jeff must have noticed and decided to take Felix

down a notch. "So what do you do for a living?" he asked him.

"I'm an animal trainer," Felix said. "These days I mostly work with dogs."

There was silence, then Jeff said, "Well, you certainly can't claim any success with Geri's new pet."

I expected Felix to protest that he hadn't had a chance to work with Pepe but he just remained silent. I remembered the training maxim he had taught me: Reward behavior you want to encourage. Ignore behavior you want to extinguish.

"What do you expect from a shelter dog?" Cheryl commented, as she came back into the room without Danielle. "No one wanted them. They're second-hand goods."

"Like Geri's furniture," said Jeff, with a smirk.

"And her clothes," Amber added.

"Hey, that's not—"

Felix put a warning hand on my leg, just under the table, and I stopped talking. Unfortunately, he withdrew it as soon as I did. Now what kind of reward system is that?

"How long have you two been—?" Amber asked the question but paused, hesitant about what word to use.

"She just picked him up in a parking lot so she'd have a date for Easter dinner," Cheryl observed. She had had a few glasses of wine by then, and her words were a little slurred.

"Actually, Geri rescued me from certain attack by her protective pup," Felix said, "and when I heard about the upcoming Easter dinner, I invited myself along. I really miss my family at Easter."

That led to a discussion of how everyone cele-brated Easter. Cheryl seemed happier with Felix when she learned he was Catholic. Turns out he had attended Mass earlier in the day, which is why he was so dressed up when he came to pick me up.

"Tell me about where you grew up," said Felix, seeing he was making some inroads with Cheryl.

"Tekoa," Cheryl said. "It's a tiny little town about fifty miles south of Spokane in eastern Washington. Population 826 in 2000."

"And your parents? Do they still live there?"

There was an awkward silence. Don got up and began clearing plates.

"No," I said, at last, wanting to break the spell. "They both died in a car accident when we were young."

"Oh, I'm sorry!" Felix said. "That must have been very difficult for you. How did you manage?"

"Well, Cheryl was already attending school at the UW, so she brought me and my younger sister out to Seattle so she could take care of us."

"You have a younger sister?"

"Yes, Theresa. My parents called us Sherry, Geri, and Terri. A cruel joke!" I tried to warn him not to go where he was going. I grabbed his hand and squeezed it but apparently that only encour-aged him.

"And where is Terri now?" Felix asked.

"We don't know," I said.

"Don't know?"

"She's been missing for ten years."

Cheryl burst into noisy tears. "Go ahead and say it!" she said. "Say it's all my fault!"

"Cheryl, you know I don't—"

"Honey, no one blames you—"

"That's what you all say but I know better," said Cheryl and she stormed out of the room.

Chapter 29

"What did you think?" I asked Felix, once we were in the car and on our way back to Seattle. Pepe was in the back chowing down on the plate of leftovers I had brought him.

"I think the ham is too dry," Pepe mumbled, his mouth full.

"You can be honest," I said.

"Okay, then the broccoli is overcooked, too," said Pepe.

"Your sister is a bit—" Felix hesitated.

"Bossy," I said. "Yes, I know. But you can't really blame her. She had to become responsible way too young."

"The Jell-O salad has a nice flavor," said Pepe. "But I do not care for the texture."

"She was only a sophomore in college when our parents died. Once she moved me and my sister to Seattle, she had to be a parent and a student at the same time."

"It was hard for you, as well," Felix observed.

"Leaving behind everything you knew and coming to a strange city." It was kind of him to notice. Cheryl has made such a big deal about her sacrifice that I had never thought too much about how it affected me. I had to leave the small town where I grew up. And transfer from a school with a total of 114 students to a big urban school with 1,600 students enrolled.

"Yes," I said, "we all adapted in our own way. I tried to not cause any trouble while my sister Terri did the exact opposite. She went wild."

"I'm really sorry I asked about her," Felix said.

"I was trying to warn you not to go there by squeezing your hand."

"Oh, and I thought you were trying to encourage me," Felix said with a laugh. "That's the trouble with unclear signals."

"No way is she going to encourage you, senor," said Pepe, who had finished up the leftovers and was now giving his full attention to our conversation.

"So you have no idea what happened to her?" Felix asked.

I shook my head. "No. She dropped out of high school but she seemed to be getting by, waitressing and such, until 2001 when she just vanished." I paused, decided to say it out loud. "We're both afraid she's dead. Else why would she never have contacted us?" My voice caught a little.

Felix reached over and put his hand on mine.

Pepe said, "Don't cry, Geri."

"I'm not crying," I said.

"It's OK if you want to cry," Felix said. He was

quiet, then asked. "Do you think that had anything to do with your becoming a private investigator?"

"Oh!" I was surprised by the question and had to think about it. "I guess that makes sense. I suppose if I had the right skills, I might be able to find her. Or at least find out what happened to her."

"Do not worry, Geri," said Pepe. "I will track her down for you. Just give me something of hers to sniff, and I can find her anywhere."

"Where did you get your training?" Felix asked. We were coasting down the long ramp of the freeway exit on our way into Seattle.

"Well, I haven't really had any," I said. "I just got a couple of books from the library."

"Your agency didn't provide training?"

"She does not need training," said Pepe. "She is working with me!"

"My boss said he would pay for classes," I said. I was feeling down as I always did when I thought of Terri. "I should follow up on that. First thing tomorrow." I gave a sigh, thinking of the long day ahead of me.

"After we rescue Siren Song," said Pepe.

"Speaking of that," I said. "What would you say if I told you I know someone who has trained her dog to dance?"

"Yes, I've seen that done," Felix said. "They call it canine freestyling. I think it looks ridiculous."

"No one cares what you think, buddy," said Pepe.

"Mostly the people, not the dogs," Felix hastened to add. "Dogs always look attractive. Even when dancing around on their hind legs."

"That is the first smart thing you have said, mister," said Pepe.

"What if I told you this person trains her dog by hitting her on the nose?"

"Ouch!" said Felix.

"Empathy," said Pepe. "That is a good quality."

"I don't approve of training methods that use punishment," Felix said. "You treat the dog with disrespect, you either get an animal that has its spirit broken or you create a nasty case of aggression."

"This *vato* is starting to make sense," Pepe said.

"So how do you train a dog?" I asked.

"I only use positive reinforcement. When the dog does what I want, I reward it. With food, at first."

"I am beginning to like this guy more and more," Pepe observed.

"Then?"

"Then with praise."

"And does that work on people?"

"You bet it does," he said with a twinkle in his eye. He had just pulled up in front of my courtyard. "Let me walk you to your door."

"I will protect her from malfeasants," said Pepe. "No need for you to do so, *hombre!*" He clawed at the screen and barked fiercely.

"Your little guy seemed to do better on the way home," Felix observed, as we got out of the car and released Pepe from the back. He sprang out and scrambled onto the parkway where he immediately lifted his leg.

"How come you're not peeing on his shoes?" I asked Pepe.

"Do you want me to?" he asked.

"No, no, it's fine," I said.

"You talk to your dog a lot," Felix observed. "It's almost like you are having a conversation with him."

"It seems that way to me most of the time," I said, tucking my arm into his.

"I will check to be sure the coast is clear," said Pepe, running ahead of us.

"You know, you really should have him on a leash," said Felix. "For his own sake. He might run into the street and get hit by a car."

"Pepe has a lot of street sense," I said.

"I could work with you on training him," Felix offered.

"I don't think Pepe would like that," I said. We had caught up with him. He was sitting outside my front door and glaring at Felix.

"Really, it's just an excuse. I want to see you again," said Felix, taking both of my hands in his. He gazed down at me with those dark eyes, and I felt a little dizzy. The yellow light from the street lamp and the overcast sky behind it made it look like we were in some noir film. He leaned in to kiss me. His lips were just brushing mine when Pepe barked.

"Geri! Watch out!" he said. "Danger!"

He was right. The kiss was dangerous. Some kisses are primarily physical, all lips and mouth and tongue. This one started out that way but then shifted into the other type of a kiss—magical, where the kiss is a portal to another world, where it is only the two of you merging and dissolving and melting together.

Felix let go of my hands and drew me closer to him, wrapping his arms around me. We could have been on a beach on a tropical island, or floating in the warm ocean waters, lapped by waves, with a velvety sky spangled with stars overhead. We could have been the only two people in the world.

Except for Pepe. He was barking furiously. "Geri! Stop this at once! Attention! I need your attention!"

I tried to block out the sound of Pepe's voice. I just wanted to fall into the sweetness of the kiss. But I couldn't ignore his increasingly frantic cries.

"Danger! Danger!" said Pepe.

"What is it?" I pulled away from Felix and looked down at Pepe, who was clawing at the front door.

"I smell an intruder!" he said. "Someone has been in our house while we were gone."

Chapter 30

"How do you know that?" I asked Pepe.

"I can smell it!" he said, sniffing all around the door.

I bent down to look at the doorknob. There were scuff marks around the door jamb and the plate, as if someone had pried it open.

"What's going on?" Felix asked.

"It looks like someone might have broken into my condo."

"Do you think they're still inside?" he asked.

"What do you think, Pepe?" I asked.

Pepe looked up. "They have gone," he said. "The scent is old. Perhaps an hour ago."

"Pepe seems to think they're gone," I said.

"I can go in and check it out for you," Felix offered. "I have training in martial arts."

"As do I!" said Pepe. "Let me in! I will defend my territory!" He scratched at the door.

I opened the door with my key and both of them charged in, almost getting tangled up in the hallway.

Pepe ran from room to room, sniffing. Felix flung open all the doors, including the door to the shower and all of the closets. He even checked under the bed. I followed behind, looking to see if anything had been disturbed. The only thing that seemed to be disturbed was Albert. He was standing in the middle of my pink chenille bedspread. His fur was all bristled up—he looked twice his normal size— and his tail swished back and forth.

"If only you could talk," I said to him. "You could describe the intruder."

I picked him up and carried him around with me, hoping to soothe him.

"It doesn't look like anything's missing," I said. My home is small. You enter directly into the living room, which has two doors—one leads into a narrow kitchen and the back porch and the other opens into my tiny bedroom and its adjoining bathroom. It didn't take long to inspect everything, even the broom closet and the cupboards under the sink.

"Perhaps someone tried to break in and didn't succeed," Felix suggested.

That made the hairs rise up on the back of my neck. But it wasn't as bad as what Pepe said next. "No, there was someone here. The intruder went into the bedroom, and into your bathroom, then looked through your closet and finally came in here."

Pepe sat down in the middle of the kitchen floor and gazed at the refrigerator.

"Hungry again, Pepe?" I asked. "You just ate."

"No, I am not hungry, Geri," Pepe said. "Well,

actually I am hungry. But that is not why you must look in the refrigerator."

"OK," I said. "I give up. Why must I look in the refrigerator?"

"Because the intruder put something there."

I set Albert down on the sofa and went into the kitchen to look in the refrigerator. I didn't see anything unusual. A carton of eggs. A loaf of bread. A box of Chardonnay. Could it be poisoned now? A half-empty can of dog food for Pepe. Maybe the miscreant tampered with that.

"It all looks the same to me," I said.

"The smell is coming from higher up!" said Pepe.

I opened the freezer, which is always a mistake at my house. I have an old pink refrigerator (one of the reasons I bought this particular condo) and it needs to be defrosted by hand every month or so. It's a task I tend to put off. A bag of frozen peas tumbled out. It hit Pepe on the head, then fell to the floor where it split open and the frozen peas came rolling out.

"Ow!" said Pepe, dancing around, and slipping and sliding on the peas. "Ow!"

I scooped him up and kissed the top of his head and each one of his little paws. That seemed to calm him down. Meanwhile Albert came running in and started hunting down the rolling peas. Felix stood in the doorway, an amused smile on his face.

"What happened?" he asked.

"Pepe thought there was something in the freezer," I said, looking back at the freezer compartment. "And it looks like he was right." I saw the glitter of gold, back behind the bag of frozen french fries and an old carton of strawberry ice cream.

I pulled it out. It was a gold case, with the initials *DPT* engraved on the cover in fancy calligraphy.

"What is this?" I asked. "I've never seen it before!"

"The intruder put it there," Pepe said.

I set Pepe down on the floor. He looked at the cat—Albert was still batting peas back and forth.

"Small amusements for small minds," said Pepe. He strolled out of the room with a swagger. I think he was still feeling sorry for himself. It is not very dignified to be hit on the head by a bag of frozen peas.

"What is it?" asked Felix, coming close, but being very careful to avoid the peas. Albert had swatted most of them beneath the cupboards.

"I don't know." I flicked open the clasp at the front and saw that it was filled with business cards. The one on top read

> REBECCA TYLER
> PRODUCER
> *DANCING WITH DOGS*

"Oh my God!" I dropped it like a hot potato. Business cards went flying everywhere, scattering into the corners along with the peas.

"What is it?" Felix asked.

"I believe it belongs to David Tyler," I said. He looked puzzled, so I went on. "The man who was murdered the other day."

"Oh!" Various expressions crossed Felix's face. First confusion, then doubt, and finally concern.

"What was it doing in your freezer?" he asked.

"Don't you see?" I asked. "The intruder must have hid it there."

"But why?"

"A warning or an attempt to blackmail you, Geri," said Pepe who was standing on the threshold. He had recovered some of his jauntiness.

I bent to pick up the cards. I did not recognize most of the names, but here and there was a name I did know: Sherman Foot, lawyer, and Stewart Gerrard, CEO of Gerrard Enterprises. Then I froze. There was my card staring up at me. Only it wasn't my old card, it was one of the new cards I had made to please Pepe: SULLIVAN AND SULLIVAN, PRIVATE INVESTIGATORS.

I went into the dining room. The box of cards was on the table. It didn't look like it had been opened. But when I handed it to Pepe to sniff, he nodded. "The intruder touched this box, Geri! It is the same horrid smell as I smelled in the bushes and on the glove!"

"I just made these cards today," I told Felix, "at a copy shop in the U District, right before you picked me up. There's no way David Tyler could have had one of these cards in his card case."

"What are you going to do?" Felix asked.

"Do you think I should call the police?"

"*No policía*," said Pepe.

"What would you tell them?" asked Felix. "That

you believe someone sneaked into your house to hide a card case that belongs to a murder victim?"

"I just don't understand why someone would do that," I said.

"To frame you for the murder, Geri," said Pepe.

"If that's true," I said, "then the police may be coming to search my house." I took the case out of Felix's hands and snapped it shut. "What should I do with it?" I looked around. "Put it back in the freezer?"

"No, that is where the police will look for it!" Pepe said. He seemed to have a good grasp of how a deviant mind would work. Perhaps it was from watching all those true-crime TV shows.

"The police have no reasonable cause to search your house," said Felix. It sounded like he watched those shows, too.

"So you think I'm safe for tonight?" I asked. And then I realized how absurd that sounded. Someone had broken into my house while I was gone. Someone who had been in David Tyler's house. Undoubtedly the person who had murdered him.

And suddenly I was shaking and crying. The enormity of all that had happened hit me. The fright of finding Mr. Tyler's body and my suspicions of his wife. The stress of the horrible Easter dinner. Even the weirdness of having a talking dog.

Felix took me in his arms. "It's OK," he said. "It's OK. You're safe now."

I leaned my head against his shoulder and let my tears fall. I felt a funny tickling feeling on my ankle and looked down to see that Pepe was licking my ankle, the only part of me he could reach.

"I'm just so scared," I said. "What if the person is still outside? Watching me?"

"Do you want me to stay?" Felix asked.

What could I say?

"No, we do not," said Pepe. "I can take care of her."

"That would be great," I said.

"Make him sleep on the couch," Pepe said.

"I can sleep on the couch," Felix said.

"Of course," I said. Although I had been imagining how nice it would be to be wrapped up in his arms.

"But first, come and sit down," Felix said. He led me over to the sofa and we settled down. Felix turned on the radio. He found a Spanish music station, with lots of slow ballads and sexy rumbas. Pepe jumped up and settled in my lap. Albert sat on the arm of the sofa, watching us out of his golden eyes.

We talked a little, trying to figure out what to do next. Felix thought I should turn the card case over to the police in the morning. Pepe thought I should sneak it back into the Tyler residence the next day. I think it was Albert who suggested I should simply give it back to Rebecca. I'm not really sure about that because by then my brain was pretty foggy. I also imagined that we wandered through a dark labyrinth, searching for a golden treasure, only to find Siren Song at the center, all alone, waltzing in a blue tulle skirt.

When I woke up the next morning, I was in my own bed, with Pepe curled up beside me and Albert snoring at the end of the bed. I got up thinking— hoping, really—that the whole day had been a dream. Except for the part where Felix kissed me. Then I smelled the scent of freshly brewed coffee. I wandered out into my kitchen to find Felix, barefoot, who looked like a dream even though his clothes and dark hair were slightly rumpled from a night spent on my sofa.

"I'm fixing breakfast," he said. "Where's the bacon?"

"A man after my own heart," Pepe murmured.

Chapter 31

Felix was pretty gracious about the lack of bacon. A lot more gracious than Pepe who complained all through breakfast, even though I sneaked him several bites of the spicy hash browns that Felix served up along with some perfectly scrambled eggs, topped with cheddar cheese.

Felix gave me another one of those long dreamy kisses before heading off for an appointment at a client's house. He offered to take the card case away for me but I had decided to return it to Rebecca and see how she reacted. Almost as soon as he left, there was a sharp knock at the front door.

"Open up, police!" said a loud voice.

"What am I going to do?" I asked Pepe, glancing at the coffee table where I had left the card case. It was gone.

"Do not worry, Geri," said Pepe. "I have taken care of it. Go answer the door."

"Open up or we'll break the door down!" said the voice at the door.

"I'm coming!" I said, moving towards the front door. I was still in my bathrobe and fluffy bunny slippers.

I opened the door to find a cop with his gun drawn on my right and another on the left side of my door. Out in the street, blue lights blinked on the top of several cop cars. I could see a little knot of onlookers gathered on the sidewalk across the street.

"Can I help you?" I asked in my most mild-mannered voice.

An older man in a suit strolled out from behind the officers. I recognized Detective Larson, the older of the two homicide detectives who had questioned me the day I found David Tyler's body. He tapped the uniform cop on the shoulder and said, "Put the guns away."

"Good morning, Miss Sullivan," said Detective Larson. "May I come in?"

I decided to avoid the question. "What's this about?" I asked.

"We got a tip that we will find evidence linking you to the murder here."

"A tip? From who?"

"I'm not at liberty to say."

"That's ridiculous," I said, trying to keep my voice as calm as possible though I was shaking. "I had nothing to do with David Tyler's death."

"Then a search would clear your name," he said in a mild tone.

"I don't think I have to let you in," I said, trying

to remember what Felix had said the night before. "Do you have a search warrant?"

"As a matter of fact, we do." He pulled some papers out of his pocket.

"Ask to look at it!" said Pepe, who had come up behind me.

"Can I see it?"

"Certainly," he said. I tried to read the pages but my hands were shaking so much, the words blurred. What to do?

"Let them in, Geri," said Pepe. "You have nothing to hide."

"You're welcome to come in and search," I said, stepping aside. In a few moments, several officers swarmed into my little house. Detective Larson went straight to the refrigerator. In fact, he went straight to the freezer. He took every item out, setting each thing on the counter, and looked puzzled when the freezer compartment was empty and he had found nothing.

Another officer had pulled out the trash from under the sink and was going through it.

"A bag of frozen peas in here," he said to the lead detective.

"Why is that?" Detective Larson asked me.

"Why is what?"

"Why the frozen peas in your trash?"

"Because you opened up the freezer compartment, and they fell out and rolled all over the floor!" Pepe prompted.

"Yes," I said. "Because they fell out of the freezer

compartment and rolled all over the floor. I didn't want to eat them after that."

"Why were you looking in the freezer compartment?" the detective asked.

"Why do you think?" I said, beginning to get annoyed. "I was looking for something to cook for dinner."

"We'd like to search your entire house," the young cop said.

"Go ahead," I said.

And so the search began. They poked through all my drawers, emptied all the wastebaskets, turned over all the cushions on the sofa. Pepe suggested I distract myself by watching old episodes of *Paraiso perdido* but it was hard to concentrate on the travails of Conchita and Hector when at any moment, the police could turn up the gold card case and I would be hauled away in handcuffs.

They noticed the scuff marks around the door and asked me about that. I told them there had been a break-in but I hadn't reported it because nothing appeared to be missing. That, at least, was true.

After about two hours, the police left. I watched out the front window until all the cars were gone. They had tried to put everything back where they found it but I knew I had a lot of work to do before I would feel comfortable in my space again.

"Where is it?" I asked Pepe, after they were gone.

"I hid it!" he said proudly.

"Where?" I wanted to know.

Pepe looked a little bit embarrassed.

"A place they would never look," he said.

"Yes, where is that place?" I asked.

"It is in your bathroom," he said.

"Let's see!" I said. Pepe trotted into my bedroom and then into the small adjoining bathroom. There wasn't much room for anything. I had managed to squeeze Albert's cat box in between the toilet and the cupboard under the sink.

"Under the rug?" I asked, pulling up the shaggy pink carpet.

Pepe shook his head.

"Not in the cupboard! You couldn't open it!" I said, pulling it open anyway to look. My hair dryer spilled out. I stuffed it back in.

"No, I can't open that," said Pepe.

"In the bathtub?" I peered in there. Nothing, except some water stains around the drain.

"Not the toilet!" I said. "That could ruin the plumbing."

"Do you consider me a dog of no brain?" Pepe asked. "The one place no one but that evil cat would ever go."

"No, Pepe!" I said. "You didn't!"

"*Sí!*" he declared, and he seemed very proud of himself. "I hid the gold case in the litter box."

Chapter 32

"Geri," Pepe said, as we drove away in the car, "I am *muy* worried about Siren Song. We should make haste to rescue her from the cruelty of Senora Rebecca."

"I agree, Pepe," I said, "but our appointment with Mrs. Tyler is not until 1 PM, and we have another case to solve as well. Have you forgotten about Bruiser?"

"That *cabrón* will never dare to show his face in Mrs. Snelson's garden again," said Pepe, "not after the lesson I taught him!"

I considered pointing out that Pepe had done nothing to Bruiser personally, but then thought better of it. The Photoshop photo was his idea after all, and I thought the photo, which was tucked into my purse, would help us close the case. I still felt guilty about using deception to frame Bruiser. After all, I knew what it was like to be framed.

Pepe had saved my bacon there, as well. "That

was very clever," I told him, "hiding the card case in the cat box. I am surprised the detectives didn't look there."

"Oh," said Pepe, "some credit is due to Albert as well. I think eating all of those peas did not agree with him."

"Yes, I noticed that," I said. "I'll have to clean the cat box when we get back home."

Pepe was standing in the passenger seat with his front paws on the edge of the window as we drove past the convenience store where we had stopped the other day.

"Look, Geri!" he said. "Do we not need supplies?"

I thought about that for a minute. The place had good memories for me, as well as Pepe, so I pulled over and went in and bought some beef jerky for Pepe and a bottle of water for me. I was hoping Felix might show up in the parking lot with his dog, but I got back to the car without any encounters, canine or otherwise.

"I have another question about last night," I said, as we continued on our journey. Pepe was chowing down on the beef jerky. "I don't remember how I got into my bed. The last thing I remember is being on the sofa with Felix."

"Do not worry, Geri!" mumbled Pepe, his mouth full. "It is true that Felix carried you to your bed—" Oh! How I was sorry I had missed that! "But then I encouraged him to leave the bedroom. Albert and I were the ones who tucked you in."

* * *

I didn't bother to hide Pepe in my purse for this visit. Mrs. Snelson, who greeted us at the door with a trowel in her hand, seemed delighted to see him.

"Here's the little hero!" she said. "He deserves a treat! Can I give him a cookie?"

"Well—"

"I am ready when you are, senora," said Pepe, heading towards the kitchen.

"Oh, he is a smart little dog," said Mrs. Snelson, sticking her trowel into the dirt of one of her larger potted plants. "He definitely understands the word *cookie!*" She hurried into the kitchen after him.

"Naturally," said Pepe, "what do you think I am? Even a child understands that word!" He sat looking up at the counter. The kitchen was full of plants, though not as many as the living room. There were drooping grape ivy plants hanging down the sides of the refrigerator and a sweet potato vine curling up from a jar behind the faucets.

Mrs. Snelson bent down to scratch Pepe on the top of his head. "Now isn't he so precious? And so good?" She was practically cooing. What had happened to change this dog hater into a dog appreciator?

"How many can he have?" she asked, sticking her hand into a ceramic container on the counter which was designed to look like a fat bumblebee. "They're my special shortbread cookies." She popped one into Pepe's mouth. He laid it down on the floor in front of him, and licked it carefully, before gobbling down every crumb.

"Keep them coming!" he said.

"I suppose one or two more," I said.

It was a lovefest in the kitchen, with Mrs. Snelson admiring the delicate way that Pepe ate and Pepe making admiring comments about her culinary skills.

"You should ask her for the recipe, Geri," he said. "These are *muy delicioso!*"

But I was eager to get my guilty errand over with and get out of there.

"Mrs. Snelson," I said, "I need to follow up with you about your case. I have evidence that will—"

"Oh! Not to worry!" said Mrs. Snelson, waving her hand at me. "That's all taken care of."

"It is?"

"Oh, yes, that beast is in jail and will be for a very long time!"

"Jail?" said Pepe. He stopped eating his current cookie.

"Yes, the Animal Control came and took him away. I doubt that he will ever get out."

Pepe looked stricken. Mrs. Snelson tried to give him another cookie but he hung his head and wouldn't take it.

"I guess he's full," she said. She popped the cookie into her own mouth. Then she remembered me. "Would you like one?"

"Sure," I said.

"They're better with milk," she said, opening her olive-green refrigerator. It was covered with magnets with garden-related themes, like a little watering can and a reproduction of an antique seed packet, the kind of gifts you would send to someone you didn't know well who liked gardening. She poured herself a glass and gave me one as well. Even the glasses were green, which gave the milk a greenish cast. Still I had to admit the cookies were delicious.

Mrs. Snelson poured a little milk in a saucer for Pepe, but he turned up his nose at it.

"What's wrong with you?" I asked.

"I do not feel so good," he said.

Had she poisoned my dog? Maybe this lovey-dovey dog act was all a ruse!

"What hurts?"

"*Mi corazon!*" he said. "My heart is heavy thinking of Bruiser in dog jail. I have been there myself. It is a rough and dangerous place."

"How did Bruiser end up at the pound?" I asked Mrs. Snelson.

"Well, after the news story aired, there was a public outcry about such a dangerous animal being allowed to run loose in our neighborhood. Then you can be sure Animal Control took action. They were out here early this morning and carted him off."

"What news story?"

"Do you mean you didn't see it?"

"No."

"It was the lead story on the eleven o'clock news!" she said.

"Well," I said, "I was pretty busy last night." I thought back to the break-in at my condo, the discovery of the card case, and the comfort of Felix's embrace.

"Yes, it was Easter," said Mrs. Snelson, "but that's what made it such a good story. You know, human interest, happy ending, all that."

"I was on the news?" said Pepe, his ears pricking up.

"So it was a story about—"

"About your little dog leading those children to safety!" Mrs. Snelson motioned me to follow her into the living room. "One of my neighbors taped it so I can send a copy to my children. Here! You can watch it with me!"

We all sat down, Mrs. Snelson and I side by side on a loveseat, flanked by two royal palms, whose fronds kept getting stuck in my curls, and Pepe between us on the green carpet. She had a widescreen TV mounted on the wall, above a tray of succulents. She picked up a remote control and punched a few buttons.

The logo for the news channel flashed across the screen in bright blue, and then the camera zoomed in on one our local commentators. She said, "And our top story tonight is about a little dog who saved Easter for a group of children."

A picture came on the screen showing Pepe clasped in the arms of the little girl in the pink dress. Her mother must have snapped the shot.

The news anchor's voice continued. "A group of children had gathered for an Easter egg hunt on the lawn of the Gladstone, a retirement center in Green Lake, when a vicious dog attacked."

The screen filled with a head shot of a woman newscaster. "And then," she said, "out of nowhere, a little white dog appeared, like an angel, and led all the children to safety." As she was speaking, a rather wobbly image came on the screen of Pepe leading the children towards the building. Apparently one of the parents had been filming the Easter egg hunt and offered the footage to the TV station.

The commentator spoke again. "The owner of the vicious animal was clearly unable to control her dog." Now the footage showed me, flapping my hands at Bruiser, trying to shoo him away, while he rooted around in an abandoned Easter basket. It was a great shot, actually, as it showed the lawn littered with abandoned baskets, like an Easter egg battlefield.

"Hey, that's not *my* dog!" I said.

"*Shhh,* Geri!" said Pepe. "I am trying to listen."

Then there was a shot of Mrs. Snelson, her white hair sticking up all over the place. She was filmed in front of her garden, holding one of her trowels like a scepter. "I've called Animal Control repeatedly for months complaining about this brutish beast, but they have refused to do anything about it. Now see what happens! Gardens ravaged! Innocent children in danger!"

The commentator continued. "Animal Control was contacted and cited the owner. The dog, a pit bull mix, was taken into custody and is currently being held for observation at the Animal Shelter.

Meanwhile, the parents of the children who were threatened wish to express their gratitude to the brave little dog who saved their children."

A man's face filled the screen. He clasped his daughter close to his heart. "That dog was a hero!" he said. "We're just all so glad he came along."

"Hey, that's my dog!" I said.

"That was me!" said Pepe.

And then they went on to their second story, about a traffic accident on the freeway.

"I am famous!" said Pepe. He got up and danced around the living room. Then he turned to me. "I want a copy of it! For my portfolio!"

"Look at him! He's so proud of himself," said Mrs. Snelson, gazing on Pepe fondly. "And he should be!"

"Do you think you can make a copy of it for me?" I asked Mrs. Snelson.

"I'll ask my neighbor," she said. "He has the gift for technology. But I'm sure the TV station would give you a copy as well. After all, it was your dog who was the star. They might even want to do a follow-up story."

"*Sí!*" said Pepe. "I will be famous! No doubt the mayor will want to present me with the key to the city!"

"I can't believe they would air the story without checking the facts," I said.

"Well, no one could find you—you departed so quickly," said Mrs. Snelson. "I tried to tell the news people that you were a detective I had hired, but they didn't seem to understand."

"Another case successfully concluded," said Pepe.

"I guess we're done," I said, with a sigh. No need to use the doctored photo. What a relief! I got up and thanked Mrs. Snelson for her hospitality.

"Yes, I've already called your boss and told him how happy I am with your services," said Mrs. Snelson. "Now that you have a reputation, I am sure you'll get many cases from other residents here at the Gladstone."

"I'm surprised by that," I said. "I would think there wouldn't be much need for a private detective at a retirement home."

"You would be surprised," said Mrs. Snelson, in a conspiratorial whisper as we approached the front door. "There is a great deal of crime here. Someone has been stealing women's bloomers from the laundry room on the fifth floor."

"That does seem disturbing," I said. "But it doesn't exactly sound like a crime wave."

"Oh, but last week someone stole Mr. Maine's boxers. He has a 45-inch waist. I don't see how they could be of use to anyone else."

"I can see that you do have a problem," I said, suppressing a smile. "I'd be happy to help you identify the perpetrator, if you decide to hire me in the future."

Chapter 33

"Now that I am famous, perhaps I can have my own reality TV show," Pepe said as we headed towards the Tyler residence. "What do you think it should be called? *Pepe el Macho*? *America's Most Courageous Dog*?"

"Perhaps, *Pepe the Most Conceited Dog*," I said.

"You are just annoyed, Geri, because the news people did not notice you." Pepe said. "But do not worry. I will give you a role on my show. You can be my assistant. Perhaps we will call it *The Pepe Sullivan Show*."

"What about *Sullivan and Sullivan, Private Investigators*?" I asked.

"Oh, that is an excellent idea, Geri. As long as my Sullivan goes first."

"How could that—"

"We will have to pitch that concept as well. Do you think Senora Rebecca will be able to get us a meeting with her producer?"

"What do you know about meetings?"

"Geri, I am a dog from Beverly Hills. I know all about how the entertainment business works. We must capitalize on our fame while our faces are fresh in the public eye."

"Perhaps Felix can help us, too," I mused. "He has a background in the movie business."

"And we will bring in Siren Song as my romantic lead," said Pepe, as we pulled up in front of the Tyler house.

"What about *Dancing with Dogs*?" I asked. "Rebecca won't want to lose the star of her show."

"Ah, but once the tabloids learn of our romance, she will appreciate the publicity. It will increase the ratings for both of our shows," Pepe said.

When I opened the car door, Pepe fairly leaped out of the car. He waited impatiently on Rebecca's front porch while I hurried to catch up.

I expected Rosa to answer the door but it was Rebecca herself. She looked as impeccable as ever in a gray linen skirt and a black chiffon blouse. But her nose was pink and so were her eyes. It was obvious she had been crying.

"Are you all right?" I asked.

Pepe ran inside before she could answer.

"No, I'm not," said Rebecca. I don't think she even saw Pepe run by. "Come in, please. I'm so glad you're here."

I stepped into the white marble foyer. Pepe was nowhere in sight.

"What's wrong?" I asked.

"Everything" she said. "Everything is going all to hell."

She led me down the hall and into an office near the rear of the house. It was obvious no decorator had been allowed to touch this room. The desk was an old corner set, designed for maximum efficiency. A gray fabric ergonomic swivel chair sat behind it. The top was crowded with several monitors and a chunky printer. Power strips and cords created a tangle of obstacles on the floor.

Brick-and-board bookshelves lined one wall, crammed with science fiction and fantasy paperbacks. On the outside wall, between the windows, a gas fire flickered behind glass.

Rebecca turned around and faced me. "The producers have given me until noon tomorrow to come up with the money for the pilot, and I still don't have it!"

"Well, isn't that why I'm here?" I asked. "To help you sort through David's papers?"

"No need for that anymore." Rebecca's said. "Stewart is taking care of that!"

"Stewart? As in Stewart Gerrard?"

"Yes. He came by to offer his condolences yesterday, and when I told him about the problems I was having, he offered to help. He and Mandy took away David's financial records and are going to look them over to see what they can find."

"How well do you know Stewart?" I asked.

"Like I told you, Stewart is one of David's oldest friends. They've known each other since college. And Stewart has been our financial advisor for ages."

"Do you know Jimmy Gerrard?" I asked.

"Isn't that Stewart's little brother?" Rebecca said.

"I think I met him once at a holiday party at Stewart's house. Quite a character. But no, I've never had a conversation with him, if that's what you mean."

"So you didn't call Jimmy G. and ask him to find your husband?"

"Now, why would I do that?" Rebecca asked.

"But he was missing, wasn't he?"

"Well, now we know why!" Rebecca said firmly.

She picked up a framed photo that sat on the mantel and threw it against the wall. The glass shattered into a thousand pieces.

"I found out why David never called me. He was having an affair!" She burst into noisy sobs and threw herself into an armchair in front of the fire.

I went over to the photo and picked it up. It was a photograph of Rebecca and David. They seemed very happy. They were in bright ski apparel, with a snowy slope behind them. She was planting a kiss on his cheek, and he was beaming.

"Toss that in the fire!" she said, looking up.

"I can't do that," I said.

"Well, then give it to me. I can!"

As I approached, she snatched the photo out of my hand and threw it into the fire. It flared up in a burst of green and blue. As it crumpled into black, sticky goo, Rebecca burst into tears again.

I sank down in the other chair, not sure what to do.

Rosa came into the room. Today she was wearing what looked like a nurse's uniform: pink polyester pants and tunic top, with pink sneakers. She held Pepe by the scruff of his neck with one hand. He was twisting and turning and seemed to be gasping for breath. I jumped up and rescued him, cradling him in my arms like a baby.

"Thank you, Geri!" he choked out.

"What happened?" I asked.

Rosa rattled off a string of Spanish in which the only words I understood were *Siren Song*.

"She says I was trying to ravage Siren Song," Pepe whispered to me, as I settled back into the chair with him on my lap. "I was only trying to rescue her. She is being held captive in a cage with steel bars."

"Clean up the glass, Rosa, *por favor*," said Rebecca, pointing at the shards on the floor. Thank God, Pepe hadn't run over them with his delicate pink paws. Rosa left the room.

"Why is Rebecca crying?" he asked me.

"She thinks her husband was planning to leave her," I said.

"Why does she think that?"

That seemed like a good question. I turned to Rebecca. "I don't understand why you think David was leaving you."

"Stewart said as much," she said, wiping at her eyes with the sleeve of her chiffon blouse.

Rosa came back in, silent in her pink sneakers, and bent down to scoop up the broken glass with a whisk broom and a dust pan.

"David had the money I needed. He just didn't want to give it to me!"

"Why not?"

"David told Stewart he thought the idea for the *Dancing with Dogs* show was stupid. And childish! And immature! But he was afraid to tell me."

"So he never intended to send you the money?"

"No. There I was in L.A., telling everyone the money was about to arrive, and he was just putting me off. There was plenty of money in our account. He just didn't want to give it to me."

Rosa finished scraping up the glass and left the room as silently as she came in.

"So this is good news," I said. "There is enough money for *Dancing with Dogs*." I didn't point out that if David had been planning to leave her, the timing of his death was awfully convenient. She would inherit everything. If he had divorced her, well, not so much.

"Yes, but David had Stewart transfer our money into a secret offshore account. You see? He was trying to hide it from me. It's obvious. It was because he was going to run off with his mistress!"

She got up and paced around the room.

"Did Stewart tell you anything about her?"

"No, apparently David didn't confide in him. Stewart just guessed that's what was going on because David asked for his help hiding our assets."

"So how will Stewart find the money you need?"

"I don't know, but the man is a financial wizard. If anyone can come up with something, he can."

"Geri, ask her about the gold case!" Pepe said.

"I have something that I think belongs to you," I said. I set Pepe down and pulled the gold card case out of my pocket.

Rebecca looked shocked. She almost dropped it. It was hard to tell if she was just surprised to see it or if she was angry. She flicked the clasp and sorted through the cards. (I had removed mine.) I could see she was puzzled by what she saw. (Perhaps David had kept them in a certain order.) She snapped it shut, then raised it to her nostrils and sniffed.

"It smells awful," she said. "Like it's been in a cat box. Where did you find it?"

"She has a good nose!" said Pepe with admiration.

"Someone left it at my house. I think they were trying to frame me."

"Or perhaps you picked it up on the day you were here."

"Why would I do that?"

"It's extremely valuable. It's part of a set I gave David for our anniversary. A solid gold pen and the card case, both engraved with his initials. David always carried them with him."

"Was anything else missing?" I asked, ignoring her insult.

"David's BlackBerry. The police thought the murderer must have taken that because it contained David's calendar and thus some clues as to his whereabouts. And the gold pen is still missing."

"But robbery doesn't seem to be the motive?"

"No, I mean, it could have been a botched robbery," Rebecca said. "What other explanation could there be?"

I could think of plenty. Maybe Rebecca had hired a hit man to kill her husband once she learned he was leaving her. Or perhaps she had come home early, found her husband with another woman, and killed him in a fit of rage. But then, who was the other woman?

"Did you ask her about pitching our show?" Pepe asked.

"No, it really doesn't seem like the moment," I murmured.

"What's that?" Rebecca's voice was sharp.

"It doesn't seem like a good time for a dancing lesson," I said, relieved at the turn of events.

"Yes, I couldn't concentrate today," Rebecca said. "Come back tomorrow. Although, if Stewart doesn't come up with the money, there won't be any point."

Chapter 34

With Pepe riding shotgun beside me, I headed downtown, hoping to get paid by Jimmy G. for the successful resolution of the Snelson case. Pepe was upset about leaving behind his lady love and the cruel fate that prevented him from rescuing her.

"We'll get another chance, Pepe," I said.

"But meanwhile Siren Song languishes in a prison," Pepe said.

"A crate, Pepe," I said sternly. "Most dogs love them. I should probably get one for you."

"Monstrous!" said Pepe. "It is the equivalent of solitary confinement. Cruel and unusual punishment."

"How would you know?"

"I have done time," he said proudly. "In a Mexican jail. The very worst kind."

"I'm sure that's true," I said, with a hint of sarcasm.

"Of course, I was innocent of all charges," said Pepe.

"Of course," I said.

I was distracted by the downtown traffic. I hate driving downtown in Seattle. One-way streets. Do Not Turn signs. Pedestrians who ignore the walk signals. Plus I can never find a parking place. I finally found a spot near the Greyhound bus terminal. I tucked Pepe into my purse to make it easier to carry him. The sidewalks were crowded, and I didn't want anyone stepping on him.

As we passed Nordstrom department store, Pepe stuck his head out of my purse.

"Wait, Geri!" he said.

"What?"

He lifted his little pink nose and sniffed the air. "Geri, I smell the smell," he said.

"What smell?"

"The stink I smelled in the bushes outside the Tyler residence. And on the gold card case. The smell of the murderer!"

I looked around. People were rushing past us, hurrying to get on buses, swinging shopping bags, carrying briefcases. It could have been anyone.

"How will I figure out who it's coming from?" I asked.

"It is coming from inside the store," he said.

"Oh!" I turned and went through the double doors, Pepe leading the way with his nose twitching. This entrance opened into the perfume section of the store, a sea of dazzling glass cases and islands full of shining bottles and metallic boxes.

"Someone nearby?" I asked.

"No, some*thing* nearby," he said. "It is one of these scents!"

"You can smell one scent out of hundreds outside the door and know it was the same scent you smelled at the crime scene?"

"*Sí,*" said Pepe, wrinkling up his nose. "Dogs have 220 million scent receptors in their noses while humans have only 5 million."

"So how will you find it?'

"We must ask a salesperson to help us," Pepe said.

"That shouldn't be too hard," I said, for as soon as they saw his white velvet head sticking out of my purse, the salespeople came swarming like bees towards flowers. Soon they were all around, petting his head and cooing over him. Pepe lapped it all up like a cat laps up cream. But after a five-minute lovefest, the crowd thinned, going back to their stations. Apparently, in some unspoken and invisible battle for customers, a young woman with blond hair pulled back in a French twist had won the competition for our business.

Her name tag said she was Eve. A perfect name for such a temptress. She wore a little black dress, which showed off her flawless milky skin and slender body, and a pair of strappy, stiletto heels. The dress and the shoes probably cost more than my entire wardrobe.

"How can I help you?" she asked.

"I'm trying to find a particular perfume," I told her.

"What's it called?" she asked with a warm smile.

"Well, that's just the problem," I said. "I don't know what it's called. It's a scent I smelled just once in . . . uh . . . at a party. I never got a chance to find out who was wearing it and ask them."

"Don't worry. We have many samples. We'll find it for you, I'm sure."

She led me over to her station, behind a glass counter, stocked with multicolored bottles of fantastic shapes and designs. "Perhaps we could narrow the selection down a bit for you. How would you describe the scent you're looking for?"

"Ugly," said Pepe.

"Ugly is not a fragrance," I told him.

"It smelled ugly?" Eve asked.

"It was ugly to me," Pepe insisted.

"No," I said to Eve. "I'm trying to think of the right words."

"Fine, then," Pepe said. "How about this? It smelled like an old *gordo* Rottweiler, heavy and musky."

"It was very heavy and musky," I told Eve.

"Ah, that helps," she said. "And how long ago were you at the party you mentioned? Where you smelled the perfume, I mean."

"Just a few days ago."

"Had you ever smelled it before?"

"No."

"OK," she said. "Why don't we begin with some of our newer fragrances? It's possible it may be one of our new lines—there are a quite few we've added recently."

She sprayed perfume from a gold bottle onto a thin strip of paper, flapped it up and down and handed it to me.

"This is called Tonal Tuberose," said Eve. "It's

a typical white flower scent but this one has a peppery top note, a green mango heart, and a creamy, yet transparent, floral drydown." I sniffed at it tentatively—I didn't smell any of the things that Eve had described. The word I would use to describe it was shrill. Then I waved it in front of Pepe's nose.

"Your little dog likes perfume?" she asked.

"He is a connoisseur of scents," I replied.

As if to illustrate my words, he sneezed. "Not this one!" he said.

"Perhaps it's too strong for him!" she suggested.

"Tell her I was a search and rescue dog!" Pepe said.

"Oh, that's OK," I said. "He was a search and rescue dog. He's used to this sort of work."

Eve looked a little worried at that. "He doesn't look like a search and rescue dog," she said.

"You really can't judge a dog by his cover," I said. Unfortunately, no one laughed at my joke.

Eve merely raised her perfectly penciled eyebrows over her stunning blue eyes. Then she offered me another splash of perfume on another test strip. "This is more in the citrus range," she said. "It reminds me of lemon cookies, with a touch of the fuzzy skin of apricots, and a light musk hovering in the background like the mist of a waterfall."

"She should write copy for these perfumes," Pepe said, his brown eyes wide with admiration.

I took a cautious sniff. All I got was the scent of pink lemonade. Hoping Pepe would smell something more, I set the strip back on the little ceramic plate on the counter but waved it under Pepe's nose as I did so.

He sneezed again. "Not it," said Pepe. "Reminds me of dishwashing detergent."

"Let's try another," I said to Eve.

And so it went until the little ceramic dish that held the used test strips was stacked high.

"How about this one?" Eve asked, offering yet another bottle. "It's very popular with our younger customers." Her perky smile had sagged a little as she had now spent over an hour with us while the other perfume salespeople had been steadily ringing up customers.

"This is our newest addition," she said. "It's called Caprice."

"Caprice!" Pepe exclaimed.

"After the actress?" I asked Eve.

"Indeed," she said. "We just got the entire Caprice line—perfume, cologne, and eau de toilette."

"Yes, I'd like to try it," I said, holding out my hand. I thought it might remind Pepe of his previous life.

The bottle was slim, and topped with a crystal swirl. The liquid inside was a violent pink. Eve sprayed it on the back of my right hand. The aroma was overpowering, something like cotton candy and cherry cola on a hot day at the state fair. I reeled back.

Pepe's reaction was even stronger. "That is *ugly!*" he gasped, and coughed.

"Does that mean it's the one?" I asked him.

"Is it?" Eve asked.

Pepe nodded, continuing to sneeze and wheeze.

He ducked down inside my purse, apparently to get as far away from my hand as he could.

"I think this is it," I told Eve.

"*You think?*" Pepe said, poking his head back up. "It is definitely the scent. But how could one as *guapa* as Caprice make a scent that is so *repugnante?*"

"I don't know," I said. "But we've found it, anyway."

"I'm so glad," said Eve.

"Take it away," said Pepe.

"Would you like the one ounce or two ounce bottle?" Eve asked.

"How much is it?'

"$125 for 50 milliliters."

"No, Geri, I would have to leave if you smelled like that all the time."

"Well," I said. "I'll have to think about it."

"Oh . . ." said Eve, disappointment crossing her pretty face. I saw her glance across the room at another salesclerk who shrugged. But being a professional, she quickly recovered. Her fetching smile back in place, she said, "Well, I'm very happy we found what you were looking for." She paused, then took a small color brochure from the counter and handed it to me. "Take this," she said. "It lists the complete line of Caprice products."

"Thanks." I took the brochure, which featured a photo of the actress in a bright pink bikini, her tan skin dripping with water as she lay back, half immersed, in the turquoise waters of a classic California swimming pool.

"Ah! I remember that pool," Pepe said, looking

at the photo. "At the Chateau Marmont. One of her friends tossed me in and I almost drowned."

"So you can't swim?" I asked. "I'm kind of surprised. You can do everything else."

"I dog-paddled to the side, but then I could not get out," said Pepe. "Caprice had to fish me out with a net. It was most undignified. Even worse, they made a video and posted it to YouTube." He gave a mighty sneeze. "But I do need to preserve my nose! It is essential to my livelihood. So get me out of here, partner!"

Chapter 35

"I'm curious," I said, as we left Nordstrom and headed towards Jimmy G.'s office. "Why do you react so badly to the scent of Caprice? Is it because it reminds you of your former owner?"

"We dogs do not use the word *owner*," Pepe said with disdain.

"What word do you use?" I asked curious.

"It depends on the dog," he said. "Some say human. I think that is too cold. Some say provider. That has merit. I prefer companion."

"OK, I can see that." I nodded my head. "My question remains . . ."

"It is not that it reminds me of Caprice," he said. "We *perros* do not like perfume."

"Really?" I thought of all the times I had carefully spritzed on my favorite scent while getting dressed.

"You did not know that?"

"I do now."

"*Bueno*," he told me. "If, however, they make a bacon perfume, I might change my mind."

* * *

"Hey, doll!" said Jimmy G. when we walked into his office. He had his feet up on his desk, as usual. He was wearing two-toned brown-and-white oxfords with green-and-blue argyle socks. His sports coat was the colors of a Creamsicle, orange and white, and his shirt was brown with a white collar.

He took his feet off the desk as we came in, creating an avalanche. Empty bags, betting forms, newspapers, and unopened envelopes slid over the edge in a waterfall of paper. Some landed in a brown puddle on the floor. An empty Styrofoam cup lay beside it, the obvious source of the spill. One of his goldfish was floating sideways at the top of the murky tank.

"Have a seat," he said, gesturing at the chair against the wall, which had a few stains of dubious provenance on the fabric. "Jimmy G. was just having a bite to eat." He held up a clear, triangular plastic container filled with some kind of sandwich. "It says it's tuna, but it looks more like deviled ham."

A piece of wilted lettuce fell out and onto his desk as he offered the sandwich to me. He left it where it lay.

"I do not eat vending machine sandwiches," said Pepe. "I learned a bitter lesson at a bus station in Tijuana."

"No thanks," I said.

"Suit yourself." He took a large bite out of it. "It

is tuna," he said, chewing thoughtfully. "So what brings you to visit Jimmy G.?"

"Money," I said.

"Just what I like. A pretty dame who wants to drop some Ben Franklins on me."

"No, I need some," I said. "I wrapped up the Snelson case, and you said you'd pay me. Two hundred in cash. The day the case was solved."

Jimmy G. took another bite of his sandwich.

"Yeah, that old broad called," he mumbled. "Was mighty pleased. Crazy old bat."

"So did she pay you?"

"No, I told her you'd send her an invoice," Jimmy G pushed around the papers on his desk.

"Why me?"

"You're my gal Friday, aren't you?"

"I am not your gal Friday!" I snapped. "And even if I was, how would I create an invoice anyway?" I might have to do it myself if I wanted to get paid. "I don't see a computer."

Jimmy G. laughed, a short bark of a laugh. "Jimmy G. doesn't need a computer! Got a typewriter right over there!" He pointed to the corner where I saw an old Royal on a rolling metal table.

"This is ridiculous," I said. "You can't run a business this way. Don't you take credit card payments? Where do you keep your receipts? How do you keep track of your accounts receivable?"

"Whoa!" Jimmy G. appeared to stagger back. "You're getting much too technical. Jimmy G. doesn't do mathematics."

"Evidently not arithmetic, either," said Pepe.

"Stewart is the numbers man. The only numbers Jimmy G. knows are the odds on the ponies at Emerald Downs."

"So Stewart takes care of your finances?"

Jimmy G. nodded. "Stewart pays the rent. Stewart pays the utilities. Stewart comes by and drops off some cash every now and then for operating expenses. At the moment"—Jimmy G's brown eyes got sad—"Jimmy G. is frankly low on funds."

"But I need the money now!" I insisted.

"Well, then why don't you head on over to Stewart's office and ask him for it. Jimmy G. will give him a call and tell him you're coming. Though come to think of it, Stewart might be a little upset when he sees you."

"Why would that be?"

"Well, he called Jimmy G. and told Jimmy G. to fire you."

"What? That doesn't make any sense. He asked me to fill out employment forms and told me he'd pay for my training!"

"Stewart is like that. Probably decided he couldn't afford it."

"This is ridiculous!" I said. "I'm going to go talk to him myself."

Chapter 36

No one responded when I rang the doorbell at Stewart's castle. I rang it again and again.

"Geri, let us reconnoiter," Pepe suggested. He darted off, running around the left side of the house. I followed him down a narrow path of stepping stones. It meandered around the carefully shaped juniper hedges, passed beneath banks of mullioned windows, and ended at the stone terrace outside Stewart's office. Gray clouds were rolling in from the south, carried by a brisk wind.

The windows of Stewart's office were finished with some sort of anti-glare product that made it impossible to see inside. So I continued around to the other side of the house and peered in the window of Mandy's office. She was there, at her desk, feeding papers into a shredder. A cardboard box full of shredded paper stood on the floor beside her and there was a stack of folders on her desk. I tapped on the window and she jumped.

Then she waved me over to the rear door, which

was located between her office and Stewart's office. She was wearing what I thought of as a sexy secretary outfit—a crisp white linen blouse, a short black skirt, and black high heels. A gold pen was stuck into her dark hair, which had been pulled back into a chignon.

"What are you doing here?" she asked.

"I rang the front door bell," I said. "No one answered."

"We're busy," she said.

"Look, I just came to drop off those papers you wanted," I said. I had the completed employment forms in my bag.

She glared at Pepe who was standing by my feet.

"Well, you can't bring that animal in here!" she said. "You know, Stewart is terribly allergic."

She glanced at the door to Stewart's office. It was closed, but it was clear she felt his presence anyway.

"Fine," I said. "He can stay out here."

I looked at Pepe. "Stay close to the house," I said. "I don't want a hawk carrying you off."

"I have been in that situation before," Pepe said. "I was able to escape by telling the bird a story that so distracted her—"

"Just get under the furniture," I said. I didn't have time to listen to another of his fantastic stories.

I pointed at the two striped lounge chairs that were on the terrace, each facing the spectacular view of the lake. Reluctantly, slowly, Pepe did as I requested, inching along until he was hunched beneath one of the chairs. I could see his dark eyes glowering out at me. He was not a happy dog.

I followed Mandy into her office. She waved me to a chair and looked over the papers I handed her. "I need to see your passport or else your driver's license and some other form of identification, like a Social Security card," she said. "The federal government requires me to make sure you are a U.S. citizen."

"Look, I just need to know what's going on," I said. "Jimmy G. told me that Stewart wants to fire me. So why are you bothering with the paperwork?"

Mandy pursed up her lips and pointed a finger at her head, waving it in circles. "Jimmy G. is loco. Haven't you figured that out by now?"

"So, Stewart didn't tell him to fire me?"

"Of course not." Mandy studied my resume. "You're an interior decorator?" I didn't like the tone of incredulity in her voice but I ignored it.

"Yes," I said, "though mainly I specialize in staging."

"I might have some work for you," Mandy said.

"Really? Are you selling a house?"

"No. But Stewart wants to redo this place. He wants something more modern that will appeal to our international clients." She set the resume down on her desk. "I'd love to get your opinion."

This was amazing. Perhaps I should consider Pepe my good-luck charm. I had been offered three jobs in the five days since had I adopted him. Of course, I hadn't yet been paid for most of them.

"Do you think Stewart will be able to pay me?" I asked. "Jimmy G. sent me over here because he said he's short on cash."

"I don't see why not," said Mandy. "We can give you a deposit or a retainer, or whatever you call it in your line of work."

"Great!" I said. "How do you want to proceed?"

"Let's start with Stewart's office."

"Won't that disturb Stewart?'

"Oh, he's not here. He's meeting with a new investor." She led me across the wide hallway and threw open the door.

As I looked around, I noticed the top of Stewart's massive oak desk was completely bare. It certainly didn't look like he was analyzing David Tyler's financial records.

"Did he finish up the work he was doing for Rebecca?" I asked.

"Yes," Mandy said. "It only took him a few hours."

"Really? I thought David Tyler had a lot of investments."

"Stewart is really good at what he does," Mandy said. She put her hands on her hips. "What do you think? Get rid of the books?"

"Yes," I said. "We can certainly make this room look lighter and brighter. Take out the Persian rug—it looks like there's a nice hardwood floor underneath. And bring in a few pieces of more modern furniture, perhaps some white leather chairs, a desk with a glass top, something with some sleek lines."

"I like it!" Mandy clapped her hands. "Let's go upstairs."

"Did Stewart find the money Rebecca needed for her show?" I asked as we headed up the stairs.

"Oh, yes, he found the money all right," Mandy said. "But he told her it was in an offshore account and he can't touch it. He doesn't want her to invest in that stupid show. It's going to be a disaster."

"That sounds unethical to me."

"Stewart is just trying to be loyal to his friend. That's what David would have wanted."

We stood at the threshold of the great room. The house was as silent as the tomb. No sounds from outside penetrated those thick walls. The light was fading from the sky and the great room was full of shadows.

"But what about what Rebecca wants?"

"Who cares?"

"You don't seem very sympathetic!" I said.

"I can't stand that woman!"

"You know Rebecca?"

"Yes, I used to work for her! She was a total bitch!"

"What? You worked for Jimmy G. You work for Stewart. And you used to work for Rebecca?"

"Well, yes," said Mandy. She seemed annoyed. "I don't know why you're so interested in my work history."

"It just seems odd," I said.

"Not really. I mean, they all know each other." She moved into the middle of the room. "What do you think we should do with this room?"

"Well, you need to make this room feel friendly and open. Get rid of all the sofas—"

"Oh, that won't be a problem" said Mandy. "They're all leased anyway."

"Is Stewart still going to use this room for talking to clients?"

"Yes, but he doesn't need to do the lectures anymore to groups. He's going for bigger fish now, and he only needs one or two people at the levels he's reaching. So if he's hanging out in this space with clients, it will be more social—drinks, conversation, maybe some catered appetizers being passed."

"Well, we can create different furniture groupings so there are places for people to sit and talk, and also room to mix and mingle. I can bring some fabric swatches and some pictures clipped out of magazines for you to show to Stewart. I think the biggest issue will be the vertical space." I looked up at the dark heavy beams looming over our heads and the shadows above them. "Maybe some big light fixtures hanging from the ceiling. I know a designer who makes custom light fixtures out of white paper. They look very Japanese."

"Stewart does have a few Japanese clients," said Mandy. She sighed and went over to the window. I joined her and we stood there for a few minutes, looking out over the waters of the lake. We could see the glowing red taillights of the cars flowing across the Floating Bridge on their way to Bellevue.

"What did you do for Rebecca?' I asked.

"I was her dog dancer," Mandy said. "Until she fired me because she thought her husband was getting interested in me. She has a problem with jealousy."

"You knew David Tyler, too?"

"Of course." Her voice was soft.

"And *was* he interested in you?"

She turned to me, her dark eyes flashing. "You've got to be kidding! David was like a father to me. He was a kind man. He took an interest in my future. He paid for my college education."

"So this must have been hard on you."

"You have no idea!" she said, and I thought I could see tears in her eyes.

"I'm sorry."

"It's OK. I've gotten used to it."

"Who do you think murdered him?"

"Probably a botched robbery," Mandy said. "I think David was alone in the house, and he heard a sound. He went to get Rebecca's gun—she kept one in her bedroom—and then went downstairs to investigate." Her voice was gathering passion as she sketched out this scenario. "He must have confronted the robber, they struggled over the gun— David was such a geek, he wouldn't have known what to do with a gun—and then the gun went off."

"If it was a robbery, then why was nothing taken?"

"I imagine the robber ran off horrified at the realization he had killed someone!"

And suddenly she was sobbing. I put my arms around her. She wasn't the easiest person to hug. She was stiff and tense and wouldn't accept the comfort I offered. I finally settled for patting her on the back as she bent over, almost double, gasping out tiny little sobs. It was quite pathetic.

I heard shouting and wild barking from down below.

"Oh my God!" I said. "Pepe! I forgot all about him."

I raced down the stairs and flung the rear door open. Mandy was close behind me.

Out on the terrace, Stewart was turning around in circles, trying to bash Pepe with his briefcase. Pepe was snarling and growling and making forays at Stewart's ankles. Stewart kicked out at him but missed. Pepe was too fast. He darted behind Stewart's back and made a lunge for his Achilles tendon. Stewart went down, almost falling on Pepe.

"What are you doing?" I shouted. I wasn't sure if I was yelling at Stewart or Pepe.

"Get this beast away from me!" Stewart screamed.

I grabbed Pepe up and held him close. "That's our boss," I whispered to him. "Why are you attacking him?"

"He smells bad," said Pepe.

Mandy went by, rushing to Stewart's assistance. She held out her hand and hauled him to his feet. Stewart sneezed.

"Did you still want to talk about the decorating?" I asked as they went by.

"Can't you see this isn't a good time!" she snapped.

Stewart sneezed again and then howled in pain as the sneeze apparently triggered a back spasm. He clutched at Mandy and they continued on their lurching way to the door.

"I'll bring by some sketches and an estimate," I said.

"Yes, why don't you do that?" It was hard to tell from her clipped tones if she was trying to encourage me or being sarcastic.

Stewart limped his way into the office, while she supported him by the shoulders.

"What about the money that Jimmy G. promised me?" I called out.

There was no response to that. Just the *snick* as the door shut behind them.

Pepe kept sneezing and shivering. "The stink!" he said.

"What stink?"

"Look!" said Pepe. "There under the lounger." He gave another mighty sneeze.

I looked and saw a gold object glittering in the sun. I pulled it out and held it up. It was a gold pen, engraved with the initials DPT.

"And it is covered with the scent of Caprice!" Pepe said. "Caprice and the scent of murder!"

Chapter 37

"Why are you not calling the *policía* on Mandy?" Pepe asked as I headed towards my car, with Pepe safely tucked into my purse.

"For the umpteenth time," I told him, "Mandy using Caprice isn't really proof of anything. There are probably hundreds of women in Seattle who wear the same perfume."

"That may be so," he said. "But I have a gut feeling about this."

"You sound like some TV detective."

"*Gracias*," he said, as usual not getting my sarcasm. "It would be too much of a coincidence that Mandy wears the same perfume. We private investigators do not trust coincidence."

"What if it was Stewart who wears Caprice?"

"Now that is an interesting possibility, Geri. Anything is possible in Seattle."

"Or perhaps Stewart was with the mystery woman who was running away with David and got her perfume on his hands or on his clothes," I pointed out. "Assuming there is a mystery woman."

"Another possibility, Geri," said Pepe. "But again, why are we not doing something about it?"

"Like what? You want me to go to the police and tell them that my dog recognized a certain perfume on a certain person, and he has a gut feeling that they're guilty of murder?"

"Something like that."

"Oh, for heaven's sake." It wasn't like I didn't share his feelings about the situation; it was just that I recognized our limitations. And maybe that was it, I thought—he was a dog and I wasn't. Dogs always act like they have no limitations. Especially Chihuahuas.

Just as we reached the car, Pepe gave a little yelp. "There is something vibrating under my butt!"

"Oh," I said. "It's my cell phone. I put it on vibrate when we arrived."

"Answer it already," he said. "Either that or rub it against my back. I could use a good massage."

I opened my car door and dumped him out, along with the contents of my purse. I was afraid the phone would go to voice mail, so I didn't bother to check the screen to see who was calling. As soon as I heard the voice, I regretted that decision. It was my ex, Jeff.

"Geri," he said. "I've got to talk to you."

"You got me," I said. "Talk away."

"Hold on a minute," he said. The line went silent as he put me on hold.

That was typical of Jeff. His needs always came first.

I was about to hang up when he came back on.

"So how soon can you get here?"

"Why would I come see you?"

"I've got something important to discuss with you, and I don't want to talk about it on the phone."

Oh, really. "Why not?" I asked.

"Look, I can't talk right now. I'm late for a meeting. Can you come to my office?"

"I'm busy, too."

"It will only take a few minutes."

And then he was gone. He hadn't even waited for me to reply. He just assumed I would come running when he called. And to tell the truth, he was right. The suggestion that he had something so important to tell me that he had to speak to me in person intrigued me.

He had told me he had fallen in love with someone else on the telephone. And he informed me he was getting married via e-mail. So I couldn't imagine what was so important that he needed to speak to me in person. But I was going to find out. I got in the car and headed for Bellevue.

Jeff's office was in one of the new high-rises in downtown Bellevue, a quick trip across the lake. Pepe quivered in my purse as the elevator gave us a stomach-dropping ride to the twenty-fifth floor.

"If this is what it is like to be an astronaut," he said, "I will take it off my to-do list."

You knew you were out of your price range as soon as you got off the elevator. The wide hallway was covered with the best wool carpet money could buy. The walls were paneled in rich, inlaid burl veneers. And everywhere you looked, you saw shiny brass fittings—moldings, picture frames, door handles, and lighting fixtures.

Jeff's company took up half of the entire floor. You gained entry through a pair of double-wide, opaque glass doors, beside which an engraved brass plaque displayed the company name:

BECKWORTH & TROUT
—INSURANCE UNDERWRITERS—
LIFE & CASUALTY/COMMERCIAL & MARINE.

Jeff had done well with the MBA I had paid for. Made upper-level management in his first year with the company. Was slated to go even higher. He had a corner office with a view out across Lake Washington.

His new secretary, the one who had replaced Amber, ushered us into his office. Kathy was a sour-faced, middle-aged woman with frizzy hair, buckteeth, and a leathery complexion. (I was pretty sure Amber had picked her out.) Kathy ushered us into Jeff's office and left us sitting on the brown leather sofa, facing Jeff's imposing desk of burnished cherry wood. Jeff was nowhere to be seen, of course. "In a meeting," she told us. "He'll be with you shortly."

I sat there, looking at his framed diploma on the

wall, the one he had earned while I slaved away at the waste disposal plant, and told myself, Geri, you shouldn't feel envious or bitter. After all, Jeff has nothing but success, a beautiful house on the East-side, a big salary, a fancy sports car, and a beautiful (if vapid) fiancée. You have . . . well, a talking dog.

As if reading my mind, Pepe said, "Geri, your ex-mate seems to have done very well for himself. He has a handsome car, a glamorous girlfriend, and it appears from this office, an important position. But he does not have, well, *me*."

I had to laugh. The little guy cheered me up. I gave him a pat on the head and said, "Thanks, *amigo*."

Jeff walked in looking rather dapper in an expensive tan suit and an eggplant-colored linen shirt. He looked at me, and he looked at Pepe, then he went out to his secretary's desk. I could hear him having words with her, probably about Pepe, because that was where he started when he came back into the office.

"Do you take that dog with you everywhere you go?" he asked.

"His name is Pepe, and yes," I said.

"Tell him I'm your partner," Pepe said.

"I can't leave him alone in the house because of Albert," I added. I hoped that would make Jeff feel guilty. Jeff chuckled. "Yes, I suppose Albert would make short work of that dog." He was proud of Albert's prowess. When we lived together, Albert was always bringing home dead birds and mice. I didn't point out that Albert always brought them to me, not to Jeff. I wasn't really too happy about it at the time.

"Hey, tell him it was I who vanquished the cowardly cat!" Pepe said, puffing up his chest a little and strutting back and forth on the sofa, tossing his head.

"I don't suppose you called me up to lecture me about my dog," I said.

"No." Jeff buzzed Kathy and asked her to shut the door to his office. That was typical of him. He couldn't be bothered to get up from his desk and shut it himself. "Hold my phone calls, too!" he added.

I wondered what was so important that he had summoned me to his workplace. Was he thinking of breaking up with Amber and asking me to try again? I hated it that my mind even went there. More likely he was going to ask me what sort of present to buy her for their first anniversary. Jeff was that clueless.

Pepe had jumped down and was sniffing around the desk.

"Keep him away from me!" said Jeff, with a slightly hysterical tone in his voice.

"Oh, it's about the shoes, isn't it?" I asked. "I can write you a check right now, if that's what you want."

"No, it's not about the shoes," Jeff said. "In fact, you can forget about paying me for them. I want you to quit your job."

Chapter 38

"You've got a lot of nerve!" I said. Pepe had stopped in his tracks and was looking at me quizzically. Then I added, "Which job?"

"Oh," said Jeff. "Are you still doing staging?"

"Yes, as a matter of fact I just got a new project. For a guy with a multimillion dollar home in Laurelhurst."

"That's good," Jeff said. "But I meant your PI job."

"Why would I quit that?" I asked.

"Yes, why would we?" asked Pepe, staring at Jeff's shoes.

"I think it is dangerous for you," he said.

I have to admit I felt a twinge of affection. He obviously still cared for me if he was worrying about me. Then again, he was being as condescending and controlling as ever. I hadn't realized how demoralizing it was to live with someone who was always telling me what to do until after we broke up. "Well, I appreciate your concern," I said, "but I can take care of myself."

"Tell him I take care of you!" Pepe piped up.

"Hush!" I said, "I can take care of myself," I told him, both of them, firmly.

"If it's because you need money, I can loan you some," Jeff said.

"That's generous of you," I started. Then I realized that he was offering me money that would have been mine if he hadn't divorced me.

"No," I said. "It's not the money."

"It's the adventure, the thrill of the chase, the satisfaction of knowing we have made the world a safer place," said Pepe.

"Wow! You really have been watching too much TV," I said.

"What?" That was Jeff.

"Sorry. It just sounded like a line from a TV show," I said. "I don't want your money, Jeff. I'm fine."

"Look, I'm not suggesting you quit your job," he said, standing up. "I'm ordering you to quit."

I stood up, too. "You can't order me to do anything," I said.

Pepe looked at Jeff and growled.

"It's for your own good," Jeff said.

"I am not a child," I said. Unfortunately, my voice got a little high and squeaky. It always does that when I'm mad, which undercuts the effect I'm trying to have. "You don't get to tell me what's good for me. I decide that myself."

"Yes, if anyone is going to tell her what to do, it is me!" said Pepe.

"Oh, hush!" I said. "You can't tell me what to do either."

"Look, Geri . . ." Jeff came to the side of the desk, but Pepe was standing at my feet growling so fiercely that Jeff didn't dare to come any closer. "I'm not trying to tell you what to do. I'm trying to protect you from getting involved in something that's illegal. I'm afraid you're in danger."

"What?" said Pepe, perking up at the word *danger*.

"Yes, what?" I asked.

"Let's just say this." Jeff lowered his voice as if his office could be bugged. "There's something funny going on at the Gerrard Agency. I don't want you there if the police raid the place. You could end up in jail for a long time."

"Good grief, Jeff!" I almost shouted. "You can't get me to back off a job to which I've made a commitment [that was a dig], when I've finally found something that fulfills me on so many levels [OK, that was another dig], by hinting at raids and jail. Either tell me what's going on, or I'm out of here. Right now!"

"You tell him, Geri!" Pepe looked up at me with admiration and added a menacing growl.

"OK, OK," said Jeff, motioning for me to sit down again. "You are so stubborn!" He glared at me. My "stubbornness" was one of his chief complaints when we were married. It just meant I wasn't doing what he wanted me to do. "I can see I'm going to have to give you more information." He leaned across his desk. "Do you know the term Ponzi scheme?"

"Isn't that like a pyramid scheme?" I asked.

"Yes," said Jeff. "An operator, under the guise of offering an extraordinary return on investments, uses the money of later investors to pay off early investors, but there's never any real investment, and eventually the scheme collapses."

"Like Bernie Madoff," Pepe said.

"How do you know that?" I asked.

"You can learn a lot from daytime TV," Pepe said.

"After Don mentioned his investment with the Gerrards, I got curious and did some investigating of my own," Jeff said. "It took a while to figure it out. There were all kinds of shell companies and bogus boards, but I finally traced it back to him."

"I don't think Jimmy G. is capable—"

"Not the younger brother. The older one. Stewart. As far as I can tell, he just uses the detective agency for money laundering. It operates at a loss, so he doesn't have to pay any taxes."

"What about Don and Cheryl's money?"

"I'm worried about that. I called Don this morning and told him to get his money out before the whole thing collapses. I'm not going to go to the authorities until he's recouped his investment. Once the police get involved, Gerrard's assets will be frozen. It might take years to get it sorted out and pay back the investors."

"Oh," I said, "but I know someone else who has money invested with Stewart—Rebecca Tyler." It made sense now that Stewart was putting her off for a few days. He didn't have the money she needed and he was trying to buy time. "She should get her money out, too."

"You can't warn her," said Jeff. "If you do, that might alert Stewart to the fact that we're on to him."

"Then what will happen to *Dancing with Dogs*?" Pepe asked. He sounded wistful.

"But she needs the money desperately," I said. I decided not to tell Jeff what she was going to use it for. He would probably consider it frivolous.

"Where's your loyalty, Geri?" Jeff asked. "To your sister? Or some woman who, for all you know, killed her own husband? That's who usually does it, you know. The wife!"

"Yes, I know," I said, "and I can see why!" I glared at him.

"All I'm asking you to do is to keep this information confidential. Don't go into the office for a few days. Wait until I tell you the coast is clear. Then you can do anything you want."

His phone rang. He glanced at the screen, then picked it up. "Yes, darling. I've got the tickets." Then a pause and, "I'll pick it up on my way home."

While he responded to Amber's demands, I pondered his demand. For some reason it did not sit right with me. I thought of both Jimmy G. and Rebecca and realized that I felt more loyalty to them than I felt to Don and Cheryl. My sister and her husband had been greedy and wanted to get an extraordinary return on their investment. But Rebecca was an innocent victim of her husband's misplaced trust. And what would happen to Jimmy G. if his brother's empire collapsed?

"What do you think, Pepe?" I asked.

"It is not for me to decide," he said. "This is a choice you must make on your own, Geri. But I hope you will make the right one." And that was all he would say on the matter.

Chapter 39

Rebecca was in the dining room, dining alone on pizza that was still in its cardboard box. It was an incongruous sight—the long, linen-draped table, the sparkling chandelier overhead, the sideboard glistening with crystal. And the woman hunched over a slice of pizza. She was wearing a purple velour track suit, and her dark hair was pulled back into a ponytail. She looked years younger without makeup.

"Yum, pizza!" said Pepe. "I hope it is pepperoni."

A bottle of champagne stood on the table in a silver bucket and Rebecca held a champagne flute in her hand.

"Geri!" She called out when she saw me. "Good news!" She lifted up her glass, and I saw the bubbles dancing in it.

"Stewart just called. I'll have the money I need for *Dancing with Dogs* by noon tomorrow."

That was the last thing I expected to hear.

"Where is Siren Song?" asked Pepe. "Can I have some pizza?"

"That's not what Mandy told me," I said. "I was just at his office, and Mandy said the money was invested in offshore accounts."

"Oh, what does Mandy know! Did you talk to Stewart?"

"No, he wasn't there."

"Well, he just called, I mean *just*. Twenty minutes max. Said he needed my bank account information so he could transfer the money into it."

"And you gave it to him?" I was horrified. Probably he was going to clean out whatever money she had in there.

"Sure! Pour yourself a glass! Want some pizza?" She waved her glass wildly in the air. I got the idea she had polished off a few glasses already.

"Yes, pizza!" said Pepe.

"I guess I will take a slice," I said.

"The plates are over there!" Rebecca waved her hand at a credenza against the outside wall, between the two windows, which were draped in white satin, edged with crystal beads.

I came back with a gold-rimmed plate and set it down at the place to Rebecca's right. She handed me a slice of pizza. It was dripping with grease and there were big gobs of sausage and rounds of pepperoni all over it.

"I can't eat this!" I said, dropping it on my plate

"What?"

"I'll eat it!" said Pepe.

"Hold on," I said to him. "Go find Siren Song!"

"Siren Song is in her crate in the kitchen," Rebecca said. "Why do you want her?"

"Pepe wants to play with her."

"Sure. Go let her out of her crate!"

I got up and went into the kitchen. I took my plate with me, hoping to have a chance to tip it into a trash can or set it on the floor for Pepe to eat. The kitchen was about the size of a small high school gymnasium. Everything was black and glass and silver—stainless steel appliances, black granite counters, and glass-fronted cabinets.

Rosa was in there, stooping down to put dishes into the dishwasher. She looked around, startled.

"Mrs. Tyler told me I could let Siren Song out," I said.

Rosa did not seem to understand me.

"Siren Song!" I said again. Rosa's eyes darted to the corner of the room, where I saw a large metal cage.

Pepe was already there, pressing his nose against the bars. His little tail was standing straight up and ticking back and forth as regularly as a metronome. As I approached, I saw that Siren Song was facing him and her fluffy tail was swishing in perfect rhythm. It was nice to know that he prioritized love over food.

"No, no, no!" said Rosa, advancing on me as I fumbled for the latch on Siren Song's cage.

"I have permission," I said. "*¡Permiso!*"

"No, no, no!" she said.

Pepe broke away from his lovefest with Siren Song to growl at Rosa. Her eyes got big and she backed up. She hurried off into the dining room, probably to tell on us.

Siren Song, once released, tore around the kitchen in big circles, sliding on the marble floor. Pepe followed at her heels, occasionally skidding into her. I set my plate of pizza on the floor and watched both dogs tear into it. It was fun to watch but I needed to get back to Rebecca.

By the time I returned to the dining room, Rebecca had given Rosa a champagne flute and poured her a glass. "Drink! Drink!" she said, pantomiming what she wanted Rosa to do.

Rosa took a cautious sip.

Rebecca handed me another empty flute and poured in a hefty swig of champagne, sloshing a bit onto the table and the pizza.

"We drink to *Dancing with Dogs!*"

I took a sip. The bubbles immediately went to my head. Champagne always does. And this was excellent champagne. It was smooth and supple and full of flavors—toast and nuts and cream.

Rebecca clinked her glass against mine and then against Rosa's. Rosa took another tiny sip and wrinkled her face. She didn't seem to like champagne. I was quite happy with it until I remembered my errand.

"I think this celebration is premature," I said.

"You are bringing me down," said Rebecca. "And that's not the right attitude to have when drinking champagne."

"I really don't like it that you gave Stewart your

bank account information. He could use it to rip you off."

"Why would he do that? He's got plenty of money of his own."

"That's not what I heard. I just was visiting a friend, well, actually, my ex-husband, and he said that Stewart is running a scam, something called a Ponzi scheme."

The dogs came running into the room and circled the table, Siren Song in the lead, Pepe right on her tail.

"So?" said Rebecca. "That doesn't change the fact that David gave him our money to invest and now he's giving it back to me!" She swayed a little in her chair and clinked our glasses again. "Drink! Drink!"

Rosa did as she was told.

I took another sip and sighed. Delicious! Or, as Pepe would say, *Delicioso!* It was hard to keep focused but my task was to give Rebecca the unpleasant facts.

"That's the nature of a Ponzi scheme. Stewart uses the money from later investors to pay off the early investors."

"And there you go! We were early investors. David has had his money invested with Stewart for over twenty years, and it's more than tripled in value."

"And don't you think that's strange in this economy?"

"Stewart is good at what he does."

There was no way to get through to this woman. I took another sip of the champagne.

"Show her the pen, Geri!" said Pepe, skidding to a halt by my chair.

"Good idea!" I grabbed my purse and took out the gold pen. I laid it down on the tablecloth in front of her. That got her attention.

"Where did you get this?"

"I found it at Stewart's."

"Stewart had it?"

"Either him or Mandy."

"I knew it!" Rebecca stood up, flinging her arms out and knocking over the champagne bottle. It went flying and almost hit the two dogs. "That little bitch! She's the one!"

"What? Who? Mandy?"

"No, no, no!" said Rosa. She set her glass down with a thump. Was she upset because of the spilled champagne? Or because of the dogs who were now lapping it up?

"I don't care if she's your daughter! She's just a little gold digger! She's been after David for years."

"What?" I was confused.

"No," said Rosa firmly. "*¡Manuela es una muchacha buena!*"

"Manuela? Who's that?"

"Her daughter!" said Rebecca, flailing her arms at Rosa. "Get out! I'm tired of looking at you. All this time, you've been plotting to replace me with her!"

"Mandy is Manuela?"

"Yes," hissed Rebecca. "We took the whole family in when they needed a place to live. We put the kids through private schools. Mandy was always batting her eyes at David. He thought it was cute. He kept buying her little presents. I told him to knock it off. He said it was totally innocent."

Rosa unleashed a string of Spanish, which ended in "*loco.*"

"What is she saying, Pepe?" I asked.

"She has a most impressive vocabulary," said Pepe, his eyes going wide. "Many swear words I have not heard since hanging out with sailors in the bars of Tijuana."

"I don't need the swear words," I said. "Just the gist of it."

"She says her daughter is a good girl. That she thought of David as her father. And that Rebecca is an arrogant, self-centered, controlling bitch."

"I can sort of see that," I said.

"I do not understand," said Pepe, "why humans use that term as one of denigration, when a bitch is one of the most beautiful things on earth." He looked fondly at Siren Song who was tottering around, in small, unsteady circles. She apparently had imbibed a bit too much of the champagne.

Rosa stomped out of the room, throwing a few more choice epithets in her wake.

Rebecca sank back in her chair.

"This explains everything!" she said, with a hysterical tone in her voice. "Mandy was the other woman! David was going to run off with her while I was in L.A.! No wonder he encouraged me to go down there and work on the show. He knew it would leave the coast clear for them to make their getaway!"

"So if they were running away together, why did he end up dead?"

"I don't know. Maybe he changed his mind at the last minute. Maybe she killed him in a fit of rage when he told her he couldn't go through with it. All I know is I'm going to kill that little bitch!"

"Do not fear, Siren Song," said Pepe, going over to her. She had sunk down on the floor and put her head on her paws. "She does not mean you!"

Chapter 40

It felt strange to leave my house without Pepe. And he made it even harder, dashing at the door as soon as he realized I was leaving, worrying at my ankles and saying, "Do not leave me! I want to go with you! Take me along!" It was heartbreaking to see how attached he was to me.

I realized with a shock that we had hardly ever spent any time apart during the five days since I first adopted him. And what a ride we had been on during those five days! Should I blame Pepe for all the drama in my life? Then I would also have to blame him for the handsome man beside me. If it hadn't been for Pepe, I would never have met Felix.

Felix had proposed going out to dinner, "just the two of us," as a way of compensating for the stress of our first date, and I eagerly agreed. I needed a break from worrying about murders and Ponzi schemes, abused dogs and bad dogs and talking dogs.

The restaurant Felix suggested was a little romantic bistro just a few blocks from my house. Despite its proximity, I had never eaten there. It seemed like a place meant for lovers, not the sort of place you would feel comfortable dining alone.

The interior was dark, a warren of little tables. The hostess led us to a table for two, close to the front of the restaurant. A flickering candle on the table cast a dramatic light on Felix's face, highlighting his prominent nose and strong jaw. I worried about what it would do to my face but Felix looked over and said, "Wow, you look beautiful in candlelight," so I guess it was good.

I could see out to the rain-soaked street and the cars splashing by, but inside it was warm and cozy. There was a constant murmur of conversation from the other diners but they seemed far away, in the dark corners of the place. It felt like Felix and I were tucked inside a secret cave that had opened up just for us.

We studied the menus, chatting about our favorite foods, before ordering. I asked for a glass of Prosecco, continuing the celebration that had been so abruptly cut short at Rebecca's house. When we left, she was on the phone with the police, trying to convince them to pick up Mandy for questioning. I had already told Felix as we walked to the restaurant about the latest developments.

"What did you decide to do with the card case?" Felix asked as the waitress, a tall woman with a long braid, arrived with our appetizers—mussels for me and calamari for Felix.

"Oh, didn't I tell you?" I asked. "The police showed up at my door right after you left. They seemed to know right where to look. They headed straight for the refrigerator."

"What did you do?"

"Well, probably the wrong thing," I confessed. I took a bite of the mussels. They were delicious, lightly tossed with tomatoes, harissa, vermouth, and leeks.

"Why do you say that?"

"I know I should have handed it over to them but I was so afraid they would just cart me off to jail. So I gave it to Pepe."

"You gave it to Pepe?"

"Yes. He hid it for me. The police searched the house but they didn't find it."

"Where did he hide it?"

"In the cat litter."

"That makes sense," Felix said. "Chihuahuas like to burrow."

"You seem to know a lot about them."

"I worked on the set of *Beverly Hills Chihuahua.* That was quite an experience. During the scene set in the Mayan pyramids, we were working with over one hundred Chihuahuas. It was a lot like herding cats."

"Oh, I loved that movie!" I said. "I think that was what influenced me to adopt a Chihuahua. That and the news stories about how many were being abandoned in L.A. It must have been a treat to work with so many of them."

"Do you know they are in the bottom ten dog breeds in terms of trainability?" Felix asked.

"You're kidding me, right?" I asked.

He shook his head. "You don't have to worry

much," he said. "Your little dog seems bright and eager to please."

"Why do you suppose they are so hard to train?" I asked.

"If you look at the breeds that are easy to train, like German shepherds and border collies and Australian sheepdogs, you realize they are all working dogs. They've spent centuries working alongside humans, being trained to do very specific tasks. But Chihuahuas? Not so much."

"What are they good for?" I wondered.

"There are a few theories about Chihuahuas," Felix said. "Including the theory that they were raised for food by the ancient Incas."

"Yes, I've heard that one." I made a face as the waiter chose that moment to bring our entrees— a vegetarian pasta dish for me, a New York steak for him.

"Another theory is that they were temple dogs."

"Oh, that's better," I said, taking a bite of my pasta. It was perfectly cooked, just a little bit chewy, and complemented by the tang of the fresh spinach and the bite of peppercorns.

Felix cut into his steak. Pink liquid oozed out. I had to look away. "Not really," Felix said. His teeth seemed to gleam wolfishly in the candlelight. "Temple dogs were sacrificed during the rituals."

"Oh, Pepe won't like that either!" I said. "Is that it? Killed for food? Or killed for the gods?"

"Well, there is another theory," Felix said. "Probably like many small dogs, they were raised to be companion animals for the nobility. And so they don't really need to be trained. They're used to being doted on."

I had to laugh. "That describes Pepe. He does think he's in charge. Of me. And everything!"

Just then my cell phone rang.

"Oh, I forgot to turn it off." I poked around in my purse. As I went to push the buttons that would make it go to silent, I realized that the call originated on my home phone. That was strange. How could someone be calling from my home phone?

"I'm sorry," I said to Felix. "I need to get this call." Even though I think it's the height of rudeness to answer a cell phone while on a date, I just couldn't resist. I got up and walked away, flipping the phone open as I went.

"Hello? Hello?" I said, as I walked towards the back of the restaurant looking for the restrooms. I found a little hallway, sealed off from the restaurant by a long, heavy, red velvet curtain. It was dark back there and quiet. Still I couldn't hear anyone on the other end. Was someone in my house? Taunting me by calling my cell phone? I felt a thrill of terror. What if they had harmed Pepe?

"Hello!" I said again.

Chapter 41

"Geri, it is I, Pepe!"

"What?"

"Yes, I figured out how to work your telephone. It is *muy* simple. Once I got access to it!"

"How did you do that?" And what was I going to tell Felix?

"I knocked it down on the floor by pulling on the wire."

I sighed. "Why did you bother to do all of this?" I asked.

"Because I miss you, Geri. I want you to come home," he said.

"Pepe, I'm in the middle of dinner. It's very rude to disturb someone when they are eating dinner."

Surprisingly that seemed to work.

"Oh, I understand that," he said. "But you have left me without any dinner."

"Forget it, Pepe," I said. "You are not going to make me feel guilty. When I left you had a full bowl of food."

"Yes, but it is now gone. And I am lonely and bored."

"Go watch TV!" I said.

"There is nothing good on tonight."

A woman came in looking for the bathroom. I squeezed against the wall and pointed her towards the door at the end of the hall.

"Well, I'll be home in about an hour. You will just have to find a way to entertain yourself until then."

"So you give me permission to entertain myself in any way I see fit."

"Yes, I mean, No! What do you have in mind?"

"You will see when you get home," Pepe said.

"You better not make a mess," I said.

"How could I make this mess worse?" he asked. I still had not picked up after the police search.

"Good point. I am hanging up now. Do not call again! I won't answer the phone!"

"Teenager?" the woman asked, her hand on the door.

I nodded. Pepe was as bad as a teenager.

"You might regret that," Pepe said.

"Why?"

"Because Rebecca called about fifteen minutes ago. She said she had important news for you."

"And you gave her my cell phone number?"

"No, I tried but she did not seem to understand me. Did you not give it to her yourself?"

I thought about that. I had given her one of my new cards earlier in the day.

"Apparently she doesn't consider it important enough to bother me at dinner time!" I told Pepe.

"What if something is wrong with Siren Song?" he asked.

"I'm sure she would not call me to talk about her dog. She would call her trainer or her vet. Good night!" And I clicked the phone shut. But when I went back to the table, there was a nagging worry in the back of my mind. What might Pepe do if he felt Siren Song was in danger? And why would Rebecca call me at nine at night?

As I settled back down in front of my now cold pasta, Felix looked up with a question in his eyes.

"A wrong number!" I said.

He looked a little doubtful at that. And I didn't want to lie to him.

"I think the dog knocked the phone off the hook," I explained. "It was my home number, which is why I answered it." I loaded my fork with the pasta but for some reason it didn't look as appetizing.

"Oh, I can see why you'd be concerned," he said. "After the break-in the other night." His plate was almost empty.

"Yes, well I could hear Pepe on the other end and he seemed fine, so I'm not going to worry about it," I said, which was actually easier to say than do. "How is Sarge when you leave him home alone? Does he ever get into trouble?"

"Sarge?"

"Yes, the dog that attacked my car."

"Oh, Sarge's not my dog. I was training him for a client," Felix said.

"Training him to attack Toyotas?" I asked, but my joke did not go over well. Felix looked puzzled.

"No, I was training him to get used to strangers. He's an extremely shy dog. Emily, his owner, wants him to get more comfortable around strangers. So I had taken him to the convenience store where there would be a lot of pedestrian traffic and every time a stranger walked by, I gave him a treat. It was working pretty well, until he went crazy on me. I still can't figure out why he did that. He's not a dog-aggressive dog."

"Can I tell you something?" I asked. I put down my fork. Now was the time to tell him about Pepe's unique talent.

"Sure," Felix set aside his fork.

"I think it was my dog's fault," I said.

"No, your dog was doing what comes naturally for a small dog. Protecting his territory," Felix said. "Don't blame yourself."

"I'm not blaming myself," I said. "It's just that my dog—"

"Are you done?" the waitress asked, coming to collect our plates. "Would you like to see the dessert menu?"

I was tempted, torn between wanting to spend more time with Felix and wanting to get home to find out what Pepe was doing.

Felix must have seen the distress on my face. "Just the bill, please," he said. I had to admit he was great at reading nonverbal signals.

"I hate to end our date early," I said, "but . . ."

"I can see you're worried about leaving your dog alone," said Felix. "Maybe we can pick up some ice cream on the way back to your place."

Wow! He really knew the way to my heart. He seemed too good to be true.

"You were saying something about your dog." Felix picked up the conversational thread as we left the neighborhood market, carrying a pint of my favorite ice cream, chocolate chip cookie dough. It had begun raining and we stood under the awning, looking out at the raindrops flashing by, illuminated by the streetlights.

"Yes," I said. "Pepe has an unusual talent . . ."

"Answering telephones?" Felix guessed.

"No, more than that."

"Turning on the TV?"

"No, it's more than that."

"I'm intrigued," said Felix.

My phone started ringing.

"Dialing the phone?" Felix guessed.

"Yes, but that's not it!" I said. I dug the phone out of my purse and flipped it open.

"What do you want now?" I asked. "I'm on my way home. If you were good, I'll give you some ice cream."

"I beg your pardon?" The voice on the other end was not Pepe's.

I looked at the screen. It said the caller was R. Tyler.

"Rebecca?" I asked.

"Yes, is this Geri Sullivan?"

"Yes, sorry about that," I said. "I thought I was talking to my dog."

There was a moment of silence, then Rebecca
spoke.

"Geri, I've got great news for you!"

"Really, what?"

"Mandy is behind bars where she belongs!" Her
voice was full of triumph. "Thanks to you!"

"Mandy murdered David?"

"Yes! I convinced the police to question her. Ap-
parently they went straight out and picked her up.
It turns out they had DNA evidence that linked her
to the crime. Something about a glove she dropped.
Also her shoes matched the shoe print they found!
Can you believe it?"

"Wow!" I said. It was hard to express my amazement.

"I can't tell you how grateful I am. You must
come by first thing in the morning so I can give you
your reward."

"Reward?"

"Yes, I offered a $10,000 reward for information
leading to the arrest of the murderer."

"But don't you need the money for *Dancing
with Dogs*?"

"Oh, that's not a problem," she said. "I talked to
Stewart. Naturally he was distracted, what with the
news about Mandy. I think he had guessed about
the affair, but who would think she was capable of
murder?"

"Yes, it's hard to imagine."

"I told him about your concerns about the money
and he assured me they were ungrounded. He put
the transfer through and we should get a confirmation

tomorrow. David's investments are safe. I don't know where you got your information, but it wasn't accurate."

"Well, that's great!" I said weakly. "Thanks for letting me know."

"Oh, and I want to draw up the contract for you and Pepe to participate in *Dancing with Dogs.* Come over at 11 AM tomorrow! Sherman will have the contract ready. You just need to sign it."

"Good news?" Felix asked when I flipped the phone shut.

"Yes," I said, still feeling dazzled. "Sullivan and Sullivan just solved their first case. And Pepe and I are going to be reality TV stars. I have to get home and tell Pepe!"

Chapter 42

In the gray light of the morning, I didn't feel as exuberant as I had the night before. It had been a weird night—the romantic dinner with Felix had been overshadowed by Rebecca's news. Felix left earlier than I would have liked. But he did promise to return the next afternoon to give Pepe a training session. I was still trying to find a way to tell him about my dog's unique talents.

I sat down on the sofa beside Pepe with my morning bowl of cereal.

"What if we were wrong?" I said to Pepe. "What if Mandy isn't the murderer?"

He was watching *Paraiso perdido*. I couldn't understand much of what was going on, but I could tell it was *muy dramático*. A close up of Conchita, her eyes wide with horror. Cut to Hector, gazing out a window with tears streaming down those gorgeous cheekbones. I felt a little flutter as I thought of Felix and the sculpted planes of his face. I indulged in a moment of fantasy, imagining my fingertips moving lightly over those cheekbones, down to his lips.

I awoke from this reverie slowly, opening my eyes just in time to see a ribbon of text running along the bottom of the television screen. It read SUSPECT IN TYLER MURDER RELEASED ON BAIL.

"Quick! Hand me the remote control!" I said to Pepe.

Pepe looked at me with horror. "Geri, you know I cannot do that!" he said.

Sometimes I forget he's a dog. "Of course you can't. What was I thinking?" I reached for the remote control, which was lying on the floor.

"No, Geri!" Pepe squeaked. "This is the scene when Hector learns the identity of his true father."

"Sorry, Pepe," I said, "but there's breaking news in the Tyler case." I clicked over to the local news channel.

The commentator was in the middle of a sentence: ". . . released on a million dollar bail." The picture on the screen showed a young woman being rushed out of the jail, a jacket thrown over her head. I recognized the man at her side, Sherman Foot, dapper and stolid in a navy blue suit.

How come he could represent her if he couldn't represent me? On her other side was a woman most people would not have noticed—a small, dark-haired woman in a nice black silk pantsuit. (I wondered if it had once belonged to Rebecca.) It was Rosa, her eyes dark with worry as she steered her daughter through the gauntlet of cameramen and reporters waving microphones.

"I find it hard to believe that they would release her," I said.

"I find it hard to believe you would switch off *Paraiso perdido*."

"Pepe, this is part of our investigation."

"I thought our case was over," Pepe said. "You told me we had earned a reward. What is left to do?"

"I'm still having trouble believing Mandy would kill David Tyler. It makes no sense."

"Murder rarely makes sense," said Pepe in a portentous voice.

"OK, you got me there. But usually there's a motive. What's her motive?"

"You wonder that, and I wonder how Hector reacted to the news that he and Conchita are sister and brother."

"What?" I switched the channel back but it was too late. The credits were scrolling across a shot of Hector, his head in his hands.

"Yes, it is *muy triste*. They will not be able to consummate their love. Unless, of course, as I suspect, it is a lie told by Catalina, the evil twin sister of Conchita, who wants Hector for herself."

"Well, that wouldn't do her much good—" I began, then realized it didn't matter. It was a soap opera, after all. Anything could happen that would make the story more interesting. Whereas the story we were in had its own internal logic. I just hadn't figured it out yet.

* * *

As we headed over to the Tyler residence to sign the contract for *Dancing with Dogs* and collect our reward, Pepe was elated. He bounced in the passenger seat, almost as if it he were on a trampoline. As I pulled into a parking place across the street from the Tyler mansion, Pepe's ears began to quiver.

"I can hear Siren Song! She is in danger!" he said.

"I can't hear anything. Are you sure?" The car windows were rolled up since it was raining.

"I am a dog. My ears can hear sounds you have never dreamed of. Open the door!"

As soon as I did, I heard what Pepe had heard—the sounds of yipping and howling.

Pepe was already dashing off across the street, like a tiny white lightning bolt.

"Pepe!" I called, but he didn't listen. By the time I had climbed out of the car, he was halfway up the stairs on the wide front porch. Then I heard another sound that chilled me to the marrow. It was the sound of a woman—Rebecca, I was sure—screaming.

It was my turn to sprint across the lawn as fast as I could. I pushed open the heavy front door and ran into the house, Pepe leading the way. We burst into the living room, fearing the worst.

To my surprise, I was greeted by an entirely different sight. Rebecca was dancing around the living room, waving her hands in the air, with her head back howling. She was dressed in what I thought were probably her training clothes—a pair of leggings and a long T-shirt with black, gold, and white stripes. Siren Song in a little gold tutu was dancing around her, turning in circles and alternately barking and yipping.

"What is it? What's wrong?" I asked.

"Nothing's wrong!" said Rebecca.

"I am so glad no harm has come to you, my darling," Pepe said to Siren Song. He got on his hind feet and circled around her, like a moon revolving around a planet.

"Everything's wonderful!" Rebecca declared, gliding over to me. She grabbed me by the hands and pulled me into an awkward waltz. It was hard to maneuver around the furniture and the dancing dogs, but I tried my best to keep up.

"What's so wonderful?" I asked as we all twirled about.

"This!" said Rebecca, waving a piece of paper that she held in her hand. She fell down onto one of the white sofas in the room. "Stewart dropped it off. You just missed him."

"What is it?"

"It's a confirmation of the wire transfer. Stewart sent the half a million dollars I need for *Dancing with Dogs* to the producers this morning!"

"What?"

"Yes, half a million dollars. The show will go on! We're going to begin filming the pilot in Hollywood next week. You'll need to do some serious training with Pepe to be ready in time."

"We're going to Hollywood?" I asked. I sank down in the chair across from her.

"Yes," said Rebecca. "Isn't it wonderful!"

"Are you sure the transfer went through?" I didn't trust Stewart.

"Oh yes, I placed a call to my partners in Hollywood. They confirmed the money is in their account. I've already got my travel agent making the arrangements."

"For you and Siren Song?"

"You and Pepe as well. We'll charter a private plane so the dogs can fly in comfort. I'll give you all of the details. We leave next Thursday."

"Ah, back to traveling in style," said Pepe, who had finally wearied of turning in circles on his back legs and dropped to all four feet. His pink tongue hung out the side of his mouth.

"You've traveled in a private plane before?" I asked him.

"*Sí*, many times with Caprice."

"Yes, as long as I can afford it, why not?" Rebecca thought I was talking to her.

"Do you know that Mandy's out on bail?" I asked.

"Yes, I know. Luis told me."

"Luis? Mandy's brother?"

"Yes, he's here helping out."

"Don't you think that's weird?" I asked.

"No, I don't. He's not involved. He had nothing to do with it. And I need help. I can't run this place by myself. Who would answer the phone?"

As if on cue, we could hear a phone ringing in the hallway and not long after that, Luis came in. He was dressed in dark slacks and a black shirt that emphasized his broad frame. His hair was slicked back and neatly combed. He didn't look like a gardener any more. Maybe a bodyguard.

"It's Channel 7, ma'am," he said to Rebecca. "They want a statement from you."

"Tell them I'll talk to them in an hour. And get Sherman! Tell him to hurry up. I need the contract and the check!"

Siren Song, intrigued by the interruption, stopped her dancing and dropped to her feet. Pepe promptly ran over to her and sniffed her butt.

A few minutes later, Sherman Foot strolled into the room. He was wearing the navy blue suit I had seen on TV, and he had a sheaf of papers in his hand.

He handed them to Rebecca, who placed them on the glass coffee table in front of her and sorted through them. I realized, with a quiver of horror, that Rebecca had already replaced the glass coffee table on which I had dropped the gun. Which might mean I was sitting on the very spot where David had been shot. I jumped up.

Rebecca didn't seem distressed by the environment. "Here's the contract, Geri," she said, handing me several pages. "And your reward check is in this envelope. You need to sign this receipt."

I took the pages over to the white baby grand piano and spread them out. The contract was seven pages long and full of legalese. It made my head swim. The receipt for the check was short and sweet. I signed that, after peeking in the envelope to be sure the check was real, and then handed it back to Sherman.

"I'll look over the contract and get back to you," I said. I hoped that sounded professional.

Rebecca didn't seem to care. She was busy discussing the statement Stewart had drafted. "I wouldn't say 'we trust the police are acting with due diligence,'" she said to him. "After all, wouldn't that preclude a civil suit if we later decide to sue them for negligence?"

"Not necessarily, but I can revise it, if you wish." He was being even more obsequious than usual.

"Why didn't they hold her? That's what I want to know. It's ridiculous that she should be allowed to go free. I want to say something like that!"

"I'll continue to work on it, Mrs. Tyler," Sherman said.

Rebecca turned to me. "I need to get dressed for the cameras." She got up and headed out the door. "You're welcome to stay if you like. We can drink some champagne and make plans for our trip."

"I think we'll be going," I said.

Chapter 43

I picked Pepe up and headed for the door. Siren Song trailed at my heels, making squeaking noises. I presumed she did not want us to leave.

To my surprise, Luis was lurking in the hall.

"I'm sorry about what happened to your sister," I said. "This must be very difficult for you."

"It is hard," he said. "I don't believe my sister would do this."

"I understand," I said.

"No, you don't." He looked angry. "Mandy is ambitious and she's greedy. She likes nice things, expensive things, things she can't afford. But she is not violent. She would never hurt anyone, especially not someone she loved."

"So she *was* having an affair with David?"

He shook his head with disgust. "No, that's not what I mean. He was like a father to her, to both of us. Our own dad died when we were young. Our mom couldn't speak English. There she was with two small children. I was eight, Manuela was six. My mother came to Seattle looking for work, and Mr. Tyler took us in. This was long before he married Rebecca." His face soured as he mentioned her name.

"So you don't like her."

"Believe me," he said, "if you had to work for her, you would not like her either." Hmm. That was too bad because I was, in a way, working for her.

"But the police have evidence against Mandy," I said.

"She will be cleared!" Luis was firm in his conviction.

"Remind him about the glove!" said Pepe.

"Her DNA was on a glove that was recovered at the scene," I said.

"Her DNA will be all over this house," Luis said. "She often helped my mother with chores. My mother could not always keep up with Mrs. Tyler's demands. So she would sometimes ask Mandy to come over and help. Mandy hated to do it. She thought housework was beneath her but still it was family, and family is important."

"And the gold pen?"

Luis looked chagrined. "That might be a problem. Mandy is totally capable of walking off with something like that. That's why Rebecca fired her."

"So she used to work for Rebecca?"

"Yes, she danced with the dog, until Rebecca accused her of—well, of many things, but among them stealing a diamond collar that belonged to Siren Song."

That was pathetic. What could Mandy do with a

diamond dog collar? On the other hand, it was an absurdly expensive trinket for a dog.

As if he could hear my thoughts, Pepe said, "I used to have a diamond collar."

"That's ridiculous," I said.

"Yes, that's what we thought," Luis said.

"And the shoe print?"

"Again, she was often here. Perhaps she was walking the dog." Luis folded his arms over his chest. "I know they will not be able to hold her. She has done nothing wrong. My mother has some money saved. She will hire the best lawyer she can afford to clear Mandy's name."

"Like Sherman Foot?" I was still annoyed that he would represent Mandy and Rebecca but not me.

"No!" Luis frowned. "Sherman was there because he was representing Stewart."

"What does Stewart have to do with it?"

"Well, he bailed Mandy out, and then offered her a place to stay. He said that way he could keep an eye on her and guarantee that she did not flee the country."

"I would think she would rather be with your mother."

"No, the news cameras have been at my mother's door since late last night. It would not be good for Mandy to be there. Besides she wanted to get back to work."

"Considering what has happened," I said. "I'm surprised you're still working here."

"Mrs. Tyler cannot function without help. And since she fired my mother, she needs me. Not that my mother would ever work for her again. She thinks Mrs. Tyler is wrong about Mandy. And she wants to hire you to find evidence to clear Mandy's name."

"Why me?" Apparently she didn't realize that I was the reason Mandy was under suspicion in the first place.

"She says you are good at your job."

I beamed. It was nice to be acknowledged.

"And you are the only private investigator we know."

Well, that was less flattering.

"Mandy said she would be willing to talk to you."

Really? I was surprised by that. But then again maybe Mandy didn't know the part I had played in her arrest either.

"I just spoke to her. She is eager to explain her side of the story."

"Well—"

"She is my little sister. I have always been the one to protect her. Now, this is the only way I can help."

"Well—"

"And if you need anything from me, if there is any investigating I can do here, just let know. I will be your eyes and ears in this household."

"That could be helpful for us," Pepe suggested. "We would know immediately if Siren Song was in danger! Until, of course, she comes to live with us."

"That will never happen!" I said.

"What?" Luis looked at me with dismay.

"Yes, that would be great," I said. "I'll go talk to Mandy."

Chapter 44

"I do not like this." Pepe glanced at me with worry in his eyes, then back at the road. "Do you not think it foolish to confront them—one an alleged murderer, the other an alleged Ponzi?"

"He's not a Ponzi," I said to Pepe. "He's a swindler, a con artist—"

"*Un ladrón.*"

"Yes, if that means a criminal."

"So I ask again. Why would we confront them?"

"Don't worry. I have backup."

"Well, you can count on me, of course."

"No, I mean Jimmy G. I'm going to call him and ask him to meet us."

I had to wait until we arrived at our destination to make the call. It's illegal to talk on a cell phone while driving in Seattle and I didn't have a head set. Luckily Jimmy G. was in the office.

"Jimmy G. here!"

"Hello, it's Geri Sullivan."

"Who?"

"I'm working for you."

"Oh yeah, Jimmy G.'s secret operative!"

"Look, I need your help. I'm at your brother's house. I'm supposed to question his secretary. And I need backup."

"What for?"

"In case something goes wrong."

"Jimmy G. will be on the way!"

Pepe and I sat in the car watching the front of the house, waiting for Jimmy G. Nothing moved. All of the houses on the street had blank windows and empty driveways. It was as if the whole world had come to an end. No sign of life anywhere.

I tried to read the contract but the lines just swam in front of my eyes. Pepe was chattering away about strategies for promoting *The Pepe Sullivan Show.*

Fifteen minutes went by. A half hour. Rain pattered on the roof of the car. Even Pepe got bored after a while and curled up and took a nap. At one point, I thought I heard a strange thump, but I dismissed it as perhaps the thud of a branch against the roof, caused by the wind. Later I would regret that.

I decided to update the notes in my casebook. Except for this last interview with Mandy, it seemed all the loose ends were tied up. I still didn't understand why Mandy would kill David but a woman scorned can be a dangerous thing. That was why I needed backup.

About an hour later, Jimmy G. pulled up in a red Thunderbird convertible from the sixties. The muffler rumbled so loud it woke Pepe out of a sound sleep. He got up and looked out the window.

"Nice wheels!" he said. "But this hombre does not know how to care for such a classic car." There were rust stains on the doors, and the convertible top was patched with silver duct tape.

Jimmy G. swung his long, lanky body out of his low-slung car, clapped his fedora on his head, and came strolling up to us.

"Sorry to be late, doll," he said, "but Jimmy G. couldn't find his gun!"

"Well, then, how can you back me up?" I said.

"You don't pack any heat?" he asked with a swagger.

"No, I don't."

"So what's the plan?"

"You're the expert! What do you think we should do?"

"I think you should knock on the front door while Jimmy G. goes around to the back, in case the suspects try to escape that way," Pepe said.

"It's not like I think they will flee," I said. "It's just that I don't want to walk into a trap."

"Tell you what," said Jimmy. "I'll stay outside and if I hear any signs of distress, I'll come to your aid."

"Without a gun?"

"Jimmy G. can be intimidating when he wants," he said.

I looked him over. He was dressed in a black-and-

white houndstooth jacket, a maroon bowling shirt,
and a pair of black and white oxfords. At least the
shoes and coat matched today. And actually the
coat matched the shirt since there was a ketchup
stain on it.

"OK. Why don't you go around to the back?
That's where Mandy's office is, and she's the one
we're going to question."

No one answered the doorbell. I rang twice and
waited for five minutes. Finally Pepe and I headed
around to the back on our secret path. If Mandy
was at work, she should be in her office. At this
point, I was glad Jimmy G. didn't have his gun
since if he did, he might have blown us away if he
thought we were sneaking up on him.

Everything seemed quiet and peaceful as we
neared the terrace. The wind swayed the branches
of the willow tree. Rain dripped from the eaves.
And then I heard peculiar sounds, like someone
was gasping or choking.

The back door flew open and out reeled Jimmy
G. He was pale and his eyes were rolling back in his
head. He fell to his knees in the grass and bent over
the shrubs. Judging by the sound of it, he was being
sick. I had no desire to verify this visually but Pepe
ran over to him and then ran back to me.

"He had a chicken burrito for lunch!" Pepe said.

"Oh, God, Pepe! I don't want to know that!"

"I thought you valued my mighty nose, partner," he said. He lifted it and sniffed the air. "*Ay!
Ay! ay!*" he said.

"What is it, Pepe?"

"There is another smell, not so pleasant. It is the smell of blood. It is coming from inside."

I took a few steps towards Jimmy G.

"Are you all right?" I asked him.

He glanced over his shoulder at me, shook his head no, and then turned back to the bush.

Pepe darted inside the house. I followed him. Jimmy G. croaked out, "I wouldn't go in there!" But it was too late. Standing in the rear entryway, I had a clear view into Stewart's office, which looked much the same as yesterday, and into Mandy's office, which was quite different.

Mandy was sprawled across her desk. Face down in a pool of blood. Blood dripped off the edge of the desk. It fell into a puddle of blood on the floor. Mandy's arms hung limp at her sides. A gun lay just beneath the fingers of her right hand. I now knew better than to touch it. It was a big gun, with a pearl handle. It looked familiar.

I wanted to check for a pulse, but Pepe shook his head. "She is *muerta*," he said. "I can smell the death. But it is recent."

"How recent?"

"Very recent. Within the hour."

I thought of that muffled thump I had heard while waiting for Jimmy G.

There was blood everywhere. Spattered on the telephone, the file cabinet, the wall, the ceiling, the window. I knew that soon the place would be swarming with cops, and they would analyze the spatter, read those intricate patterns, analyze trajectories and angles, and form a picture of what had occurred. But what had occurred seemed obvious, especially when I found the paper.

It was lying on the floor, just a little beyond the gun. You couldn't miss it when you walked in the door. It was a typed note. It said merely:

I loved him.
I couldn't live with the guilt.
I'm sorry.
Please forgive me.

It was signed *Manuela*.

"Pepe, come here," I said. "Smell this for me!"

He sniffed around the edges of the paper, being careful not to step on it.

"It has the stink of Caprice," he said. "But there is a faint odor of another person."

Chapter 45

"I should call 911!" I said. I fumbled in my purse for my cell phone. My fingers were stiff and didn't seem to work right. It took me a while to figure out what numbers to push.

"Nine one one. What's your emergency?"

"I just found a dead body."

"Can you give me your location?"

"Yes, I'm—" I tried to remember the address.

Pepe rattled it off for me. He had a gift for memorizing addresses.

"What happened?" The operator asked.

"I don't know," I said. "I just got here and found a woman dead. And there's a suicide note."

"Do you know the victim?"

"Yes, her name is Mandy." I realized I didn't know Mandy's last name. And that seemed unbearably sad.

"Ma'am, stay on the line. We've got emergency vehicles on the way."

I went out into the back yard. Jimmy G. was sitting on one of the lounge chairs. He looked green around the edges.

"I think I found your gun," I said to Jimmy G.

"What?"

"Come and look!"

"Jimmy G. doesn't think he can handle the sight of all that blood." The poor guy—he was really rattled.

We heard sirens in the distance.

"Come and look at this gun! See if it's yours."

Jimmy G. followed me back into the house. He could hardly bring himself to look at the body but he sneaked a sideways look at the gun on the floor.

"Oh my God! That *is* Jimmy G.'s gun," he said. He reached out for it.

"Don't touch that!" I said. "It's evidence. Don't you know anything about crime scene investigation?"

"Good one, Geri!" said Pepe. He had come back in from outside. He hesitated, swiveling his head from side to side, his ears pricked. "I think there is someone at the front door."

And then I heard it, too. A key turning in the lock. The sound of footsteps in the hall. A man whistling cheerfully.

We all froze as if we had been caught doing something illegal.

"Mandy! I'm back!" sang out a voice. I recognized it as Stewart's. In a few minutes, he appeared in the hall. He looked like he had been out jogging.

He wore a pair of dark blue sweatpants and a dark blue hooded sweatshirt.

"Miss Sullivan!" he said, peering at me in the dim light of the hall. "James! What's going on? Where's Mandy?"

I stepped forward. Jimmy G. was shaking too hard to talk. "I hate to tell you this, but Mandy's dead."

"What? No! That's impossible. She was fine when I left. She was talking on the phone. To her brother, I think. What happened?"

He pushed me aside, but then hesitated on the threshold of the blood-spattered room.

"Oh my God!" He staggered back a little. "Who could have done this to her?" He turned around to glare at his brother. "Was it you? You couldn't stand it that she preferred me."

"Why would I kill her?"

"Isn't that your gun?" Stewart reached out for the revolver on the floor in the puddle of blood.

"You can't touch that!" I said. "It's evidence."

"For all I know, you stole it when you and Mandy came over the other day!" Jimmy G. shouted.

"Why would I steal your gun?"

"The same reason you stole my gal Friday. You always have to be on top!" Jimmy G. launched himself at his brother, punching at him.

"Hey!" said Stewart, shoving him back. "I didn't steal her. She begged me to rescue her from you!"

"Watch it, you guys," I said, trying to squeeze in between them. They were going to contaminate the crime scene. "No one killed Mandy. She killed herself."

That stopped Stewart. "But why?" he wailed. "I know she was humiliated by being in jail, but I told her we would fight the charges. She had every reason to live. Oh, Mandy!" He fell to his knees and buried his face in his hands.

Chapter 46

It was almost 7 PM before the police released us. This time they caught Pepe up in their dragnet, and he was not too happy about that. Detective Sanders and Detective Larson were not too happy to see me either. They told me if they caught me practicing private investigation without a license again, they would throw me in jail. I told them I wasn't really a private investigator, but Jimmy G's girl Friday. I crept home, too depressed to make dinner.

So it was great that Felix, who I had called from the police station, offered to bring me food. He gave me a choice of Thai or Mexican, and I picked Thai, against Pepe's objections. He was very grumpy about being locked in an interrogation room for hours and told to stop investigating. It turns out he has a lot of his ego invested in being a PI. He plunked himself down in front of the TV and flipped through the channels.

I took a shower and washed my hair, then changed

into black yoga pants and a pink tank top. I was just sitting down at my makeup table to put on some lipstick when I heard footsteps behind me.

Thinking Felix had let himself in, I said, "Wow, that was fast!"

Then I caught a glimpse in my mirror of the man who had entered the room. It wasn't Felix. It was Stewart Gerrard, in a dark suit with a red tie. My first thought was he must have gone home and changed after the police had questioned him. Then I noticed he was holding a gun in his hand.

"Get up!" he said.

I got up, slowly, keeping my eyes on him in the mirror.

"We're going for a ride!"

"Can I at least put on my makeup?" I asked.

Stewart kept his pistol trained on me. "Why would you want to do that?"

"If you're going to kill me," I told him, "I don't want to be found looking any worse than I have to."

Stewart laughed. "Just like a woman," he said. "Sure. Go ahead. But no tricks."

I laughed. "That sounds like a line from a million old detective novels."

"I suppose it does," he said. "But this time there won't be a happy ending."

My mind was in overdrive trying to figure out some way to stay alive. As long as I kept him talking, I'd be OK. Failing that, I'd fight. I wasn't going to be one of those women who whimper and whine and fall apart when some bad guy was about to do them in. I'd go down swinging—or at least trying to kick him in the crotch.

"Hurry up," he said. "I've got a dinner date to keep."

"Who are you having dinner with?" I asked as I retook my seat at my makeup table.

"What do you care?"

"Oh, I don't know." I picked up my mascara wand, while watching him in the mirror behind me, his pistol inches from the back of my head. "I'm just naturally curious when somebody's going out on a date."

"Business," he said. "Not a date."

"Another investor you're going to rip off?"

"Yes, actually. Coming up with that money for Rebecca wiped me out. Not to mention the bail for Mandy."

"So you're looking for a new sucker who will give you money to invest."

"Yes, and I already found him. You'll be happy to know who it is. Your brother-in-law, the dentist!"

"What? Don? But he was going to call you and ask for his money back!"

"Right! He did, and I talked him into investing more. How do you think I paid off Rebecca?"

"That's sick!" I said.

"It's their own greed that gets them," said Stewart, a smug expression on his face. "A 30 percent return on their money? In *this* economy? Who are they kidding?"

"It doesn't bother you?"

"What would bother me is *not* having new investors. But that won't ever happen considering my reputation and people always wanting more. It's a sweet deal."

"Unless somebody wants to cash out their whole investment and you don't have it. Like David."

"Screw him!" he yelled, smacking the back of my chair with his free hand and startling the wits out of me. "He pulled a gun on *me*. Said he was going to force me to give him his money. I was just trying to take the gun away from him. It was self-defense."

"Self-defense," I said, eyeing him in the mirror. His face had turned bright red like he was going to have a stroke. "That's a laugh."

I suddenly realized what had bugged me about Mandy's supposed suicide. It had been staged. Mandy would never have fallen forward on the desk if she had shot herself in the head. The blast would have pushed her to one side and the blood spatter indicated that as well. She had been shot and then arranged with her arms dangling and her face on the desk. Even Stewart couldn't bear to look at what he had done.

"You killed Mandy, too, didn't you?" I asked.

Stewart shrugged. "It was all her fault. She interfered. David's death was an accident. But Mandy saw it happen. She was watching through the window. She convinced me we should try to cover it up. She was the one who washed the glasses and wiped my fingerprints off the gun. She decided we should frame Jimmy G. and called him, pretending to be Rebecca, and sent him to the house. Obviously, it was a stupid plan. I should have gone straight to the police, instead of taking her advice."

"So you weren't trying to frame me. You were trying to frame Jimmy G."

"Yes, but you got in the way, so then we decided to make it look like you were involved. That's why Mandy broke in and hid the card case in your freezer. But by the time the police followed up on her anonymous tip, you had gotten rid of it somehow."

"And then when the police arrested her, you realized she might tell them the truth. So you bailed her out. You took her home. You wrote the suicide note. You made her sign it. And then you killed her!"

"Get up!" He grabbed me under the arm and jerked me to my feet.

"But I haven't finished my lipstick," I said, feeling stupid for pushing him too far. I had thought if I could delay him long enough, Felix might show up at the front door with the Thai food. On the other hand, did I really want him walking into this scene?

"You're done."

"But—"

Just then, Albert jumped up beside us on the makeup table.

"That is one big cat," said Stewart.

"Watch out," I said. "He's an attack cat."

"Sure he is." Stewart smiled. "It just so happens I like cats, and they like me." He let go of me with his left hand, kept his gun trained on me with his right, and reached out to pet Albert, saying, "Hey, big guy—"

Albert raked his hand from wrist to knuckle in a flash.

"Ow! Shit!"

Simultaneous to his cry of pain, Albert laid a second swipe across his hand, filleting it even more before Stewart could jerk it back, dripping with blood.

"Sonofabitch!"

I saw my opportunity and took it. While Stewart was preoccupied shaking his bloody hand, I stepped up and put my left knee straight into his balls.

Well, maybe not so straight . . . and maybe not really into his balls . . . I must have missed them, because, contrary to what they say is supposed to happen, all Stewart did was let out one tiny, little, insignificant grunt, then smashed me against the makeup table.

Stewart's eyes narrowed and a terrible, malevolent look contorted his face as he raised his pistol, cocked it, and aimed at me.

Chapter 47

This was it. I was a dead woman for sure. At least my cat had tried to save me. My dog, Pepe the Macho, woman's best friend, had remained remarkably out of sight. Probably hiding under the coffee table, out in the living room. He hadn't even barked when Stewart had somehow broken into our home. It was just as well, I thought, as I closed my eyes and waited for the end—maybe Pepe would be able to stay hidden and safe until Stewart left.

Loud voices came from the living room!

"Drop the *pistola*, gringo!" somebody yelled in heavily accented English.

"We've got you surrounded!" another man hollered.

"What?" Stewart mumbled, sounding as confused as I was.

"You can't murder one of our women, you dirty *cabrón*!" screamed somebody else.

"Somebody's in the living room," said Stewart,

nervously pulling me a little closer to the bedroom door. "Who the hell's out there?" he asked me.

"Must be the police," I said. "And they've got you surrounded."

"Impossible," said Stewart, his tone worried.

"If you know what is good for you, you will lay the *pistola* down and come out with your hands up, gringo!"

We got right to the door. It was slightly ajar.

"Give up!"

Stewart threw the door wide open. "Never!" he screamed, pushing me ahead of him into the room, his left arm tight around my neck, holding me close. "I've got a hostage! Back off or I'll kill her!"

Of course, there was nobody in the living room to hear his threat. The room was empty except for Pepe, who sat on the floor next to the remote control. The TV was tuned in to the Spanish channel, its dialogue blasting at full volume.

"What the hell?" Stewart stammered, as if he couldn't believe what he saw. Then he let out a relieved laugh. "Ha! It's just the TV, for crying out loud! There's no one here!"

"I wouldn't say that," I told him, noticing the look in Pepe's eyes. They were smoldering, mean, scary—a look I'd never seen in them before.

"What are you talking about?" Stewart asked.

"Get away from Geri!" said Pepe, advancing on Stewart. "Drop your *pistola* and release her."

Stewart stiffened. "He talked," he said to nobody in particular. His grip on me loosened a bit as he repeated himself. "The dog *talked*!"

"Of course, I talk!" said Pepe, getting even closer.

"No!" said Stewart, moving back a pace. "It can't be! I don't believe it!"

"You better believe it," said Pepe. "And you better believe that I will bite you, bite you, bite you!" He charged at Stewart, his teeth snapping.

Stewart tried to aim his pistol at Pepe, but Pepe had already found his target and was latched onto Stewart's right ankle.

"Ow! Shit!" screeched Stewart, trying to shake Pepe off. He totally lost his grip on me.

Big mistake. I wheeled about and clocked him right in the Adam's apple. Fortuitous, as I was actually aiming for his nose, but this worked even better. He let out a choking, gurgling sound, and his gun went flying when he reflexively reached for his neck with both hands.

Every ounce of my being told me to run, but then I thought of all those stupid women on TV shows who knock their assailants down and then run and the creep gets back up and catches them and kills them. And, anyway, I couldn't leave without my dog, who was attached to Stewart's ankle.

"Get him from behind!" I yelled at Pepe. Pepe knew immediately what I meant. He let go, circled around Stewart, and lunged for the back of his heel.

"*Argh!*" shrieked Stewart, as Pepe sank his fangs into his Achilles tendon. At the same time, I picked up my favorite lamp, the bulbous glass collectible on the end table, and swung it at Stewart's midsection. He went down in a flurry of flailing arms and shattered glass. Pepe sprang out of the way just in time. Stewart's head hit the edge of the coffee table with a thunk. He lay there, dazed, staring up at the ceiling.

I picked up his pistol and trained it on him. Pepe jumped onto Stewart's chest and looked him straight in the eyes.

"We captured you, you murdering *puerco*!" said Pepe.

"What?" gasped Stewart. He tried to lift himself up, but gave a mighty sneeze and fell back down.

"You heard me," said Pepe.

"He talked," Stewart said. "The dog talked."

"You can hear him talk?" I was puzzled by that.

Stewart was even more puzzled. "You mean, he really does talk?"

"*Sí, hombre*," said Pepe.

"I don't believe it," said Stewart. A look of amazement crossed his bloody face. "A talking dog!" And then he fell back down. His eyes went all glassy, and he passed out.

"He is out cold," Pepe told me. "We've done it, Geri."

"Yes," I said, thinking that Pepe, still standing on Stewart's chest, looked like he'd just bagged a hunting trophy.

"Thanks, in no small part to my brilliant maneuvering," said Pepe. "And, of course, my detective partner's bravery."

"Well, *gracias*," I told him. "I'm glad you remembered my part in it."

As usual, Pepe did not notice my sarcasm. "*De nada*," he said, jumping off of Stewart's prone body.

"Well, before we get swelled heads, Pepe," I told him, "I should point out that we didn't really solve anything. Stewart thought we were a threat and came after us."

"That is because we poked our nose into places and stirred up trouble and interviewed suspects and asked the right questions. That is what detectives do. And you cannot dispute the fact that we did catch the murderer."

Pepe seemed proud of himself but I was still feeling shaky from almost being killed. We'd have to study up and learn everything we could about being PIs and do it fast. I didn't want to ever be in this situation again.

I looked over at Stewart who was sprawled on my carpet, still not moving.

"I guess I should call the police," I said.

"*Sí*," said Pepe, "but before you do, could you do one small thing for me, *por favor*?"

"Sure. What is it?"

"Could you hold me?" he asked, his brown eyes seeming larger and warmer than usual.

I bent down and picked him right up. I noticed he was shivering as I held him in my arms.

I must say, I was shivering a little, too, what with everything that had happened.

"Well, partner," he said to me. "Everything has worked out *bueno*—we have caught the murderer and solved our first case together. Even so, there is still one thing that is kind of a bummer."

"Really? What's that?"

"That *cabrón* Stewart was only the second person in the whole world who ever understood what I was saying. And he turns out to be a murderer. *¡Ay caramba!*"

Acknowledgments

Mucho kudos to Waverly's daughter, Shaw Fitzgerald, who found and adopted the charming Chihuahua known as Pepe Fitzgerald, thus bringing a lot of joy and amusement into our lives and inspiring the character Pepe Sullivan.

We also want to acknowledge Judy Schachner and her clever books about a frisky kitten who thinks he's a Chihuahua. Many years ago Curt read these stories to children at a local library and the character of Skippy Jon Jones entered his consciousness to surface later in the personality of the adventure-seeking, Spanglish-speaking hero of *Dial C for Chihuahua*.

Shaw Fitzgerald was our first and best reader, pointing out problems and making suggestions that improved the story. Our writing group—Linda Anderson, Rachel Bukey, and Janis Wildy—responded to every chapter with the proper amount of amusement and encouragement.

Thanks to King County Library for publishing an early version of the first chapter. Also thanks to Krista Brooks of RetroPets® for her unflagging enthusiasm and donation of her artwork to adorn our Web site (and thanks to Judith Gille for introducing us to Krista's fabulous retro portraits of dogs).

The Shipping Group was instrumental in helping hone the query letter and develop a strategy for submission. And The Playground, a heavenly projectizing environment created by Havi Brooks of The Fluent Self, was the haven where the rough draft was polished into a submittable manuscript.

We appreciate the efforts of our fabulous agent, Stephany Evans, and her staff, who provided excellent suggestions for improving the manuscript and found it a great home with Kensington.

When we were considering publishers, Karen Allman of Elliott Bay Book Company introduced us to Kevin O'Brien, author of many best-selling thrillers published by Kensington, who answered all of our questions and showed us how to put on a dynamic book launch.

Our editor at Kensington, Michaela Hamilton, is a valuable part of our creative team, coming up with the title, developing exciting promotional ideas, and smoothing out our sentences. A book is a collaborative effort, no book more so than this one, and we are grateful for all the members of Team Pepe.

Turn the page for an exciting preview
of the next irresistible mystery
starring Pepe the Barking Detective
and his human sidekick, Geri Sullivan:

Chihuahua Confidential

Coming soon from Kensington Publishing!

Chapter 1

My counselor insisted I come in for an appointment before I left Seattle. She wanted to discuss my talking Chihuahua, Pepe.

I could totally understand her concerns. There were times when I questioned my own sanity.

Two hours after I adopted a cute white Chihuahua from a Seattle shelter, he started talking. And he hadn't stopped since. Even as we drove to the appointment, Pepe was chattering away about all the things that he wanted to show me when we got to L.A.

He claimed he had once lived there, as the pampered pet of Caprice Kennedy, the ditzy blond starlet famous for her love of small dogs.

I really didn't believe this story. He had dozens of stories, all preposterous. He claimed to have fought a bull in Mexico City, raced in the Iditarod in Alaska, and wrestled an alligator in an Alabama swamp. It pained him that I didn't believe his stories. And I could appreciate that, since no one believed me when I said my dog talked.

If anyone was going to believe me, I had high hopes for my counselor. Susanna is the sort of woman who sees auras and talks about chakras. Her waiting room is cluttered with crystals (to channel energy) and overflowing with plants (to detoxify the environment). She dyes her hair a shocking shade of red and wears chunky jewelry.

"So, Geri," Susanna began, after waving me and Pepe to a seat on the dark gray velour sofa in her office, "is your dog still talking to you?"

"Of course, I am still talking to her," said Pepe. "Who else would I talk to? She is only one who can hear me."

"That's not true," I pointed out to him. "Stewart could hear you, too."

"It is of little merit," Pepe said. "That *ladrón* is in jail."

Susanna was quick to jump in. "So you believe he spoke to you just then?"

"Yes," I said, "and he pointed out that there was one other person who could hear him talk."

"Oh really?" Susanna asked. "Who is that?"

"Stewart Gerrard."

"Your new boss?"

"No, Stewart is Jimmy G's brother."

I had already told Susanna about getting a job working for an eccentric PI who likes to talk and dress like a detective from the forties. Pepe had insisted on going with me to my first appointment with a client, where we stumbled over the corpse of millionaire, David Tyler.

"It turns out Stewart was the one who killed David Tyler. And when he realized we knew that, he tried to kill me, but then—"

"I saved you," said Pepe with great satisfaction. He was leaving out the part where I whacked Stewart in the stomach with a lamp but like most Chihuahuas, Pepe likes to pretend he is bigger than he is. So I let him take the credit.

Susanna looked disturbed. "That's quite a story, Geri."

"You say that as if I made it up."

"Now you see what it is like when you scoff at my stories," said Pepe, with some satisfaction.

"I heard the police made an arrest in the Tyler murder," Susanna said, "but they didn't mention you."

"What do you expect?" I asked. My counselor knows the story of my life. I've been going to her ever since she started seeing clients at the clinic associated with the college where she got her master's in counseling. The clinic offered a sliding scale, and I needed that after my divorce since I was only making enough money to make ends meet. So she knows that after I put my husband through business school, he left me for his secretary at his first job. And that just as my career as a stager was taking off, the real estate market crashed. I never get credit for my accomplishments.

"What does she mean, Geri?" Pepe asked. "Are we not heroes?"

My dog loves the limelight. Perhaps he once lived in Beverly Hills after all. It was theoretically possible, since he was one of a group of Chihuahuas who had been flown up to Seattle because the shelters in Los Angeles were overflowing with them.

"The Seattle police wanted to take credit for the arrest," I said. Actually they had threatened to arrest me for practicing as a PI without a license.

"That is outrageous!" declared Pepe. "When it was I who brought the *bandido* down!"

"It's OK with me," I said. I really don't like center stage. Which is why it was so annoying that my dog kept putting me right in the middle of the most ridiculous schemes. For instance, we were about to leave for L.A. to participate in the pilot episode of a reality TV show called *Dancing with Dogs*. Rebecca Tyler, David's widow, was producing it and said it was going to be a cross between *So You Think You Can Dance* and *Dancing with the Stars*. Pepe was thrilled, but I was terrified.

"By the way, I'm going to have to cancel my appointment for next week. Pepe and I are going to be in L.A. filming a TV show."

Susanna shook her head. "You should be checking yourself into a hospital, not going on a trip."

Pepe, who had been lying down, sat up abruptly.

"No way, Geri!" said Pepe. "I need my partner." It was unclear whether he meant for dancing or for investigating. He has this delusion that we are partners in a detective agency called Sullivan and Sullivan.

"I can't abandon my dog," I said.

Susanna's eyes grew dark with worry. "Geri, this is all so unlike you. Stories about catching a murderer. An invitation to perform in a reality TV show. A sudden trip to L.A. Do you realize what this sounds like?"

"No," I said. "What does it sound like?"

"Mania," said Susanna.

"Fun!" said Pepe.

My dog, like most dogs, knows how to have fun. And there's something contagious about being around that kind of joy. Which may be why we adopt dogs in the first place.

And Pepe was definitely enjoying himself. He spent the two hours of the flight from SeaTac to LAX running around the private jet with Siren Song, the golden Pomeranian belonging to Rebecca Tyler who had chartered the plane. Pepe and I met Rebecca after her husband was killed, and we helped her locate the missing money she needed to fund *Dancing with Dogs.* This was her pet project: a reality TV show featuring dog owners dancing with their pets for cash prizes. Rebecca spent most of the flight on her phone, talking with her casting director and her agent. She was busy trying to line up sponsors and celebrity judges for the show.

In the Los Angeles airport, everyone stared at our entourage. Rebecca looked stunning as usual, striding through the terminal in a chic black dress and sparkly high heels, with Siren Song trotting at one side, her hunky gardener-turned-bodyguard, Luis Montoya, at her other side carrying her luggage.

I trailed behind with Pepe tucked in the crook of my elbow. I felt very self-conscious in an outfit that was perfect for Seattle's rainy climate—black jeans, a violet-colored sweater, and a black velvet jacket. It was apparently all wrong for L.A. Most of the women in the airport were wearing low-cut, brightly colored tight tops and tiny skirts that showed off their long tan legs and strappy high heels. Their hair was sleek and styled and mostly blond (or highlighted if not blond), while mine was curly and messy and very dark. And their nails gleamed in various shades of red and pink and even orange. Mine were bitten down to the quick.

Still I held my head high as I passed through the gauntlet of their stares. I assume they thought I was Pepe's handler. He certainly acted like a star, gazing out over the crowds with a little smile on his lips and a proud tilt to his head.

"Ah, Los Angeles," he said. "The City of Angels."

A Hummer limo was waiting for us at the curb, and we settled in. Rebecca got back on the phone while Pepe positioned himself at the window, gazing out and keeping a running commentary on various landmarks we passed.

"There is Century City, Geri," he said, pointing out a cluster of skyscrapers. "I attended a big premiere there with Caprice. Those were the days when she took me everywhere with her. She dyed my fur to match her gown."

"Geri?" asked Rebecca. She and Siren Song and Luis were sitting in the back of the limousine, which was about half a mile from where we were sitting. "Is Pepe all right? He's making quite a racket."

"He's fine," I told her. I tend to forget that nobody can understand him but me. "He's just excited, Rebecca," I added. "For that matter, so am I."

"Well," she said with a smile. "You'll be even more excited when you find out who just agreed to be our last celebrity judge."

"Really?" I asked. "Who?"

"*Sí*, who?" asked Pepe, his long ears pricked forward.

"Caprice Kennedy!" Rebecca said, and she practically squealed, which is unusual for her as she is one of the coolest characters you will ever see. She didn't even cry when she found out her husband was murdered. For a while, I thought she might have killed him. I still didn't totally trust her, though I had agreed to go to Los Angeles with her. But that was mainly because of Pepe. He really wanted to be a star. Also he didn't want to let Siren Song out of his sight.

"Yes," Rebecca continued. "Isn't it wonderful? Having such a famous movie star and dog lover on our show is going to guarantee that the networks will pick it up!"

"Dog lover," mumbled Pepe. "Or dog discarder."

Poor Pepe. Caprice had ditched him for another dog. I'd been ditched myself a few times and could understand how he was feeling.

"And she'll be meeting us at the hotel for a photo shoot," Rebecca went on.

"She will?"

"Yes. Isn't it exciting?"

"I wonder if she will remember me," Pepe said softly.

"Of course she will," I told him.

Rebecca leaned toward me. "It's great publicity for *Dancing with Dogs*. The best! And great publicity for Caprice, too. She needs it! After the troubles she's had. A few DUIs. That impulsive wedding in Las Vegas. Then dropping out of rehab. This will cast her in a much better light. That's part of the reason she agreed to be on the show. Her agent said as much when I talked to him."

"Caprice is young," said Pepe. "It is only natural for her to sow some wild oats."

"Why, Pepe," I said, "sounds to me like you still have a soft spot for her."

"Everyone makes mistakes," he told me.

"Wake up, Siren Song." Rebecca gave her sleeping Pomeranian a shake. "We're almost there, my little darling. You've got to be at your best."

The limousine rolled to a stop under a striped awning. Someone opened the door from the outside and before I could stop him, Pepe hopped out.

"Pepe!" I jumped out after him, afraid he would run into traffic. He was always doing this to me, getting me into all sorts of predicaments. If it hadn't been for him running into Rebecca Tyler's house, I wouldn't have gotten mixed up in her husband's

murder. On the other hand, if Pepe hadn't antago-
nized a Great Dane in a parking lot, I wouldn't have
met the handsome animal trainer Felix Navarro,
who I reluctantly had to leave behind in Seattle.

I only had a few minutes to take in my surround-
ings: the blue sky full of puffy white clouds, the
palm trees swaying above, the towering gray bulk of
the old hotel, and on the steps of the hotel a pha-
lanx of photographers all grouped around a pretty
blond woman in a pink sundress.

It was Caprice Kennedy. Her hair was so blond
and so teased it looked like cotton candy. Her nails
and her lipstick matched the exact pink of her dress.
She clutched a small white and brown Papillon with
pink ribbons on its fluffy ears.

Pepe had gone charging into the midst of the
photographers and now skidded to a halt right at
Caprice's polished pink toenails.

"Caprice! Caprice!" He was squeaking. I had
never heard him so excited.

She looked down at him and frowned. "Get that
strange dog away from me!" she said, kicking at him
with her sandaled foot.

Pepe's big brown eyes got even bigger.

"But Caprice—" he said. "It is I, Pepe!"

"Shoo, dog!" said one of the photographers, flapping his hands at him.

"You're my little Princess," Caprice cooed to her
Papillon, holding it up to her lips and giving the
dog a kiss, which incited a round of camera clicks.
"Mommy won't let that ruffian get near you!"

Pepe came back to me, wobbling a little. His ears were down and his tail curled between his legs. He seemed to be in shock. I picked him up.

"Geri, she did not remember me!" he said. He sounded so pathetic I thought my heart would break.

Chapter 2

Pepe was quiet during the photo shoot, which was unusual for my blabbermouth of a dog. He did seem to know how to handle the publicity, though. He managed to work his way into the front of every picture; I did my best to stay in the background. Unfortunately, Caprice's little Papillon did not appreciate Pepe hogging the limelight. At one point, she snapped at him, which made Caprice chide her.

"Be nice, Princess," she said, with a little wag of her finger. It made for an adorable photo. Even more so, when the paparazzi snapped photos of Pepe gazing up at Caprice with longing. I heard one of them say, "That Chihuahua has real star quality."

The little star was not so happy with our lodgings. While Rebecca swept Luis and Siren Song off to a bungalow by the pool, Pepe and I were ushered into a room on the fifth floor of the hotel at the end of a long hallway.

I thought it was rather charming, furnished with a shabby chic aesthetic that evoked the old days of Hollywood: faded gold satin draperies, a gilt-edged mirror on the wall across from the bed. But Pepe grumbled as he inspected the tiny bathroom and the contents of the small refrigerator tucked into a corner. According to him, he and Caprice had always stayed in the penthouse suite.

"Do you miss living with Caprice?" I asked, expecting an answer that would crush me.

"Oh no, partner," he said with a straight face. "I far prefer our rather cramped and humble condo in chilly Seattle to living the life of luxury in Los Angeles."

Rebecca didn't even give us time to unpack before she herded us back into the limousine for a trip to the sound stage to check out the set. Caprice drove off in her low-slung convertible red Ferrari, saying she'd meet us at the studio.

"I remember that car well," said Pepe. "I spent many happy days tooling around in that macho machine." He sounded wistful.

"Perhaps you would rather ride with Caprice," I said. I couldn't stop myself from sounding sulky. I was flashing back to my childhood and arguments with my sisters about who would ride in the front passenger seat. Being the one riding beside Mom or Dad meant they loved you best.

"Not if it means being in the same car as that diva," Pepe said. For a moment, I hoped he was talking about Caprice, but then I realized he was probably referring to Princess. "Anyway, a Hummer limo suits my style." He jumped up onto the back of the seat and curled up behind me, where he could see out the window and keep an eye on his true love, Siren Song, who was snoozing on the seat beside Rebecca.

In Seattle, if you drove down the street in a Hummer limo, most people would stop and stare. (Some of them might even throw eggs.) In L.A., no one batted an eye as our long white limousine cruised down the crowded streets.

"What is all that racket?" asked Pepe, as we turned down Santa Monica Boulevard. We had made slow progress through the mid-afternoon traffic—sometimes it took three lights before we could proceed through an intersection.

"I don't hear anything," I told him.

"You are not a dog," he said matter-of-factly. He had made that statement more than once since we'd been together, and I sometimes wondered if he was just stating a simple fact, or if he was being patronizing: like someone explaining a complicated theoretical formula, and when you say you don't understand it, they say, "Well, you're not an astrophysicist."

"I believe we are approaching the cause of the disturbance," said Pepe, craning his neck forward as our limousine slowed down. "It appears to be a protest."

"What?"

"*Sí*, a protest," Pepe continued. "Many people carrying signs and yelling and blocking our way."

The limousine had come to a complete stop as it attempted to turn right into a driveway. There was a little booth at the edge of the sidewalk and behind it a barred gate. The archway above the gate read METROLAND STUDIOS. A few people were marching back and forth on the sidewalk, carrying signs that read NO DOG SHOULD DANCE! and STOP CANINE SLAVERY.

"What's going on?" I asked.

"It must be that damned PETA!" said Rebecca.

"What does the Greek bread they use in making gyros have to do with any of this?" Pepe asked me.

"It's not that kind of pita," I told him.

He gave me a quizzical look.

"This is *PETA*," I explained. "People for the Ethical Treatment of Animals."

"Oh," he said. "Well, that is a good thing, is it not?"

"Not in this case," I told him. "I think they might be trying to stop us from doing *Dancing with Dogs*." I turned to Rebecca. "Why are they doing this?"

"They think making dogs dance is cruel and unusual," she said.

"Why would they think that?" Pepe asked.

"I can't believe they organized this fast!" Rebecca said.

"Did you know this was going to happen?"

"Oh, we started getting threats as soon as the *Hollywood Reporter* mentioned we were going to begin filming. These people are fanatics!"

The chauffeur pulled as far as he could into the driveway, and we could see the demonstrators better. Most were in their twenties. Some of the young women were almost nude and had painted their bodies to make them look like Dalmatians and springer spaniels. They wore dog collars around their necks with leashes dangling down.

"I must say I like their costumes," said Pepe thoughtfully. "You should try that, Geri. I think it would be a good look for you."

"I guess my publicist is worth the money I'm spending on her," Rebecca observed.

"You arranged this?" I asked, aghast.

"Publicity is publicity," Rebecca shrugged. "Look!" She pointed out the window. I saw a TV cameraman and a reporter thrusting a microphone toward the young woman whose lithe body was painted white and covered with the black spots of a Dalmatian. "We'll probably make the evening news."

The chauffeur was talking to the guard in the booth and in a few minutes, the gate slowly slid open and our limousine began to ease through it into the studio.

As we passed through the demonstrators, they shook their signs like so many leaves in a storm. The messages were weird: DOG IS GOD SPELLED BACKWARDS! and LET MY ANIMALS GO! and YOU'RE REALLY DANCING FOR DOLLARS! and PEOPLE ARE ANIMALS, TOO! and EAT TOFURKEY, SAVE A TURKEY! The strange mix of slogans made me wonder if they'd brought some signs that were left over from a previous demonstration.

"What is a Tofurkey?" Pepe asked me. "Is it better than turkey? I very much like turkey."

"I'll get you one later," I promised him.

"Yum!" he said. "A new taste treat!"

The studio was quite impressive. There was a tall office building, which Rebecca explained was used for interior shots, like the office scenes in *Mad Men*, plus it also contained the studio offices, some editing suites, and a café where we could get lunch.

"We were lucky there was a sound stage available here," Rebecca said as the chauffeur pulled up in front of the building. "Unfortunately I couldn't get the one with the in-stage pool."

"How would we have used that?" I asked.

"I thought it might provide a nice twist. We could have had the dogs perform some synchronized swimming," Rebecca said.

Pepe shuddered. He has a fear of water that he claims comes from being thrown into a swimming pool by one of Caprice's friends.

"The only problem is the tight schedule," Rebecca said. "We have to be in and out of here in a week."

"Look at all the *caliente* cars!" said Pepe, checking out the parking lot. "And there! That is Caprice's car parked ahead of us." He pointed to the red Ferrari parked in a handicapped spot.

"Are the other judges meeting us here?" I asked Rebecca.

"Yes, all three of them. I want to do a run-through,

just to see if the setup works. That way they won't have to come back until we start filming tomorrow afternoon."

"Who are the other judges besides Caprice?"

"Oh, didn't I tell you? I've lined up animal psychic Miranda Skarbos and Nigel St. Nigel."

"Nigel St. Nigel?" That was quite a coup. Nigel St. Nigel had been the mean judge on the popular *So You Wanna Be a Star* show for four seasons. Then he disappeared. No one was sure why, although there were many rumors.

"Yes, we have to have one mean judge. Otherwise, the show won't work."

I shuddered, already anticipating his scathing comments.

We transferred to an electric cart to get to the sound stage. Apparently they restricted the number of normal cars and trucks on the lot—the vibrations of too many heavy machines could rattle lights and wobble cameras.

As we rolled along the asphalt, down a narrow alley between the sound stages, I began to enjoy myself. The sun on my skin felt good after weeks of Seattle's gray skies and constant drizzle. Puffy white clouds floated in a sky the exact color of a sky blue crayon. Pepe seemed happy, too, with his tongue hanging out of his mouth and his eyes closed.

The sound stages resembled the hangars where Boeing builds its jets in Seattle. They were made of corrugated steel, painted dull beige and punctuated by red doors with numbers on them. We didn't see any other people, just empty carts parked outside the doors. One could imagine all the fantastic worlds going on inside. I would have to Google MetroLand and find out what shows were currently being filmed here.

Our sound stage was number thirteen. I thought the number was ominous, but Rebecca didn't seem fazed.

She tried the knob and it turned. "I guess one of the judges must have gotten here before us," she said.

The inside was cavernous. The ceiling towered overhead, laced with grids of metal and dripping with cables and ropes. The walls were painted black, which gave the impression that we were standing in infinite space. A little light came in through the open door illuminating a swath of concrete floor that was cluttered with snaking cables, but beyond that was only a dense velvety blackness. A few exit lights glowed green. They seemed to be miles away.

"Hello? Is anyone here?" Rebecca called out. Her voice died away. She sighed, exasperated. "Where are the lights?" She fumbled around on the wall for a switch.

Suddenly a light flickered in the darkness. Ahead of us, like an apparition, a stage appeared. The floor was a dull black but it was surrounded by a white plastic surround that cast an eerie glow in the dark space. A flight of glittery stairs, also lit from underneath, led down to the dance floor between two bright red fluorescent fire hydrants.

"Oh, it's just as I pictured it!" said Rebecca, with a little gasp of admiration. "Our set designer did a great job."

"I think the fire hydrants are a mistake," said Pepe. "A dog is a creature of instinct, and when I see a fire hydrant, it is not dancing that comes to mind."

Rebecca hurried towards the stage, with me and Siren Song and Pepe following close behind. As we got closer, I could see that there were bleachers for the audience members rising up on either side of the stage and a sort of booth in front of the stage for the judges. A man sat in one of the judge's chairs, gazing out at the stage.

"Nigel? Is that you?" Rebecca asked. He did not respond. But then no one really expected that of him. He was known for his long silences during which the contestants would squirm.

"Wait, Geri!" said Pepe, coming to an abrupt halt. "Something is wrong! Do not go any closer."

Rebecca reached his side and put out a hand to tap Nigel on the shoulder.

"I'm so honored to be working with you, Nigel," she said.

And then she began screaming. Ignoring Pepe's frantic attempts to stop me, I ran forward, just as Nigel St. Nigel toppled sideways and fell into a pool of blood on the floor.